BROKEN
BONES

ALSO BY ANGELA MARSONS

DETECTIVE KIM STONE SERIES
Silent Scream
Evil Games
Lost Girls
Play Dead
Blood Lines
Dead Souls

OTHER BOOKS
Dear Mother (previously published as *The Middle Child*)
The Forgotten Woman (previously published as *My Name Is*)

Angela
MARSONS

A D.I. Kim Stone NOVEL

BROKEN
BONES

bookouture

Published by Bookouture

An imprint of Storyfire Ltd.
Carmelite House
50 Victoria Embankment
London EC4Y 0DZ

www.bookouture.com

ISBN: 978-1-78681-303-9
eBook ISBN: 978-1-78681-302-2

This book is dedicated to my Granddad, Fred Walford,
who was taken from us far too soon.

I would have liked to have known you better.

PROLOGUE

Black Country: Christmas Day

Lauren Goddard sat on the roof of the thirteen-storey block of flats. The winter sun shone a grid onto her bare feet dangling over the edge. The cold breeze nipped at her wiggling toes.

The protective grate had been erected some years ago after a father of seven had thrown himself over. By the time she was eleven she had stolen a pair of wire cutters from the pound shop and fashioned herself an access point to the narrow ledge that was her place of reflection. From this vantage point she could look to the beauty of the Clent Hills in the distance, block out the dank, grubby reality of below.

Hollytree was the place you were sent if Hell was having a spring clean. Problem families from the entire West Midlands were evicted from other estates and housed in Hollytree. It was displacement capital. Communities around the borough breathed sighs of relief as families were evicted. No one cared where they went. It was enough that they were gone and one more ingredient was added to the melting pot.

There was a clear perimeter around the estate over which the police rarely crossed. It was a place where the rapists, child molesters, thieves and ASBO families were put together in one major arena. And then guarded by police from the outside.

But today a peace settled around the estate, giving the illusion that the normal activities of robbing, raping and molesting were on pause because it was Christmas Day. That was bollocks. It was all still going on but to the backdrop of the Queen's Speech.

Her mother was still slurring her way around the cheerless flat with a glass of gin in her hand. Her one concession to the event was the line of tinsel wrapped haphazardly around her neck as she stumbled from the living room to the kitchen for a refill.

Lauren didn't expect a present or a card any more. She had once mentioned the excitement of her friends. How they had enjoyed presents, laughter, a roast dinner, a chocolate-filled stocking.

Her mother had laughed and asked if that was the kind of Christmas she wanted.

Lauren had innocently nodded yes.

The woman had clicked the television to the Hallmark Channel and told her to 'fill her boots'.

Christmas meant nothing to Lauren. But at least she had this. Her one piece of Heaven. Always her safe place. Her escape.

She had disappeared unnoticed up here when she was seven years old and her mother had been falling all over the flat pissed as a fart.

How lucky was she to have been the only one of the four kids her mother had been allowed to keep?

She had escaped up here when her mother's drinking partner, Roddy, had started pawing at her groin and slobbering into her hair. Her mother had pulled him off, angrily, shouting something about ruining her retirement plan. She hadn't understood it when she was nine years old but she had come to understand it now.

She had cried up here on her sixteenth birthday when her mother had introduced her to the family business and to their pimp, Kai Lord.

She'd been up here two months earlier when he had finally found her.

And she'd been up here when she'd told him to fuck right off. She didn't want to be saved. It was too late.

Sixteen years of age and already it was too damn late.

Many times she had fantasised about how it would feel to lurch forward onto the wind. She had envisioned herself floating to and fro, gently making the journey like a stray pigeon feather all the way to the ground. Had imagined the feeling of weightlessness of both her body and her mind.

Lauren took a deep breath and exhaled. In just a few minutes it would be time to go to work. Heavy rain, sleet, snow, Christmas – nothing kept the punters away. Trade might be slow but it would still be there. It always was.

She didn't hear the roof door open or the footsteps that slowly strode towards her.

She didn't see the hand that pushed her forward.

She only saw the ground as it hurtled towards her.

CHAPTER ONE

'Are you kidding me?' Kim screamed at the dashboard of her eleven-year-old Golf. 'I mean, really?' she cried, turning the ignition key once more.

Any slim hope that her tantrum had persuaded the car to start was lost as the battery squealed its last few painful breaths before dying completely.

She sat for a moment, rubbing her hands together. She shouldn't really be surprised at her vehicle's refusal to move. It had been sitting on the car park since 7 a.m. in temperatures that had not nudged above -2 °C. The Golf had had fourteen hours to plan its revenge.

'Damn you,' she said, opening the driver's door.

She'd have to go back into the station and call a taxi. Oh, she could imagine the satisfied expression on Jack's face after she had smirked at his inability to get any sense from a drunk who insisted his name was Santa Claus. Two weeks too late but the guy was insistent.

She prepared herself for his glee as she reached out to open the door to the station.

Suddenly, the door flew out towards her as two black clad uniforms exploded from the building. One continued running while the second slowed and apologised.

'Sorry, Marm,' he said, 'five car pile-up on the motorway slip road.'

She nodded her understanding and stepped aside.

They slid into the squad car, hit the blues and tore off the car park. Their journey would meet little resistance from other vehicles even though it was Saturday night. Most sensible people were home watching television with a warm, comforting drink. It's where the rest of her team were and where she'd hoped she was heading. Damn car.

Luckily, Barney was enjoying the four-bar gas fire at Charlie's after their recent walk. On long work days her seventy-year-old neighbour stepped in and took care of Barney for her.

Coming to get you soon, boy, she promised silently as she crossed the space left by the speeding squad car.

She frowned as she saw an alien shape against the wall of the building. She knew what it looked like, *but surely not*, she thought as she moved warily towards it. Nestled in the corner the object had gone unnoticed by the distracted officers tearing out of the station to a multi car pile-up.

The external temperature was suddenly forgotten as ice ran through her veins.

'No bloody way,' she whispered, taking two steps forward. 'Oh shit,' she said, as she stepped into the light.

CHAPTER TWO

Kelly Rowe walked along Tavistock Road trying to remain visible while avoiding the snowflakes that had thickened over the last two hours and now aimed diagonally for her.

The cold wind swirled around her bare legs. The denim mini just about protected the skin to her mid-thigh.

The rest of the girls had dribbled away slowly since ten o'clock. Only Sally Summers, one of the older prostitutes, remained hopeful at the top of the road.

Snow was not good for business.

She took out her phone and made a call. Her mother answered on the third ring.

'Hey, Mum, everything okay?'

'Yeah, Lindy was in bed finally by ten. Kept insisting she just needed another biscuit.'

Kelly allowed the warmth to spread through her. For a four-year-old Lindy had a devious streak, and she used it to full effect on her nanna. Oh, how she ached to go home and snuggle in bed next to her little girl. Feel the plump, small hands in her own. Nothing in the world was as bad when she was holding Lindy.

She wanted to but she couldn't.

Part of her had been secretly hoping that her daughter was awake, unsettled so she could speak to her, reassure her she'd be home soon. Just hear her voice.

'Club busy tonight, Kel?' her mother asked, filling the silence.

Kelly crossed her fingers and closed her eyes. Her mother thought she spent three nights each week bartending at a night club in Stourbridge. The truth would break her heart.

'Yeah, still a few left in. Just popped out for a quick fag break.'

'All right, love. Well, be careful getting home. It's coming thick and fast now.'

'Will do, Mum, thanks,' Kelly said, ending the call.

Had she stayed on the phone any longer her mother would have heard the tears thickening her throat and for the hundredth time she cursed herself for her own stubborn streak. If only she'd swallowed her pride eighteen months earlier she might not be in this situation now.

She hadn't expected to find herself single and pregnant at seventeen and, God forgive her, she had been an hour away from a termination. But at the very last minute, against her mother's wishes, she had chosen not to go through with it and not one second of regret had passed through her mind since.

She had been absolutely determined to take care of her daughter and had been doing okay. She'd secured an administrative job and a small two-bedroom flat in Netherton which was big enough for her and Lindy. The rent had just about been affordable as long as she shopped clever, picking up discounted goods at the end of the day.

Two and a half years in and she'd lost her job as a care home administrator. The debts had started to mount up and every envelope that dropped on her mat was coloured red. Total desperation had gripped her when the electricity was finally turned off.

It was her neighbour, Roxanne, who had come to her aid and suggested she accept a loan from Kai Lord. The enigmatic West African man had offered her much more than she'd needed, but he was insistent she take it, for 'the little one'.

She had briefly considered asking her mother for help but the woman had been critical of the decision to leave home so soon.

She had believed Kelly incapable of taking care of her daughter on her own. To have turned to her for money would have been admitting defeat.

A dour-looking man with body odour at the benefits office had helped her with her claim before explaining it would be at least a couple of weeks before the regular two-weekly payment of £200 would begin landing in her bank and no emergency payment was available.

So, with no electricity, her rent late and barely any food in her cupboards, she had taken the money from Kai, all £1,000 of it, and got all her bills up to date. Three weeks later the loan had been called in. Payment in full with interest. A total of almost three thousand pounds: triple the amount she'd borrowed.

When she'd been unable to pay, Kai had become angry. He'd told her that his associates would not be pleased and, although he himself would never harm the 'little one', he couldn't guarantee her safety from the people to whom he would sell the debt. He had offered her a way out and she'd had no choice but to take it.

The first punter had been the worst but necessity and desperation meant she had to see it through.

After the first few she had found a way of disconnecting herself from the actual act and taking her mind elsewhere.

It had all been for nothing anyway as she'd been forced to move back in with her mother after her failure to secure a job before the loan from Kai Lord had run out.

But every time she got into a car she was one step closer to being free. She already had a plan for the future. Stay with her mum for as long as it took to get a respectable job, save some money and move out when she was properly prepared.

A car turned into Tavistock Road. The speed of the vehicle was indicative of a punter on the crawl.

She stepped out of the doorway, looking right and then left. The punter would see her before Sally at the end.

She stood tall against the biting wind, the snowflakes melting against her bare skin. She sauntered to the kerb and tipped her head suggestively.

The car pulled to a halt beside her.

She smiled and got in.

CHAPTER THREE

'Err… it's a baby, Marm,' Jack said, from behind the safety of his glass partition.

'You do know you're wasted as custody sergeant?' Kim snapped. She already knew what it was. What she wanted to know was what he intended to do about it.

'Well, I know one thing, Marm, you didn't have it when you left ten minutes ago.'

She narrowed her eyes. 'Very funny, Jack. Now, buzz me through so you can—'

'Can't have it back here, Marm,' he said, cutting her off.

'Jack, stop pissing about and take this…'

'Seriously,' he said, shaking his head, 'I've got two squad cars and a van on the way from a fight that got out of hand at the chippy.'

Fair enough, she thought. That would definitely keep him occupied for the next few hours.

'Okay, well just call someone down to…'

'Of course, Marm. I'll just ring the twenty-four hour crèche on the third floor.'

'Jack…' she warned.

He opened his hands and shrugged expressively.

She wasn't sure what she wanted him to do either but the car seat handle was beginning to dig into her hand.

'Buzz me through,' she snapped. 'And call social services right now.'

'Will do, Marm,' he said, picking up the phone.

She headed up to the office she'd left in darkness less than fifteen minutes earlier.

She placed the car seat on Bryant's desk and switched on the radiator. Luckily the heat had not yet totally disappeared from the room.

'Okay, now what?' she asked, standing in front of the desk with her hands on her hips.

The small face wrinkled its nose and continued sleeping soundly.

Kim tipped her head. 'Okay, I'm gonna search you for clues,' she said, quietly.

She peeled back the white lace shawl that had been quadrupled and tucked around the baby's legs and arms encasing it like a mummy. Beneath the shawl the baby was zipped into a lemon all-in-one suit that had feet, hood and ears. She felt around its body but there was nothing else in the chair. She gingerly opened the car seat clasp and touched the zip of the suit. She paused as the baby made a chomping motion with its mouth as though chewing on a steak.

Don't wake up, she prayed silently, as her hand stilled on the fastener. She'd felt less anxious when dealing with hardened criminals. A morning raid on drug dealers, a two-mile foot chase in the dark to apprehend a rapist and entering the scene of an armed robbery were all incidents she'd recently dealt with and none had induced the levels of stress she was feeling right now.

The baby's eyes remained closed, so she continued her investigation. As the zip lowered she saw that the child was dressed in another all-in-one suit but this was an inside garment.

Suddenly it stirred and kicked out its legs. Kim stepped back, and held her breath.

The phone rang, startling her.

'Please tell me they're here, Jack,' she said, knowing it would be a social services record.

'Ha, you wish,' he sniggered. 'The on-call team is currently trying to place a mother and five kids after her estranged husband issued a death threat.'

'Jesus,' Kim said. The season of goodwill appeared to be well and truly behind them. 'How long?'

'Not a clue; they wouldn't commit, but a wrapped-up baby in the safety of a nice warm police station is not their top priority.'

'Come on, Jack. There must be something you—'

'Gotta go,' he said, as a sudden rush of shouting filled the earpiece.

'Thanks for nothing,' she growled, slamming down the phone.

'Oh great,' she said, as the baby's eyes and mouth opened at the same time.

She looked around apologetically as a loud wail filled the room. She wasn't sure who she was trying to tell that she hadn't harmed it in any way. There was no one around. That was the whole bloody point.

It wailed again. The sound managed to dance on her nerve endings. Shit, what was she supposed to do now?

She took out her mobile phone and pressed on her contacts. The phone was answered on the second ring.

'What's up, guv?' she heard in her ear and never had she been happier to hear his voice.

'Bryant, I need you at the station, right now.'

She looked at the baby who was screaming accusingly right at her.

'And hurry, Bryant, this is an emergency situation.'

CHAPTER FOUR

Andrei cried out in pain with each movement of the van. Every corner, bend or dip shot the blinding agony from his leg around his body like an exploding firework.

The sound he made was deafening in his head but muted against the cloth that had absorbed all the moisture from his mouth. He had tried to use his bound hands to clutch the metal floor of the van to steady himself and keep his leg still but the suspension was tossing him around like a rag doll. He tried to convince himself that he was on his way to hospital, that the restraint and gag were just a precaution as they travelled.

The man driving the vehicle was not known to him but he had seen him at the farm now and again. It occurred to Andrei that the black van always came after a bad accident.

Suddenly the vehicle stopped and then shuddered into silence.

Andrei listened keenly.

The side door was opened and he was hauled out like a sack of potatoes. His eyes watered as he screamed his agony into the damp cloth.

The snowfall had thickened since they had left the farm. The flakes were not fluttering around his head but smashing cold and icy onto his skin. An inch layer had already formed on the ground.

'Please,' he spluttered.

The sound was ignored as he was dragged down a ditch at the side of the canal. The pain in his leg was causing red darts to cloud his vision.

'Please, take me to the hospital,' he begged, hoping that his words would somehow be understood.

'Shut up, idiot,' he heard, even though there wasn't a soul around to hear his pleas.

The male dragged him away from the bridge and along the towpath. Every movement ignited the pain in his broken bones.

He saw the man look to the left. They were fifty feet away from the bridge which already had a snow ledge on top. The man looked to the right. There was no other bridge or access point onto the canal in sight.

Andrei followed the man's gaze up to the factory wall with cracked and broken panes of glass.

Seemingly satisfied, he pushed Andrei to the ground, ripped the gag from his mouth and tore the bindings from his wrists.

He leaned down and whispered conspiratorially. 'Listen, the boss wants you dead and I gotta make it look good. I ain't the murdering kind, so if you stay here I'll come back for you when I can. If you move from here, we'll both be fucked. Got it?'

Andrei nodded. Not sure what else he could do. The searing pain in his leg meant he was powerless to argue or move anywhere without help.

The man wiped the snow from his eyes before turning and heading back towards the bridge and the slope.

As another shot of pain brought tears to his eyes, Andrei prayed the man would be back for him soon.

CHAPTER FIVE

'Thank goodness you're here,' Kim said, as Bryant entered the squad room.

Her repertoire of silly faces had been exhausted within minutes and her current activity of pushing the car seat to and fro appeared to be making them both nauseous.

Bryant assessed the situation, shook his head and placed a carrier bag on the spare desk. He nudged her out of the way. 'Have you not taken it out of the seat?' he asked, unfastening the belt.

'My dynamic risk assessment and knowledge of my own capabilities strenuously advised against it,' she said, drily.

In one fluid movement, the baby was in Bryant's arms and against his outdoor jacket. His arms began moving up and down rhythmically. The baby bounced a few times and began to quieten.

Kim felt the tension begin to drip out of her body.

'Bryant, you are an absolute—'

Her words were cut off as Dawson strode into the room.

'Kev, what are…'

'Like I'd miss this,' he smirked, heading for the baby. He placed a carrier bag beside Bryant's.

She looked at her colleague accusingly. 'You told him?'

He viewed her as though it was a no-brainer. 'Hell yeah. You and a baby? Couldn't keep that to myself.'

She shook her head as Dawson tickled the baby under the chin.

He shrugged. 'Thought I'd better get here before you hauled it into interview room one and started to question it.'

'Great, all we need now is—'

'Hey, boss, what's gooin on here?' Stacey said, placing a third carrier bag on the desk.

Kim threw up her hands in despair.

'Bryant, tell me you didn't call all of the armed forces out too just in case.'

'No, that's pretty much everyone,' he said, without apology. 'Now if I'd had the chance to send out invitations…'

'What's all this?' she asked, nodding towards the carrier bags.

'Nappies,' said Bryant, laying the baby on the desk.

'Milk,' Stacey said.

'A toy,' Dawson answered.

'From the three wise bloody men,' she said. 'Sorry, Stace. But for your information the kid isn't moving in. We're minding it for a few hours not adopting it.'

Bryant began to remove the baby's suit as Dawson looked thoughtful.

'So, if we're the three wise men, doesn't that make you the virg?—'

'I dare you to finish that sentence, Kev,' she snapped, as Bryant turned towards her.

'Congratulations, guv. It's a boy,' he said, with a smirk.

Kim looked around at the three of them thoroughly enjoying themselves and began to wish she'd just handed the baby over to Jack and ignored his protests.

She looked at the baby's face gurgling happily up at Bryant. No, she'd done the right thing. The child was safe and warm and that was all that mattered.

'Stace, can you pass me one of those nappies,' Bryant said, as Kim reached for the coffee jug. It was going to be a long night.

'I'll get that, boss,' Dawson offered.

She began to shake her head as her mobile began to ring.

'Stone,' she answered.

Her face changed as she listened carefully.

'Okay, got it,' she said, ending the call.

'Bryant, hand over the baby. We've got a body on the Burton Road,' she said, grabbing her coat.

It was never a good call to receive but as she threw a backwards glance to the writhing small person on the desk, it was at least a situation she could deal with.

CHAPTER SIX

Kim arrived at the cordon tape eleven minutes after she'd received the call. The snow was still falling freely but had not yet frozen to the gritted roads.

The row of shops backed onto an alleyway that led under a railway tunnel and then disappeared into the east side of Hollytree.

She stood for a moment with her back to the crime scene. If people were curious about the commotion they were prying at a distance. As yet members of the public had not congregated at the crime scene, eager for a front row seat to an image of a dead body.

Bryant offered his warrant card as Kim donned the plastic shoe coverings offered to her.

Halfway along the alley a familiar voice greeted her.

'Detective Stone. I was hoping you would be the OIC called from your bed on this fresh, crisp morning.'

'Keats, it's almost two a.m. and I have not seen my house or dog in almost twenty-four hours. Feel free to bait me some more. I dare you. Now, what have we got?'

Keats was the local pathologist whose mood rarely elevated beyond obnoxious. He was a short man with facial hair only on his chin, which appeared to compensate for the sparseness on his head. His humour was dry, sarcastic and usually aimed at her. Most days she liked the man a lot. At this hour, she did not.

'Ah, Bryant, thank goodness,' Keats said, as her colleague appeared behind her. 'A much more accomplished conversationalist.'

Bryant groaned. 'Don't tempt her, Keats. Not while I'm the closest one to her.'

Although Kim heard their banter she tuned it out.

The alley was dark, illuminated only by a street lamp at the cordon. The police photographer took a snap. The flash illuminated the whole alley.

'Jesus Christ,' Kim said. 'Do it again.'

This time she was ready and took her own mental snapshot. She was looking at the body of a female in her early twenties. The blonde hair was tied back in a ponytail revealing a face not yet ravaged by time. The eyes were open and stared up into the sky.

'Do it again,' Kim said.

Snowflakes were landing on her eyelashes, holding for a second before disappearing. It was eerie to see that the eyes didn't blink as flakes fell onto the open eyes.

She wore a short denim skirt, no leg coverings and black stiletto heels. The top of her head to her neck and her thighs to her feet looked relatively normal.

'And again,' she said.

Kim could not identify the colour of the upper body garments. The entire area was stained red.

'And again.'

This time Kim could see at least three tears in the fabric.

'Here, take this,' Keats said, offering her a Maglite torch.

She took it and aimed it at the torso. The blood had soaked into the snow around the body. It looked like training day at the butcher's.

'How many stab wounds?'

'I've counted four so far but I'll confirm that once I get her back.'

Kim nodded. 'Timing?'

'Liver tells me she's been dead for around three hours but you already know—'

'It's difficult to be more precise because of the weather,' she finished for him.

'Good to see you're learning, Inspector.'

Kim ignored him as she cast the torch over the body again. She fought the urge to lean down and close the eyes as though shutting the doors on the woman's suffering and sending her towards peace. A final act of kindness.

She could have guesstimated the approximate time Keats had given her without the aid of the liver probe. The snow had started falling around nine o'clock and had grown heavier around eleven. With the smattering of snow evident on her upturned hands Kim would have guessed at around three hours.

'Is that a handbag underneath her right arm?' she asked.

Keats nodded and then looked at the forensic photographer, who stepped back.

'Go on,' Keats advised, giving her permission to move it.

Kim leaned down and lifted the right arm gently. She used the torch to lift the flap of leather so she could see inside. At the top of the handbag was a bunch of notes.

'Last punter?' Bryant asked, opening an evidence bag.

'Yeah, and not too long ago.'

Kim dropped the notes into the bag. 'She didn't even have a chance to fold it in with the rest.'

A small roll of notes lay at the bottom of the bag, pitifully thin for a night out working in these conditions.

Other than condoms and a set of house keys on a smiley key ring there was little else in the main section of the bag. She felt into the side pocket and found what she'd been looking for: a driving licence and a mobile phone.

She shone the torch at the driving licence.

'Kelly Rowe.' She peered closer. 'Aged twenty-one, address in Wordsley.'

'Not robbery then, guv?'

Kim shook her head. She had known that immediately. The handbag had been underneath the body, so the victim had fallen on top of it. Had the bag been the motive it would have been subject to a tussle or struggle and would more likely have been forward of the body or to the side. Additionally, very few robbers then re-closed the handbag after emptying it.

'Think that top batch of cash is important?' Bryant asked.

'Not as much as we'd like,' she answered. 'That money came from the last customer who was happy to pay for her services. The killer would have kept the money.' She thought for a minute. 'Pass that evidence bag again.'

'The cash?'

She nodded, and examined it under the light of the torch. She was guessing it was forty or fifty pounds but however much it was, the money appeared to be in denominations of £5 notes.

'Whoever paid with this may be able to tell us which direction she went but that's probably about it.'

She turned. 'Keats, when—?'

'Monday morning and I won't be bullied into any earlier. We have three expired pensioners at the mortuary at the moment and I'm sure you'd like me to take care of this lady personally, and I have just worked eleven days straight.'

Kim opened her mouth and closed it again. He had recently assisted in another county with a house fire that had claimed the lives of four children under the age of nine.

Keats clutched his chest. 'What's this, Inspector, no arguments, no coercion, no threats?'

Just to play with his head she smiled at him and walked away. Two officers passed her carrying a privacy screen. The narrow alleyway would not contain a white tent. Common sense should have dictated that few passers-by would be interested on a cold winter's night and yet macabre fascination knew no season.

She removed the shoe coverings and placed them in the box beside the two officers guarding the cordon.

'What is it?' she asked Bryant as he took his phone from his pocket.

'Baby was collected from the station ten minutes ago by social services. Kev's dropping Stacey back home.'

Kim acknowledged the relief that flowed through her. She spoke to Bryant across the roof of the car.

'Let them know we're briefing at seven. Get a message to the notifying officer that nothing is to be mentioned of Kelly's profession to her family, got it?'

Bryant nodded and looked at his watch. 'So the day starts again in about five hours, guv?'

Kim opened the driver's door and was half bent into the vehicle when a movement to the right of the cordon caught her eye. She straightened and narrowed her eyes, staring past the darkness.

The figure had disappeared.

But she knew for sure it had been there.

CHAPTER SEVEN

Kim seated herself at the spare desk in the squad room. She'd been in at six and already managed a quick meeting with Woody. There was no need to share the entire agenda of that meeting with her team quite yet.

'Okay, guys, our victim, Kelly Rowe, was a sex worker. Stace, get the board.'

Stacey took the marker and transferred the information to the board.

'She was twenty-one years of age, a single mother who lives with her own mum in Wordsley. The night's takings were still in her purse, so definitely not robbery and there were at least four stab wounds to the torso. Time of death was around eleven last night.'

'We looking for her last punter, boss?' Dawson asked.

Kim shook her head. 'I'm not convinced her last punter did it,' she admitted, still questioning the wad of notes sitting at the top of Kelly's handbag.

'We've got no post-mortem until tomorrow as Keats is taking the day off. Bryant and I will be starting with the family and I want you two looking at CCTV to see if you can identify the person who left the baby last night.'

It appeared to be an example of finders' keepers as Woody had already allocated them the abandoned baby case in addition to the murder investigation.

Dawson's head shot up. 'Isn't that something Stacey can do on her?—'

'I want you two working together on this one,' Kim said.

'But surely you need me on the real—'

'That baby looked pretty real to me,' Kim snapped.

She understood that Dawson would see an abandoned baby as a lower priority and would want to be involved in a murder case but the baby was theirs whether they wanted it or not.

'I get to leave the office?' Stacey asked, widening her eyes.

'Yes, once you've taken a look through these witness statements from last night.'

'And I get a partner again?' Dawson joked.

Stacey frowned at him.

He smiled. 'But that's okay seeing as it's you.'

Kim checked Stacey's expression for any hint of hesitation or reservation. She found none. It had only been a couple of months since the constable's traumatic experience at the hands of a bunch of racist bastards. Kim had kept her deskbound ever since but she knew she had to loosen the reins and allow her to do her job and not only the data mining. Yes, that left a gap in the team but it was a situation she had already addressed with Woody.

'If you come up with anything, give me a call on the mobile,' Kim said, grabbing her jacket from the desk. She was halfway down the stairs before Bryant caught up with her.

Kim hadn't called a press conference. She hadn't needed to. She fought her way through reporters three deep to leave the building.

Reporters and photographers stood in huddles. She recognised a few of the locals from the *Express* and the free papers. A Central News reporter and a BBC *Midlands Today* cameraman were sharing something on their mobile phones. A Sky *News* correspondent was busy texting, and Tracy Frost from the *Dudley Star* was front and centre.

'Okay, gather round,' Kim shouted. A bunch of microphones appeared before her face and tape recorders were activated and thrust forward. God, she hated this.

The appetite of the beast would not be sated but they had to offer something. It was only a matter of hours before their victim would be identified as a prostitute, sparking a whole series of media debates before the family had been given the opportunity to draw their breath. This lot were not going to wait for the press liaison officer before they got something in print or online.

'Is she a prostitute?' Frost shouted, quickly.

Kim ignored her and started speaking.

'The body of a young woman was found last night in the Brierley Hill area—'

'Is she a prostitute?' Frost shouted again.

'She will be formally identified once her family has been informed and—'

'Is she a prostitute?' another reporter called out.

Kim stared forward. 'West Midlands Police will be doing everything to—'

'Is there a reason you're ignoring the question?' Frost challenged.

Kim met her expression squarely. 'Is there a reason that's the only question you've asked?' she said, stepping away from the microphones.

News reporters and journalists she could live with, and in some cases, even respect. Headline hunters made her sick.

'So, you gonna throw the full weight of the law behind this one, Stone?' Frost asked, sarcastically, once they were away from the baying crowd.

Kim stopped dead causing Tracy to land two steps ahead before she realised.

'Really, you of all people ask me that?' Kim said with disgust. 'If I championed only the public perception of worthy you'd be dead meat right now.'

'Fair enough,' Tracy conceded. 'You gonna confirm later?' she asked, still seeking a response to her only question.

'Confirm what?' Kim asked, innocently.

'Jeez, Stone, you're hard work,' Frost said.

'But so worth it in the end,' Kim said, raising one eyebrow.

Tracy chuckled. 'Anyway, heard you had a young new recruit in there last night,' she said, nodding towards the station.

The smile disappeared from Kim's face.

'Don't you dare even think about it,' she warned. She did not want anything to do with that child splashed over the front page. Thank God the woman had waited until they were away from the rabble to throw that one at her.

Frost shrugged and sauntered away.

'Bryant,' Kim said, across the roof of his car. 'Remind me why the hell I bothered saving her life.'

He followed her gaze to the swishing blonde hair and the five-inch heels. 'Beats me,' he said, getting in the car.

She headed out of the car park, onto the ring road, and sighed.

She was missing one family for a child and she was about to make another family's day a whole lot worse.

And there was something she still hadn't told her team.

CHAPTER EIGHT

'You almost ready?' Dawson asked, glancing towards Stacey. It had taken them less than half an hour to work through the few witness statements they had. 'I mean, if you need more time...'

'I ay left the building in the last two months, Kev,' she said, tetchily. 'You really gonna ask me if I need more time?'

'Yeah, I know. Just trying to be the supportive colleague,' he offered with a smile.

'Well, stop it. You're freaking me out.'

He glanced back down at the desk. In that case it was a good job she didn't know the whole truth. Stacey's abduction seemed to have hit the rest of them harder than it had her. He knew she'd been in counselling since it happened. At first, she had moaned at him about the psychologist and had denied the need to speak to someone. Then she'd said it wasn't all that bad, and now she was saying nothing at all. He suspected she was missing appointments.

The boss had done what they had all wanted to do: protect her and keep her locked in the office. But now she was giving Stacey some freedom and she was entrusting Stacey to him. And he wouldn't have wanted it any other way.

'So, what are your thoughts?' she asked, as they headed down the stairs.

'On what?'

'The baby,' she said. 'Where it came from, who left it, why the mother felt driven to panic and do such a terrible—'

'Bloody hell, Stace. A few assumptions in there. How do you know it was the mother? Why do you already say it was a terrible thing to do and why a panic?'

'Okay,' she accepted. 'Maybe not the mother but why would any parent choose to leave their child outside a police station?'

'There are a hundred reasons. Young mothers are frightened, teenage mothers panic but this wasn't a newborn. That boy was around three months old so we're not looking for a teenager trying to hide the new arrival from her parents. The child has been somewhere since it was born.'

'Well, doe that just make it all the weirder?' Stacey asked.

Yes, he silently agreed. It certainly did.

CHAPTER NINE

Ellie Greaves stepped off the bus and headed to the front of the station. The argument with her mother still rang in her ears, primarily because it was the same argument they had every time they were in the same room.

Her mother had gone back on her word and Ellie felt betrayed.

Discussions about college had surfaced a couple of months ago, a week before her sixteenth birthday, and it was a discussion Ellie had been dreading.

Having been bullied for her entire school life because of a stutter, which had corrected itself in her second year of high school, Ellie had no wish to continue within the education system. A chart in her bedside cabinet had marked the days until she could escape the misery.

As a single parent who had never claimed a welfare benefit in her life, Ellie's mother was passionate that she would gain a decent education. She wanted Ellie to see that college was the key to her future. That she would go on to university and secure a job that would ensure she was financially independent for the rest of her life.

Except Ellie couldn't see the stretch of her whole life. She could only see that day on the calendar, marked with gold stars, exclamation marks and glitter that signalled the end of the torture.

During the last few months the arguments had become more frequent. Often they were about tidying her room or because she was playing her music too loud or she'd left the mayo out of the fridge.

It didn't matter what the surface arguments were about. The underlying battle was the same every time. A month before, Ellie had goaded her mother into an agreement. If she found a job with real prospects her mother would forego the college rule. Two weeks later Ellie had presented her mother with a written job offer as an apprentice mechanic to start as soon as she left school. Her mother had been incensed and had thrown the job offer in the bin, claiming it wasn't a proper job and therefore didn't count.

Ellie had barely left her bedroom since discovering her mother's deceit and the realisation that the deal had been on her terms only, in a career she deemed fit for her daughter.

During those two weeks she had thanked God for Roxanne. Just before Christmas Ellie had stumbled onto a Facebook page entitled, 'Teen Angst'. It was little more than a message board designed for venting. After reading the other posts Ellie had taken full advantage of the page and vented her heart out. Afterwards she had felt much better, even cleansed.

That same night, she'd received a personal message from the page administrator thanking her for the valuable contribution and offering personal support should she need it. There had been something in the brief message that had spoken to her. Just a no pressure response from someone claiming to have been in the same situation ten years earlier.

Messages back and forth had ensued, each one longer and filled with more detail. One thing that Ellie had warmed to was that while understanding her plight Roxanne had offered calm reassurance without once dissing her mother. In fact, Roxanne often offered an alternative view of their arguments and presented her mother's opinion in a reasonable, measured way that always managed to calm her down.

The previous night, after their worst row yet, Ellie had immediately taken to Facebook and told Roxanne she was considering running away.

Roxanne's response had been immediate, urging her to reconsider. Instead she had offered to meet with her for coffee and a chat. Some cooling off time. Ellie had felt special being singled out. And going for coffee felt really mature.

She had considered leaving a note for her mother but at the last minute had decided it would do her mother good to wonder for a few hours.

* * *

Two short bus rides had led her to the front entrance of Cradley Heath bus and train station.

Roxanne had said she would be waiting but Ellie could see no woman standing around. Ellie took out her phone and scrolled down to the number Roxanne had sent her in case anything should go wrong. As she pressed the button to call she felt a presence loom up on either side of her. Her breath caught in her chest as the two guys startled her. Perhaps they had bumped into her accidentally.

'Hey, sweetness, what you got there?' the taller guy asked, snatching her phone.

She instinctively reached for it but he was too quick for her.

He laughed as he held it high above her head.

Ellie felt her heart lurch inside her chest. She looked frantically around but there was no one.

'P-please, give it—'

'Nice phone,' said the black guy appraising it and nodding.

She tried to swallow the fear that had dried her mouth. Her tummy was turning but she had to try and get it back. If she lost her phone her mother would kill her.

As she turned, the second guy grabbed for the small rucksack. She hunched her shoulders forward trying to keep it on her back but his strength was too much for her. He swung her against the wall so that her shoulder crashed against the brick.

'Let go, bitch,' he growled, as her weakened arms slid out of the straps.

Although her heart was beating fast she made another grab for the phone.

'Give me back—'

The smaller one holding her rucksack slammed her against the wall of the building and thrust his hand between her legs. He squeezed, hard.

She cried out.

He threw back his head and laughed. His breath smelled of beer and stale smoke.

She tried to control the trembling and the sudden swell of tears that rushed to her eyes. She just wanted them to take the phone and go, terrified of what they might do to her.

'Be grateful this is all we're after, gorgeous,' he said, with another squeeze between her legs.

Within seconds they had disappeared from view around the side of the building and across the railway tracks.

Ellie was stunned and frightened. It had all happened so quickly. She looked around to see if anyone had seen anything. A woman was sprinting towards her. She was reed thin, wearing skinny jeans, inch high boots and a sweatshirt. Her long red hair was tied in a ponytail.

A look of horror shaped her face.

'Ellie?' she asked.

Ellie nodded dumbly, feeling the tears again sting her eyes.

The woman took her hand. 'I'm Roxanne. I just saw what happened as I got out of the car. Are you okay?'

Ellie nodded not trusting herself to speak.

Roxanne walked around the building but the thugs were long gone. The woman placed an arm around her shoulders, protectively, and began guiding her across the bus station to a car park on the other side

'Come on, sweetie, let's get you back to mine and sort out what we're gonna do.'

Ellie allowed herself to be guided and fought back the tears. Although only a few miles from home she suddenly felt much further away. She allowed Roxanne to place her into the small silver car and pull the seatbelt around her.

She realised that without her purse or mobile phone, she really had very little choice.

CHAPTER TEN

The home of Kelly Rowe's mother was unremarkable. It was a red-brick terrace with no front garden. A step up led to the front door that was opened by the family liaison officer.

She stood aside to allow them in and closed the door quietly behind them.

She offered her hand. 'Louise Nash.'

Bryant took it and introduced the two of them.

'Got here about two hours ago. She hasn't yet stopped crying but I get the impression she doesn't know about her daughter's profession. Keeps mentioning the name of a club I've never heard of. And I've kept the television on the kiddie channels for Lindy.'

A good ploy for keeping the woman away from the news.

'Other family members?' Kim asked.

'Doesn't seem to be a father in the picture. Audrey has said nothing about a husband or any brothers and sisters. I'm pretty sure Kelly was her only child.'

Kim nodded and took a step towards the door to the other room.

The space was darker than the front room with only a small window that looked out onto a six foot fence that separated it from the next property. The woman on the sofa had a head full of tight brown natural curls. Kim guessed her to be early fifties. She wore plain blue trousers and a buttoned-up cardigan.

The red raw eyes turned to Kim as she entered. They held what Kim had seen a hundred times: hope that a mistake had been made and that her daughter was alive and well.

'Hey, Lindy, want to help me make breakfast?' Louise asked.

The child turned from her position in front of the TV. She frowned but nodded and left the room.

Bryant stepped forward and touched the woman's shoulder gently.

'Mrs Rowe, we are so sorry for your loss.'

The hope in her face died and a fresh wave of tears rolled into her eyes.

Kim and Bryant both sat on the two-seater sofa. Bryant sat closest.

'Mrs Rowe, we understand how difficult this must be for you but we need to ask some questions.'

Audrey dabbed at her eyes and nodded bravely. Some part of the poor woman thought that if she cooperated fully time could be rewound and the death could be undone.

That her daughter had been brutally murdered was not bad enough. That the child who now pottered in the kitchen was going to grow up motherless was not sad enough. That this poor woman was going to have to bury her daughter. They were now also going to have to inform her that her child had lied and kept secrets. And that she'd slept with men for money. Not a vision any mother wanted but the headlines would scream that fact soon enough with remorseless brutality. It was best she heard it from them first.

'Can you tell us about Kelly's habits?' Bryant asked.

Audrey nodded. 'She lost her job almost two years ago. It wasn't a well-paid job but it was enough for her and Lindy to get by. She got a job cleaning offices, which she does a few mornings a week, and she works at a club Thursday, Friday and Sunday.'

Kim said nothing at her use of the present tense. The past tense would come soon enough and would then stay with her for life.

'And what did she do at the club?' Bryant asked.

Audrey shook her head. 'Bartending, I think. She was always there late so I don't know if she had to lock up afterwards.'

Kim caught Bryant's eye. Painful as it was he was going to have to tell her the truth.

'Did Kelly talk about any trouble she was having with anyone? Did she mention any names of people she'd argued with?' Bryant asked.

Kim understood that her colleague was attempting to get information before breaking the news that would render her incomprehensible.

Audrey's grief temporarily made way for confusion.

'You can't think this is personal. That someone intended to hurt her?'

'We can't rule it out, Mrs Rowe.'

Audrey shook her head. 'But surely it was a random robbery?'

Kim would have loved nothing more than to leave that picture in her mind. That her child had been leaving work and been in the wrong place at the wrong time and she had bravely fought her attacker. The real, lingering picture was going to be much harder to bear.

'Have you not talked to the owner of the club or the other staff members?' she asked.

And the game was up. Audrey had forced Bryant into a position from which he could not escape.

'Mrs Rowe, I need to tell you something that is going to come as a shock to you. I'm afraid your daughter was not working at a bar. She was involved in the sex trade.'

Bryant's phraseology allowed Audrey a few more seconds of ignorance before her own brain fitted the pieces together.

Kim wished it was a fact that they didn't have to reveal but she preferred the woman to hear it from them. The news headlines would scream her profession at every opportunity and Kim wanted her to be ready.

The tissue fell from Audrey's hand.

'Are you trying to tell me she was a…' She shook her head in disbelief. 'You think she was a prostitute?'

Bryant said nothing but held her gaze.

Audrey started shaking her head from side to side.

'No, no, no… you have it wrong. Kelly doesn't do that. She works at a bar. She makes good tips. She would never…'

'Audrey, we need to give you the whole picture before you read it in the newspapers. Your daughter was stabbed multiple times and we don't feel that robbery was the motive.'

Audrey rose and paced the small room looking for somewhere to hide where the truth wouldn't find her.

'It's just not possible, officer.'

Kim knew what was coming next and she was ready for it. Denial of part of the truth allowed the woman to deny the whole truth.

Audrey turned and focussed red, stricken eyes on them.

'You have to be mistaken. You have it all wrong. This is not Kelly you're talking about. You obviously have the wrong girl.'

Kim thought back a few hours to when she'd opened Kelly's bag and inspected the contents properly.

'Mrs Rowe, the three of you recently went to see Santa at the safari park?'

'Yes, but how could you…'

Her words trailed away.

'The photo was in Kelly's handbag,' Kim said, gently.

Audrey folded to the ground. A keening sound came from between her lips.

Bryant immediately knelt to comfort her.

Kim stepped into the kitchen.

CHAPTER ELEVEN

It was almost lunchtime when Stacey followed Dawson out of Sedgley police station. So far it had not differed from a normal working day. She'd been sitting in a room, staring at a computer screen.

They had shared out the possible cameras that might have offered them a lead and trawled through them in virtual silence.

They had agreed to break for lunch after a potential sighting had been obscured from view by a gritting lorry.

Stacey was unsure how this worked out in the field. Normally she either ate a sandwich at her desk or snuck down to the cafeteria for a portion of guilty chips. Did they separate for a while or stick together and discuss what they'd learned or, in their case, what they hadn't? She was just about to ask when a blonde woman in high heels stepped right in front of Dawson, blocking his path.

Although she'd never met the woman, it didn't take Stacey long to work out who it was.

'What do you want, Frost?' Dawson asked, attempting to step around her.

'Hear you had a new recruit at the station last night. Bit young for active duty, eh?'

'How'd you know about that?'

She shrugged as she took a last draw on the cigarette she was smoking.

'I have sources,' she said, discarding the cigarette and thrusting her hand at Stacey.

She had no choice but to take it.

'Nice to meet you,' she said, with a smile that wasn't really a smile. More an automatic expression change that accompanied the handshake.

'Not now, Frost,' Dawson said wearily.

'Wanna do an appeal?' she asked.

He offered her a derisive look. 'I'll pass on that.'

They all knew what had happened the last time Dawson had appealed for information. He had been played by a trainee reporter and had gone against the direct instruction of the boss. His mistake had led to hours of sifting through and eliminating piles of useless information.

'It's going live on the website in less than an hour and will be in the afternoon edition of the paper.'

'Then you don't really need anything from me, do you?' he said, finally stepping around her.

'Jesus, that bloody woman…'

'Hey, Dawson. Cute little bugger, isn't he?'

Dawson stopped dead and turned.

'How the hell do you know?'

She smirked. 'Got a photo as social services were heaving him out of the car.'

Dawson took a step towards her. 'You dare use that photo and I swear…'

'Untwist your knickers, Dawson, I was just saying.'

Stacey saw the amusement in her eyes. Clearly the reporter knew how to wind up her colleague.

'Fuck off and get your information from the press office like everyone else,' he growled, walking away.

'And where's the fun in that?' she called after him.

Stacey followed her colleague to the end of the car park.

'Oh, and Dawson,' Frost called from beside her car, 'if I didn't bug you I'd never get to find out all your terrible secrets.'

Frost looked at her, smirked and walked away.

Stacey glanced at her colleague expecting his expression to be one of weary toleration but it appeared this woman had a knack of crawling under his skin like no one she'd met before. His gaze followed her as she tottered away, his face full of murderous thunder.

CHAPTER TWELVE

'Everything okay?' Kim asked the liaison officer over the top of Lindy's head.

The child was busy beating a bowl of batter into submission for a cake that no one would eat.

'She's asking when?'

Kim understood. Lindy was beginning to realise that her mummy wasn't home yet. It was not their place to explain to the child that her mummy would never be coming back again. And for that she was truly thankful.

'Anything to note?'

Louise shook her head as she lined up mugs and dropped in teabags.

Kim thought it took a special kind of person to be a family liaison officer. This woman was never going to be called to a family about to embark on a celebration. When Louise answered the phone in the middle of the night it was a request to immerse herself in the grief of a family.

'Nothing yet. She made one call to her sister in Glasgow stating there'd been an accident, so I think she'll be here later today.'

'This okay?' Lindy asked of the gloop in the mixing bowl.

Kim marvelled at how quickly children could adapt to new situations. And very shortly she would need to. The finality of death would be lost on Lindy. Four-year-olds didn't understand the concept of for ever.

For a while Lindy would be a bystander to the imminent events. Strangers would pass through the house. There would be tears, anger, denial. There would be a funeral and Lindy would attend the burial and still she would wonder when her mummy was coming back.

And through it all Louise would grow closer and closer to the child. And then she would have to leave.

'How do you do it?' Kim asked, nodding towards the child.

Although not specific Louise understood the question.

'Bonds form, especially with small people. I have a feeling we'll be cooking a lot,' she said as Lindy tried to squash a lump of flour against the side of the bowl.

'Good girl, you keep getting those lumps out for me.'

Lindy nodded again and stirred some more.

'But how do you keep distance?' Kim asked.

Louise smiled. 'You don't in cases like this. I know that the people I'm around were not responsible, so I don't have to listen for any inconsistency or mistake. I don't have to watch the family dynamics looking for nuances. In this case my role is to offer support.'

'And when it's over?'

'I'll go home, hug my kids hard, cry and then move onto the next family that needs me.'

It was a world that Kim could not comprehend.

'It's no different for you,' Louise said, pouring hot water into the row of mugs. 'You put everything you have into each case and then it ends. And you move on to the next.' She looked saddened for a second. 'And, unfortunately for both of us, there will always be a next.'

'No lumps,' Lindy cried, pointing to the globs of flour mashed against the side of the glass mixing bowl.

Well, Kim reasoned, that was one way of removing the lumps.

Louise put her arm around the child's shoulders. 'Well done, Lindy. That's excellent work.'

As Lindy smiled up into the police officer's face Kim caught Louise's eye.

'No, it's not really the same at all.'

'All right, guv,' Bryant said, entering the small kitchen. Immediately it felt cramped. 'We can go take a look around.'

Kim looked to Louise who nodded her understanding that she would need to try and keep both the child and the grandmother downstairs. They had no idea what they might find and watching strangers examine her daughter's possessions would not be a positive experience for Audrey.

* * *

'On the left, guv,' Bryant said, as she neared the top of the stairs.

The room was at the front of the house and was the larger of the bedrooms. Two windows offered a light and airy space. Beneath the left window was a three-quarter-sized bed covered by a quilt with the Manhattan skyline. Beneath the other window was a small single bed with a pink, flowery bed set.

A picture of the two of them late at night shushing each other formed in Kim's mind. She pushed it away. It wouldn't help the investigation.

'I'll start this side, guv,' Bryant said, indicating the back wall that was occupied by two wardrobes and a dressing table.

Kim nodded and opened the top drawer of the dressing table.

They worked in silence until Bryant called her over.

On the left-hand side of the wardrobe, beneath a pile of jumpers, was a carrier bag, half filled with packets of condoms.

'Bag 'em,' Kim instructed.

Although they would not help further the investigation it was not something Audrey needed to find when sorting through her daughter's possessions. It would put pictures into her mind that would do her no good.

Bryant took evidence bags from his jacket pocket and a black marker pen.

'Bloody hell,' Kim breathed as her eyes moved across the wardrobe rail. The far left held a selection of workwear from her previous job. Two navy skirts and two pairs of smart black trousers. Long-sleeved shirts and two suit jackets suitable for her previous office job. That they were still in her wardrobe told Kim she had hope of changing her own future.

Next were furry pyjamas and a dressing gown. Kim could easily imagine Kelly snuggled up on the single bed reading a story to four-year-old Lindy. Beside those were jogging bottoms, jumpers and jeans.

And finally, right at the end of the rail, was another short skirt and three tops similar to the one Kim had seen on her dead body.

'What?' Bryant asked.

'The entire gamut of her personalities on one bloody rail.'

She was a good girl, Kim thought, as she returned to the bed and looked beneath it. Only a few pairs of shoes and a couple of handbags met her gaze.

She lifted up the mattress and found a small book. Kim took it out and leafed through it. It was a red pocket-sized book used for household budgets.

At the front of the book was an initial amount of £1,000 as a brought forward balance, followed by an entry of almost two thousand pounds marked up as interest and fees.

Kim sat on the edge of the bed and studied the dates and amounts. Payments were made weekly for the first month of eighty to a hundred pounds. As each payment was registered on the left-hand side an amount was entered on the right. She continued through the book and saw that six months before the weekly payment had increased to an average of two hundred pounds.

Kim did a quick calculation to find that £2,750 had been paid with a balance still outstanding of over eight hundred pounds.

She whistled. What an interest rate.

Kelly Rowe had owed somebody a lot of money and Kim had a good idea who it was.

CHAPTER THIRTEEN

'Nothing so far,' Dawson said, ending the call to social services.

'Calls have been placed to local GP surgeries and walk-in centres but they don't hold out much hope. Normally only works if the mother has given birth very recently. The baby is still in hospital being checked over but no bruises and no obvious injuries.'

'And no helpful clues,' Stacey offered.

Dawson agreed. The child appeared well-nourished, healthy and well taken care of. Right up until he was abandoned outside a police station on a freezing cold night. There was just no getting away from that fact.

His gaze passed over every female on the screen of the time-lapse video running from outside the petrol station a mile away from the police station. The child could belong to any of the women passing by. She could be any age, any circumstance, any income bracket. Working, not working. He had no clue how they were going to narrow it down.

He heard Stacey's loud sigh as his phone began to ring.

'Yo,' he answered, seeing it was the station.

'Dawson?'

'Hey, Phil, what's up?' he asked the custody sergeant.

'Where are you?' he asked.

'We're just at Sedgley checking—'

'Yeah, it doesn't really matter,' Phil said, cutting him off. 'Wherever you are I need you back here, right now.'

'Can't it wait until—?'

'Dawson, I need you to come back to the station, right now. I have three women in my reception yammering away about that abandoned child…'

Dawson frowned. 'Well, just take details and we'll—'

'No chance. They're not leaving. Every one of them is saying she's his mother.'

CHAPTER FOURTEEN

Kim stamped the snow from her boots on the mat inside the coffee shop. The seating area was not highly populated and her eyes found their target immediately.

'Go on, then, Bryant, you've twisted my arm,' she said, nodding towards the counter.

Bryant rolled his eyes as she headed for the window table. She pulled out a chair and sat.

'Mr Lord, I hope I'm not disturbing you.'

He glanced up from his phone and fixed her with a cold stare.

Kim smiled in the face of his irritation. Any inconvenience to this man was a job well done in her view.

Kai Lord was now twenty-seven years of age and had taken over as boss of the Hollytree multiracial gang two years earlier following the imprisonment of the previous leader for attempted murder.

His dress sense had elevated from his early days as the boss. Gone were the low-slung jeans and hoodies favoured by his minions. Kai Lord now dressed with style in plain black trousers and a crisp white shirt. No jewellery adorned his body except for an expensive-looking watch on his left wrist.

His rise to power had been calculated and shrewd, building on loyalty of gang members until the perfect moment presented itself and he became the natural successor.

In his two-year reign he had clamped down on the gang's involvement in violent crime and focussed his attentions on the real money: drugs and prostitution.

Seven months earlier she had been called to the bedside of a fourteen-year-old boy from Hollytree who had fallen into a comatose state after being given a freebie drugs sample from Lord's supply chain. She had learned that the gang was offering freebies to kids to hook them young.

She had eventually persuaded two witnesses to testify against Lord when one of his underlings had stepped into the station and admitted to feeding the kid a free dose. The Crown Prosecution Service had happily ripped the confession from the kid's hand knowing that her two witnesses against Kai Lord himself would probably never make it to court. She had fought them on it, wanting to get the real drug pusher behind bars until fourteen-year-old Jackson Booth had died and then she had accepted that someone needed to pay for his death.

So while twenty-one-year-old Lewis Harte spent the next seven years inside for manslaughter the real killer sat here eating his lunch.

He had also been responsible for Dawson being badly beaten by four of his underlings. It was safe to say she wanted this particular low life residing at Her Majesty's Pleasure.

'And you is?' he asked, in a voice that was as deep as the colour of his skin.

'We is Detective Inspector Stone and that is my colleague at the counter, Detective Sergeant Bryant, as you well know. May we get you another coffee?'

'Nah, blud,' he said, placing his phone on the table.

'I'm not your blud, Mr Lord,' she said, calmly. 'So, please don't call me that. And I'm pleased to see that the death of Kelly Rowe hasn't interrupted your appetite too badly.' She looked pointedly at the large plate with an egg stain and a dollop of tomato ketchup.

He smirked. 'Gotta keep up my strength, officer,' he said, emphasising the last word.

Kim waited for Bryant to place the drinks and sit before she continued.

'So, Kelly Rowe was one of your girls?' she asked.

'We was colleagues,' he said.

'And how did Kelly become one of your "colleagues", Mr Lord?'

He shrugged. 'My colleagues come to me for many reasons. And I take very good care of them all.'

'Except she's dead,' Kim stated.

He cared about his 'colleagues' so much they were out on the streets in sub-zero temperatures trying to reduce a debt that would never be paid off. A real contender for Employer of the Year.

He shrugged.

Kim took the payment book from her pocket and held it aloft.

'And I can see your generosity right here.'

Kai reached for his cup and took a sip. There was no tremble to his hand, and Kim didn't expect any.

'She came to me, officer. She needed dollar to help feed her child. Would you have me turn her away?'

'Mr Lord, I would hate to doubt your genuine intention of philanthropy but not at an interest rate of 59 per cent APR.'

Amusement passed through the expressionless eyes. 'I have expenses,' he said with a lazy smile.

And those expenses included kitting himself out from head to toe in Ralph Lauren designer clothing.

She sat back, and smiled in his direction.

'You know, you can dress a pig in Prada but at the end of the day it's still a pig.'

'But a very wealthy pig,' he replied, taking another sip, and dropping the gangster speak all at the same time.

'How did you meet Kelly?' she shot at him.

'I don't recall.'

'When did you meet her?'

He shrugged. 'My apologies but I don't recall.'

'Have you so many "colleagues" that you recall so little about them, Mr Lord?'

'Not at all, officer,' he said, leaning forward. 'I know everything, and I mean, everything, about my girls but I'm just not very good with dates.'

Kim sat forward and took a sip of her latte. And like him, there was no tremble to her hand either.

'I note that you charged Kelly a weekly management fee. Could you explain that?'

'My time is chargeable and I make no apologies for that.'

'And what does that "management fee" include, Mr Lord?'

'Introductions to clients, of course.'

'And your clients are risk assessed, are they?'

Kim knew that there were pimps out there that did take reasonable care of their girls. Clients were vetted and conditions were imposed. But Kai Lord was not one of those people.

'I have never used force, officer.'

Kim thought that was probably true. Entrapment, however, was a whole different story.

'And are you quite so diligent in vetting clients for girls who are desperate to pay you off?'

'Kelly was aware of the risk involved and if she chose to be out on a night…'

'You know she was just trying to pay you off as quickly as she could,' Kim said.

'A colleague's motivation is not my concern.'

Of course it wasn't his concern, it was his insurance. The more the girls owed him the longer they were trapped into earning him money.

Personally, Kim had no problem with prostitution, providing it was a conscious choice, not born of fear, intimidation, addiction. A woman's body was her own providing her mind was in full working order.

'So, where were you at around eleven on Saturday night?'

Kai reached into his pocket and handed her a card.

'This is my solicitor. He's very, very good. I would suggest you give him a call if you wish to ask me any further questions.'

Kim looked at the card. He was right. This solicitor was very good. And very expensive.

'So soon, Mr Lord. I didn't have you down as the scaredy-cat type. What exactly are you trying to hide?'

He smiled widely and opened his arms expressively. 'He really enjoys making fools of the police, officer, so I like to help him out when I can.'

The sudden sound of her mobile signalling a text message startled her and she found herself suddenly tired of the polite, cordial conversation that was taking place at surface level.

She reached for the phone and clumsily knocked her latte forward. Bryant managed to get out of the way in time but Kai Lord not so much. He jumped back and stood looking to the area of his trousers that now looked as though he'd pissed himself.

'You fucking bitch,' he growled as his face ignited with the rage that kept his girls in line.

Finally she was in the company of the real Kai Lord.

Kim smiled and moved away from the table towards the door.

'Well, this has been lovely but I have to go,' she said, pleasantly.

His eyes bored into hers with hatred and Kim was gratified to find that she could elicit some genuine emotion in him after all.

She couldn't help the smile that touched her lips as she stepped out into the cold.

She read the text message and put her phone away as Bryant appeared beside her.

'Matey boy wants to know where to send the dry cleaning bill?'

'I'll pay it myself. It was worth it.'

Bryant nodded. 'Yeah, I'll go halves.'

They headed back towards the car. 'So what was the text?'

'Nothing important,' she said, looking away.

'Seriously, though, guv, that guy is some serious pond scum.'

Kim shook her head. 'No, Bryant, Kai Lord aspires to be pond scum but he's not gonna give us the answers we need. There's only one place we can go for that.'

And only one person she could think of to ask.

CHAPTER FIFTEEN

Stacey found herself struggling to understand how they had returned to the station to find an additional woman claiming to be the mother of their abandoned child.

They now had four prospective mothers milling around the reception area.

She had immediately headed to the office, logged into her computer and begun assembling the news reports. The *Dudley Star* article had been shared a dozen times. The national news had given the abandoned baby a mention in between weather-related catastrophes and the inauguration plans for the new President of the United States.

It still amazed Stacey how priorities shifted depending on the current news cycle. On another day, another week, the national press would have been camped outside the station for the duration of the case, already vilifying the mother of the child. But not this week.

There was a part of her that hoped one of these women was the child's mother and that whatever had prompted her to abandon her child had magically been resolved and everyone could live happily ever after.

She was fully aware that social services would not view the situation with the same level of simplicity. And if one of them was the child's mother, how were there three additional claimants? What would possess a woman to come forward and try to claim a child that was not their own as though it was a rescue puppy they'd seen on the news?

'Why would you want to try to claim a child that's not your own?' she asked Dawson as they waited for the next potential mother.

Dawson shrugged in response. 'Mental illness, sterility, desperation.'

'Still doe ger it,' she said, taking a sip of her diet Coke.

So far they'd interviewed a forty-seven-year-old woman who couldn't recall exactly where she'd left the baby and another who was late twenties insisting she'd had the child snatched while shopping. For just a split second Stacey had been hopeful until she described in detail the pushchair the child was in.

And what now? she wondered as a light tap sounded on the door.

PC Bellamy appeared and guided in a woman in her early thirties. Stacey took a moment to appraise her as she walked around to the other side of the desk. Her jeans fitted snugly and she wore sensible, flat boots. She unzipped a Barbour Icefield jacket as she sat to reveal a tartan jumper beneath. Her hair was short and stylishly cut and two simple stud earrings adorned her earlobes. She uncoiled the scarf from her neck and placed it on the table.

Stacey noted the single gold band on her ring finger.

Dawson offered her a brief smile before opening his mouth. 'So, Mrs?—'

'Miz,' she corrected, quickly. 'Jane Sheldon. Please call me Jane,' she said, pleasantly, looking from one to the other.

Stacey was immediately struck by the woman's calm demeanour. The two previous interviews had been full of hand-wringing, face-touching, palpable anxiety and tension reaching them across the table. In contrast, this woman presented as calm, controlled and eager.

'So, Miz Sheldon, you claim that the baby currently in the custody of social services is yours?' Dawson asked.

She nodded, amicably. 'Yes, yes, he's my child.'

Dawson lowered his pencil and sat back.

'So, please tell us about your situation,' he urged.

The woman sat forward and met his gaze confidently. She sighed heavily.

'I couldn't cope any more. My husband is away, you see, in the military. I've been on my own. I have no family nearby and it all got a little too much for me. What I did was completely wrong and I knew that the minute I got home but by then I was frightened of the repercussions of my actions. I really am sorry for the inconvenience but if you could just tell me where he is, I'll—'

'Was it anything in particular that prompted such an extreme action?' Dawson asked.

She shook her head and closed her eyes.

Stacey found herself entranced by the emotion emanating from the woman. Instinctively she wanted to reach across and reassure her that everything would be okay.

'It was a culmination of things. Not enough sleep. He kept crying and couldn't settle. I hadn't left the house for days. I made sure he was wrapped up, though,' she said, narrowing her eyes.

'Of course,' Dawson said, sitting forward.

He pulled the list of bullet points towards him but Stacey felt real hope that this seemingly respectable woman had acted rashly in a moment of panic.

'So, did anyone pass you as you left him by the double doors?'

'I left him outside. No one passed me.'

Correct, Stacey thought.

'And what time did you leave him?'

'Nine o'clock,' she said.

Within the time frame. Stacey saw a flash of irritation as Dawson's phone vibrated in his pocket.

'And what type of carrycot?'

'It was a car seat,' she answered.

Correct, Stacey thought.

'And what colour is the baby's hair?' Dawson asked, and Stacey began to get a feel for where he was going.

So far he had asked only questions that could have been answered from reading all the articles or just a clever deduction.

This woman was assured, confident and convincing.

'The baby's hair is fair,' she answered.

Correct.

'And what colour was the baby's playsuit?' he asked, as Stacey felt the vibration of his phone again.

'Oh, please, officer, I had changed the baby's suit so many times that day through sickness and soiling.'

Dawson nodded. 'Understandable. So, what about the baby's coat?'

Stacey could feel him gearing up for the all-important question.

'The baby was wearing—'

'Miz Sheldon, what is the baby's name?' he asked, going in for the kill.

The sudden question caught her off guard. Two full, long seconds passed before she answered.

'Peter,' she blurted as colour flooded her cheeks.

Dawson had continually referred to 'the baby', awaiting her correction, which had not come. She had been too busy keeping her composure in place and her story straight that she had forgotten the most basic information.

'Why would you do this?' Stacey asked, unable to contain herself.

'I don't understand your question, officer. It's my child, it's my son. I want him—'

'It's not your child,' Stacey snapped. 'So why would you waste valuable time that we could be spending trying to reunite him with his real family?'

Dawson placed his hand against his vibrating pocket. By her count that was four attempts. Someone someone wanted to speak to him badly.

The woman's demeanour was now polar opposite. There was a hardness in her eyes and thin line to her mouth.

'I'd be a much better mother than the one that dumped him out in the cold.'

'You don't know the circumstances,' Stacey replied, unable to understand this woman before her.

'I know that…'

'Thank you for coming in, Miz Sheldon, PC Bellamy will show you out,' Dawson said, opening the door.

'Shouldn't we be charging these women with wasting police time?' Stacey asked.

'And waste even more time making a case that CPS will never take to court?' Dawson asked reasonably.

Stacey tried to swallow her irritation as the door closed and Dawson's phone vibrated again.

'Jesus, Kev, just bloody answer it,' she said.

'Frost,' he said, frowning at the screen. He put the call on speaker phone.

'Yeah,' he answered.

'What you doing, officer?' she drawled.

'Interviewing every woman that claims to be that little boy's mother,' he snapped.

'Aah, that's why I'm ringing, as a matter of fact. I suggest that if none of them are Romanian you might as well knock it on the head.'

CHAPTER SIXTEEN

The heavy snow of the last couple of hours had slowed to a haphazard falling. Flakes landed on the windscreen but quickly melted despite the plunging temperature.

'Did you put the jackets in the car?' Kim asked.

Bryant nodded.

Kim took a detour and headed through Lye. She turned left into the McDonald's Drive Thru, and ordered four lattes with lots of sugar.

'Not that thirsty, guv,' Bryant said as she passed the cardboard carrier to him.

'Lucky they're not for you, then.'

'Aah, bribery and corruption.'

Kim said nothing. A cup of hot coffee wasn't enough to bribe or corrupt the people they were going to see.

She drove to Brierley Hill and turned into Tavistock Road.

'I count three,' she said.

Bryant nodded as they walked towards the small huddle of women halfway along the strip.

'Evening, ladies,' Kim said, stepping into the middle. 'Coffee?'

'Jesus, that's all we fucking need,' said Sal, clearly the oldest of the three.

'Don't be like that, Sal. It's been a while. Haven't you missed me?'

The other two females looked at each other.

Most local police officers had had dealings with Sally Summers. She'd been on the circuit for many years and had been hauled in and charged by most police constables for petty theft and soliciting. But Kim's path had crossed with Sal's way before her choice of career in the sex trade.

The woman's make-up was heavy. The harsh light of the street lamp did her no favours and no amount of make-up could cover the red lines in her eyes. The wrinkles around her eyes were premature and not from laughter. Sal had smoked twenty or more a day since she was twelve years old.

'What's that gonna cost us?' Sal asked, looking down at the drinks.

'Just take one. It's cold out here.'

Sal did so and the other two followed.

Kim guessed the short blonde girl to be mid-twenties. Her hands shook but it had nothing to do with the cold. Kim could tell that she was clucking. Sudden withdrawal from heroin brought the trembles, hot and cold sweats, nausea, diarrhoea, and confusion. Kim guessed she hadn't had a fix for a while. Heavy snow, weather warnings and poor driving conditions dented most economies.

The third girl had mousy brown hair and looked like she was of Eastern European descent.

'Well, thanks for the drinks, now fuck off. You're bad for business,' Sal said.

Kim laughed. Sal was hard as nails. And she always had been.

The Eastern European woman gave Sal a look and then walked away.

'She don't much like you lot,' Sal said.

'Sorry if we're getting in the way,' Kim said, not really sorry at all.

Sal shrugged and took a small bottle of Bell's Whisky from her bag. She emptied half of it into the coffee. Unlike many of the others Sal had never touched drugs. Her addiction was to alcohol. Sal had always frustrated Kim. She was not a stupid woman, and although alcoholism was not a choice, her failure to seek help was. Sal's addiction had started young and Kim knew exactly why.

'So, what are you ladies doing out when you know there's a killer about?'

Sal shrugged and used her free hand to extract a pack of cigarettes from her bag. She took one and lit it, passing it to the other girl.

'Here, Donna,' she said.

Donna's hands would not have been able to hold a flame to a cigarette end if her life depended on it.

Sal lit one for herself and then offered the pack to them. Kim's was an instant head-shake but Bryant's held that millisecond of hesitation that comes from a reformed smoker.

'Gotta earn, Kim. Couldn't get out last night. Too bloody cold.'

Bryant looked at her sideways. Sal had never used her rank or title. And Kim never expected her to.

'What do you know about Kelly Rowe?'

'That she's fucking colder than me, right now.'

'Come on, Sal,' Kim urged.

A car turned into the street and slowly headed towards them. Twenty feet away the car sped up and passed them by. Bryant wrote down the registration number.

'For fuck's sake,' the blonde growled.

Kim was guessing that punters were sparse this evening.

'Look, give us a couple of minutes of your time and we'll get out of your way.'

Sal cut her eyes. 'Look, I didn't know her very well. We never went for coffee or did lunch and she always hogged the top of the street. Hard worker for her own reasons.'

Kim knew that 'hard worker' meant she'd take almost any old shit to get as much money as she could.

'Obviously it was temporary,' Sal said.

And of course it was, for all of them. Very few prostitutes set it out as their retirement plan. Woman were driven to the trade for a hundred reasons all of which were grounded in survival of some kind.

'She didn't talk all that much but she seemed decent enough. She had a kid, I think.'

'Any new weirdos about?' Kim asked.

Sal shook her head but Kim knew she was lying.

'You sure?'

'I'm sure.'

Kim turned and raised an eyebrow at her partner. 'Bryant, it's a bit chilly out here.'

He nodded and turned, jogging back to the car.

Sal watched him go and eyed Kim suspiciously.

'What you up to, Kim?'

'Just a bit cold, that's all,' she answered.

'Yeah, sure, it'd take more than the fucking elements to bother you.'

Kim saw Bryant approaching with two high-vis jackets.

'Are you fucking kidding me?' Donna asked, walking away.

The West Midlands police logo emblazoned on the back would kill trade on the street for weeks.

'So, any new punters around?' Kim asked Sal.

Sal threw her cigarette to the floor and ground it out.

'There's this one guy, northern accent. Likes 'em young. Pays very well for it. He pays the pimps direct and then picks up the kid from the corner.'

'And how do you know this one is different?' Kim asked.

'Always with a minder so they can't get away.'

Kim felt the rage surge around her body. Oh if only she could guard this street twenty-four hours a day. And every one like it.

'Nothing to do with Kelly, though?' she asked.

Sal shook her head. 'Nah, way too old,' Sal said.

'That it?'

'Yeah, that's it,' Sal said, biting her lip.

'Come on, Sal, I'm really feeling the bite in the air now.'

'Jesus, Kim, you always were a devious bitch.'

Bryant gave her a questioning glance.

'Come on, Sal.'

A car turned into the street and moved slowly towards them.

'Jacket, Bryant?' Kim said, holding out her left hand.

The car began to speed up. Donna was already tottering quickly to the top end of the road to try and catch the car at the Give Way sign.

'Jesus, Kim. Okay, there's this one guy. I can't tell you why he's weird but he just is. Works with kids and there's something about him that just makes me uneasy.'

'Name?' Kim asked.

Sal laughed out loud. 'You'll put that fucking coat on and hold an open day on this street before I give you any names and you know it.'

'Is he a regular?'

Sal nodded and then held up her hand. They were getting no more.

Kim glanced to her right, to the top of the street. Both Donna and the car were gone.

'Okay, Bryant, we're done for now. Go ahead, I'll be with you in a minute.'

Bryant eyed the two of them before walking away.

Kim looked into a face that was only two years older than her own. 'Jesus, Sal, when are you gonna give this up?'

'Don't fucking start. I know what I'm doing.'

'Can't you at least stay safe until we catch the bastard who killed Kelly?'

Sal smiled but there was no joy in the expression. 'My landlord don't like safe all that much. Especially when the first of the month comes around.'

Kim was frustrated. The low value placed on life on the streets sickened her.

'D'ya know what, Kim? I remember this kid once, hardened little thing she was. She came to the children's home when she was six.'

Kim looked to the ground.

'Terrified little mite but you wouldn't have known it. Offered her half my apple I did and she just wouldn't have it.'

'Not the only time you helped me out, was it Sal?' Kim said, meaningfully.

Sal ignored her response. 'It didn't matter how many times I tried to be her friend she just wouldn't have it.'

'Look, Sal…'

'No, Kim. You gotta accept that there's times you just can't mend the world. I don't take your help 'cos I don't want it. You know what I mean?'

Kim nodded, knowing there was no more to be done here.

'Okay, I got it. Just be careful, okay?'

Sal nodded and lit another cigarette.

Kim turned back to the car with a heavy feeling in her stomach.

'Hey, Kim,' Sal shouted along the pavement. 'No need to rush off right away, eh?'

Kim paused and tried to read her expression. It was closed and so was her mouth but her message was loud and clear.

Something was going down.

CHAPTER SEVENTEEN

'Can we really trust this tip-off from Frost?' Stacey asked him, rubbing her cold hands together. 'How the hell did she identify the shawl as Romanian?'

'Cleaning lady saw the photo of the baby on her desk and commented on having a shawl just like it handed down from her Romanian grandmother. Intricate design, hand-knitted with some crochet work, whatever the hell crochet is,' he shrugged.

After the phone call from Frost they had visited a greengrocer's in Cradley Heath High Street and a chippy in Quarry Bank, both owned by Romanian immigrants. The woman at the greengrocer's, through eye-wateringly broken English, had confirmed Frost's theory that the shawl was likely to be of Romanian origin, and the chippy owner had pointed them towards a bag factory that he should have recalled himself. He'd been there before.

'So, where are we going now?'

'Robertson's,' he answered and watched as her teeth clenched in frustration.

'Who or what is Robertson's?' she asked.

'Jeez, it's like working with a newborn,' he sighed. 'Robertson's is a small factory in Lye. Been done in the past for manufacturing copy designer handbags. Took to court five years ago and now produce cheap, poor-quality stuff for a couple of quid. Workforce is primarily Romanian and female.'

He took a right onto Hayes Lane and then a sharp left and pulled onto a car park.

'Bloody hell,' he said, switching off the ignition.

'Thought yer said small factory,' Stacey said.

'It was five years ago,' he said. 'Looks like they've taken over the units either side.' He noted that two thirds of the building appeared to be factory space with the final third converted to a glass-fronted showroom.

'Healthy market for cheap shit, then?' Stacey quipped as they headed for the door marked 'Reception'.

They were met by a young blonde girl with a tan at odds with the outside temperature. Dawson caught the surreptitious movement of her hand as it pushed the mobile phone out of sight. Her hands came back into view displaying nails that would have struggled to press any key.

'May we speak with Mr or Mrs Robertson, please?' he asked, leaning his elbows on the curved desk.

The receptionist, badged as 'Melody', leaned forward slightly and tipped her head.

On closer inspection Dawson could see that the heavy make-up masked countless bobbles of skin on a face that wasn't being helped underneath the stifling layers of cosmetics.

'Do you have an appointment?' she asked, pleasantly.

He shook his head and smiled. 'We were just hoping for a quick chat with one of the owners.'

'Is it regarding an order… an enquiry?' she asked.

Dawson shook his head, and opened his mouth.

'We're police officers,' Stacey butted in, breaking the spell he was trying to weave across the reception desk.

Melody frowned and retreated just an inch or two.

'There's no problem,' Stacey reassured quickly. 'We just have a situation that the Robertsons may be able to help with.'

'May I see your identification, please?' she asked.

Stacey obliged and Dawson followed suit. She glanced at them both before picking up the phone.

'Shame on you, Kev, using your sexuality and charm to get what you want,' Stacey whispered, frowning at him.

'Hey, I'm a modern man, equality and all that,' he said, smiling as Melody replaced the receiver.

'Steven will see you in a minute, if you'd like to take a—'

'Who is Steven?' Dawson asked, perplexed.

'Mr Robertson,' Melody answered. 'You asked for Mrs or Mr…'

'I thought his name was Alec.'

Understanding dawned on Melody's face. 'Oh, you meant Mr Robertson, senior. I'm afraid he's no longer with us.'

'Oh, I'm sorry,' Dawson offered. 'I had no idea he had passed…'

'He hasn't,' Melody replied. 'He's just not here any more,' she said with an air of finality and a look of distaste.

Dawson raised his eyebrows in Stacey's direction. There was a story there, he could feel it.

'It's Mr Robertson, junior that's—'

'Right behind you,' said Steven Robertson coming into view.

He remained behind the reception desk but offered his hand to Dawson first and then Stacey. His grip was firm but warm. The gold Rolex brushed against his wrist.

'How may I help?' he asked, looking from one to the other.

'It's regarding a current case we're working,' Stacey offered while Dawson observed.

He guessed Steven Robertson to be mid-thirties. His dirty-blonde hair was cut tidily around a good-looking face. His light blue shirt was open at the neck and his sleeves rolled part way up his forearms. Dawson detected an athletic build beneath the expensive but understated clothes.

'You may have seen on the news that a baby was recently abandoned at the police station in Halesowen?'

He nodded but looked confused.

'Of course, but I'm not sure how we might assist with that.'

'We have a suspicion that the mother of the child is Romanian.'

'There was a note?'

Dawson smiled. 'Nothing as helpful as that,' he said.

'So, what would lead you to believe…' his words trailed away. 'You can't tell me?'

Dawson nodded. They had agreed to keep the link to the shawl out of any questioning as it could prove to be a valuable form of identification later.

'And you'd like to know if any of our employees know anything about it?'

Dawson nodded again. 'If we could speak to any of the ladies here they may know of someone who—'

'I can definitely understand your logic but that would be impossible right now. We are all working flat out to complete an urgent order.'

'Not even for just a few minutes?' Stacey asked.

'I'm afraid the freight ship to China won't delay for even a few moments, abandoned child or not,' he offered.

'And there's no other reason you don't want us coming out back?' Dawson asked, not unkindly.

Steven Robertson grinned. 'If you're referring to our previous working practices you know that we now only manufacture quality merchandise at affordable prices.'

Yeah, cheap shit, he thought, recalling Stacey's apt description.

'You are more than welcome to come take a look,' he said. 'We have nothing to hide.'

Dawson nodded and followed the man through the door behind the reception desk.

The corridors were formed of narrow stud walling that didn't reach the ceiling, reminding Dawson of a maze. They reached a metal staircase interrupted by a turning landing halfway up. Three pairs of footsteps traversing together rattled in his ears. They exited the stairway onto a mezzanine that overlooked the factory floor.

Three glass-fronted offices glared down at three rows of sewing stations. Dawson counted at least fifteen heads bent over machines. Their hands were busy expertly turning and stitching different coloured fabrics as their feet tapped on pedals below.

'My mother,' Steven Robertson said, opening the door to the largest office at the centre. 'Janette Robertson.'

Clearly taken by surprise the woman looked to her son for some kind of explanation.

'Police officers, mother. Detective Sergeants Dawson and Wood.'

Dawson didn't correct Stacey's rank.

Janette Robertson's gaze lingered on him. 'Have we met?'

Dawson smiled at the well-kept, attractive woman. 'Let's just say I've been here before.'

It took only a nanosecond for the sharp brain to put it together. She removed her glasses and frowned.

'We don't do that any more.'

'I know, Mrs Robertson. That's not why we're here.'

Steven stepped in and explained the reason for their visit.

A range of emotions passed over her face ending with understanding.

'Please sit,' she said. 'Although Steven was correct in telling you that we can't really spare anyone to speak to you right now. This order…'

'We understand, Mrs Robertson,' Stacey offered. 'But do you know of any workers with a newborn, maybe a young, frightened girl who might have taken such action?'

She slowly shook her head. 'I'm sorry, I don't. I try not to get involved in the personal lives of my employees.'

Dawson thought of all the heads bowed beneath them on the factory floor and wondered if the woman even knew their names.

'Isn't there someone, anyone, you could spare for just a few minutes?' he asked.

Mrs Robertson turned to her son. 'Nicolae may be able to help.'

Steven nodded and stepped out of the office. He approached the railing at the end of the mezzanine and called down.

'Nicolae is our foreman,' Janette Robertson explained. 'He knows the girls better than we do. He may be able to help.'

'Things have moved on a bit since I was here last,' Dawson observed, looking around the stylish office.

'Yes, a six-figure fine and the threat of a prison sentence will do that to you,' she said, ruefully.

'Doesn't seem to have done you any harm,' he responded.

'I don't complain,' she said, as the glass door opened.

Behind Steven Robertson was a rugged-looking man in his early fifties. His piercing blue eyes added a gentleness to the weathered face. The stubble on his chin was 60/40 in favour of the grey. He wore a black, short-sleeved shirt, and plain black trousers.

'Hello, how may I help you?' he asked, pleasantly.

While his colleague filled the man in on the details, Dawson observed his body language and movement as he listened carefully.

Robertson's hands slid idly into his pockets as though that was his natural relaxed stance. There was no head bobbing or fidgeting, or licking or any other kind of tic that offered anything other than transparency.

When Stacey finished Nicolae thought for a few seconds and then began to shake his head.

'None of m… these girls have newborns that I know of. Natalya has a little girl aged ten back in Romania and Daniela a teenage boy but not newborns,' he said.

Just a trace of accent hung onto his perfect English. Dawson wondered how long he had been in the country.

'Would any of the employees here be able to offer—'

'I think we've covered that,' Steven said from the doorway.

'Nicolae,' Dawson said, turning to the foreman. 'Is there anywhere else we might try, anyone who might know?'

'Nail bars,' he offered. 'Try local nail bars.'

'Thank you,' Dawson said. It had been a long shot.

'I'll show you out,' Steven said, following Nicolae to the door. They bid farewell to Mrs Robertson and followed her son.

Of course, they should have thought of that sooner. Only last year almost a hundred people had been arrested as part of operation Magnify, an initiative aiming to tackle exploitative employers who provide low-paid jobs to illegal immigrants. The initial stage of the operation had focussed on construction, care, cleaning, catering, taxi and car wash industries. Nail bars had been highlighted as a particular workplace for exploitation.

It suddenly begged the questions in his mind:

Was the mother of this child an illegal immigrant?

Had she been pressured into giving up the baby?

Or was it more difficult for her to stay under the radar with a child?

Had the sacrifice been for the child or herself?

But those weren't the only questions on Dawson's mind. Allowing Stacey to lead the conversations was beneficial to him for a number of reasons. Her expertise and experience out in the field was severely limited but she was a fast learner. She watched carefully and soaked in all new data like a sponge giving him the chance to observe.

And right now he found himself wondering why, throughout that entire exchange, Janette Robertson and Nicolae had not looked at each other once.

CHAPTER EIGHTEEN

'Guv, did I do something to really piss you off?' Bryant asked, rubbing his hands together.

'Not yet, but I'm sure it's only a matter of time,' she said, from the other side of the doorway.

The smell of fresh meat wafted through the locked door of the halal butcher's shop.

'Only, I'm sure Kev and Stacey feel like they're really missing out on these field trips.'

'Yeah, well they're a bit busy trying to find the mother of an abandoned child right now,' she said, glancing left.

'What are we doing still here anyway?' he asked.

'Not quite sure, Bryant,' she said, glancing at Sal a few doorways down. 'But we need to get these registration numbers, and if you can offer a better suggestion I'm all ears, so get your notepad out.'

Sal's suggestion to stick around had not come easily to the woman. Donna had returned from the guy she'd caught at the Give Way sign and was now beside Sal halfway along the street in the doorway of a charity shop.

Of course, this was a task Kim could have delegated to members of her team. Standing in a shop doorway taking registration numbers of punters for follow-up was not her idea of a good night out. But she'd never been the type to ask her team to do something she was not prepared to do herself.

'Got one,' she said, as a car turned into the strip and slowed down. The aptness of the term 'kerb crawler' instantly sprang into her mind.

Suddenly the street came alive as a few more girls stepped out of the doorways and moved closer to the road. Gone was the shivering, hand-wringing and foot stamping to keep warm. Now it was Game On. The movements and poses reminded Kim of a body-building championship with each girl standing in a way to show off their best assets.

The vehicle gradually came to a stop near the end of the road.

A figure that Kim recognised stepped forward to the open passenger window.

'Damn it,' she breathed, fixing her eyes on the short curly hair of the girl dressed in jeans and trainers.

Bryant followed her gaze.

'Is that…'

'Gemma,' Kim answered when he hesitated over her name.

Kim wouldn't forget her name in a hurry. Four months before the girl had been sent by her sociopathic nemesis, Alexandra Thorne, to kill her and had it not been for a tortured, broken soul named Shane the girl might have had a shot.

Alex had spotted both the vulnerability and rage in the girl while she'd been visiting her mother who had been residing off and on in the same prison as Alex for most of Gemma's life.

Kim could easily imagine how Alex had manipulated the girl's need for a caring parental figure, evidenced by the prison visits despite the fact her mother had never managed to go straight for the sake of her own child. Alex had used that basic information to maximum effect.

Guided by Alex, Gemma had cleverly wormed her way into Kim's home. Kim had seen so much of herself in the spirited, angry kid and had even cooked her a meal. Hell, she'd never even cooked Bryant a meal, she thought as she continued to watch the transaction taking place.

Negotiations were brief and the girl got in the passenger door.

Watching the car drive away Kim couldn't help the swell of sadness that inexplicably rose within her.

'You liked her, eh?' Bryant asked as the car disappeared from view.

'I understood her,' Kim said, quietly.

And she had. Gemma's mother had been in and out of prison all her life. Eventually relatives had grown tired of taking in the spirited kid who played up because she never knew where she was going to be living from one month to the next. Once she hit thirteen she was left to fend for herself when her mother was put away. She had taken to the street to fulfil the most basic of needs. To eat.

And yet there was still a little girl inside who ached for her mother's approval, direction, discipline which had prompted the visits to prison and right into the waiting, manipulative arms of Alexandra Thorne who had spotted every similarity to Kim and every weakness the girl had before she'd even sat down. Gemma hadn't stood a chance.

'You never even mentioned her in your statement of what happened that night?' Bryant said.

She heard the accusation in his tone. The girl had tried to kill her, and Bryant would have been happier seeing her behind bars. Her choice not to bring charges had not gone down well with her colleague.

Kim shrugged. 'You think she's leading any kind of charmed life because I didn't?' she asked. Gemma's mother was still in prison and Alex would have forgotten her name by now. Gemma had failed and Alex didn't remember people who failed.

What had the experience earned her? She was back on the street selling her body for a warm meal.

As though reading her mind Bryant spoke quietly.

'Could you ever do it, guv?' he said, nodding to the females all returning to the doorways following the punter's choice of Gemma.

Kim opened her mouth but then closed it again. It was much too easy to say no. It was the moral answer, the expected response. The instant answer that kept this lifestyle away from respectable people. Realistically, that choice, that very decision, should have been much closer to her than it was. Her early years had dictated a propensity to self-destruction and addiction. Events had shaped her and prepared her for many versions of her future and not one of them included being a police officer.

Most people felt that a moral code was present from birth but in Kim's own experience that was not the case. She remembered reading a quote about a notorious killer – a child who had murdered two boys when she was eleven years old. Asked why she had done it she had stated 'because I didn't know it was wrong'.

Most people would find the simplicity of that statement unbelievable but Kim did not. Morals were formed by example, a learned behaviour, reinforced by continual practice and correction.

'Bryant, I have the luxury of not having to make that decision. But I'd ask you the same question.'

He thought for a moment. 'In all honesty, guv, to take care of and protect my family, there's probably not all that much that I wouldn't do if I needed to.'

Kim smiled at his honesty.

'Hey, here comes another,' she said.

The car slowed and stopped at the first girl. Donna Hill sashayed towards the car. Three feet away she raised her hand and shook her head. Kim watched with interest as Donna turned away. The heroin addict wasn't normally that fussy.

She turned again and stepped back towards the car. This time she leaned in closer and then shook her head. She stepped away and headed back into the shadows.

The car crawled slowly to the end of the strip but was not approached by any other girls.

Kim's stomach began to churn.

'Bit weird,' she said to Bryant. 'Put an asterisk by that one.'

They watched as Donna returned and re-took her place close to Sal.

Kim stepped back further into the doorway as a couple passed by. The man was much taller with his right arm draped around the shoulders of the woman. She watched their progress along the street. Not the normal area for a late-night stroll, not to mention the weather conditions.

As the couple passed the charity shop, Sal stepped forward and lit a cigarette, and then stepped back.

Kim looked again and saw that the hand of the man was not draped around the shoulders of the woman but was clutched over her shoulder like a claw.

'That's one,' Kim whispered, as the male deposited the girl at the Give Way sign and stepped back into the shadows.

This was the young girl tipped off to her by Sal. She had known it was happening tonight and the reason she'd encouraged Kim to stick around.

Kim took note of the jeans with a butterfly design on the pocket. The flat, patent shoes and the pink bubble gum puffer jacket.

Bryant nodded his agreement. 'Our northern guy shouldn't be too far away.'

Kim stared at the young girl whose shoulders were hunched against the cold. She knew that, regardless of any other fact, they were looking at a girl who had probably been hand-picked for the pleasure of some sicko because she was a virgin.

'This might be him,' Bryant said.

Kim turned her head towards a dark blue BMW 5 Series. As it passed them by Bryant took the private plate registration.

The car travelled slowly and didn't pause as the other girls stepped forward. The driver headed straight for the end of the strip.

Kim felt the anger begin to rise inside her. There was something authentic about a transaction that took place between two willing parties. A business arrangement between two consenting adults, but this was no such thing.

'Guv, I can see from that muscle in your cheek what you're thinking but there's nothing we can do.'

Right now they were gathering useful intelligence that could help further their investigation into the murder of a young prostitute named Kelly Rowe. Compromising their position for one young girl was not in the greater interest of the case.

'Jesus, Bryant, how stupid do you think I am?' she said, right before she stepped out of the doorway.

CHAPTER NINETEEN

Ellie woke to a dull thudding pain in her head. She groaned as she turned onto her back and opened her eyes. It took a few seconds for her to realise she was not in her own room. The ceiling was covered with some kind of bobbling effect. Her own ceiling was white with a few dark patches following her mother's attempt to paint over a night sky mural.

She sat up and instantly wished she hadn't. The nausea swirled around her stomach as bile bit the back of her throat. She covered her mouth and swallowed it back down.

First she looked down at herself. Her body was clad in cotton pyjamas bearing poodles. It took her a further few seconds to realise they were not hers. The room was pleasant but sparse. A dressing table and a wardrobe lined the walls along with a couple of framed photographs Ellie had seen in a dozen bargain shops. Finally, she realised she was definitely in someone's spare room.

She raised herself to a sitting position and closed her eyes, focussing on what she last remembered. She recalled getting off the bus at Cradley Heath station. But when that was she couldn't be sure.

Her heart quickened as she recalled the two men who had robbed her.

She remembered Roxanne guiding her to the car and pulling onto the drive of a semi-detached house with a garage.

She remembered Roxanne had told her to drink some liquid to calm her nerves. The drink had burned, she'd coughed and Roxanne had laughed.

Ellie remembered sitting at the kitchen table while the radio played gently in the background. She had felt so grown up, drinking coffee and talking to an adult that was not her mother.

Roxanne had been so understanding. She had listened for hours, pausing only to refill her drink, while Ellie had talked about her problems.

Her eyes widened and her hand flew to her mouth. Her mother would be worried sick.

She scrabbled from beneath the covers at the exact second that the bedroom door opened.

Roxanne entered wearing leggings and an oversized jumper.

'Hey, sleepy head, how are you feeling?'

'I don't… I'm not…'

Roxanne sat beside her on the bed and chuckled.

'You fell asleep right in front of me. I was just coming to check for a pulse. I let you sleep because you had quite an ordeal earlier. Shock can sometimes do that. But you're awake now so—'

'My mum, I need to let her know…'

'Don't worry, it's all fine.' Roxanne patted her knee and smiled. 'Come down when you're ready and we'll get you sorted. The bathroom is on the right.'

Roxanne stood and left the room.

Ellie looked around for her clothes. All she saw was her watch beside the bed. It told her it was almost eight p.m. She'd left the house at nine o'clock that morning.

She slipped her feet into a pair of moccasin slippers and padded to the bathroom. Once outside the room her nostrils were overpowered by aromas from downstairs. The smell of meat roasting and vegetables steaming hit her in the stomach. She mustn't have eaten all day.

Before she left the bathroom she threw cold water on her face. She followed the trail of the smells to the kitchen.

'Umm... Roxanne... my clothes?'

'Just next door in the washer. They'll be freshly ironed and ready for you to wear in about an hour.'

Ellie instantly felt that was really thoughtful.

'So, you're not gonna leave me to eat by myself, are you?' Roxanne asked as she took a dish of roast potatoes from the oven and shook them. They were browned and crispy and Ellie's mouth began to water.

The radio was still playing quietly in the background. The washing machine rumbled in the utility room next door and the meal being cooked smelled positively delicious. At this moment in time, Ellie had no wish to be anywhere else.

'It's just my mum...'

'Don't worry about that, right now. I've taken care of it. Now all I need to know is should I reach for one plate or two?'

'Two,' Ellie said, bravely.

She was already in a whole heap of trouble with her mother. She would be grounded for the next ten years, so one more hour would hardly make the difference.

Being around Roxanne was like being in a dream. She was tall, slim and glamorous. And she was now Ellie's friend.

Ellie sat back and watched as Roxanne carved two slices of meat for them both. She carved a third small piece, turned and popped it in Ellie's mouth.

'Nice?'

The beef was succulent and tasty and melted in her mouth. At home she normally had gristle-laden pork that she chewed for most of the afternoon.

Roxanne added a portion of broccoli to Ellie's plate.

'Enough?'

Ellie nodded as Roxanne put the pan to the side. 'I can't stand the stuff.'

She took the roasters from the oven and spooned a liberal amount onto each plate. The kettle boiled and Roxanne added the hot water to a jug of gravy granules.

'Can you stir this a minute while I get the star of the show?'

Ellie stirred the thick brown liquid as Roxanne opened the door of a second oven on the other side of the room. She wasn't sure what else could fit on the plate.

'Ta dah, what do you think?'

Ellie gasped at the tray holding the two largest Yorkshire puddings she'd ever seen.

'Home-made,' Roxanne said, proudly.

Ellie's stomach growled in response and they both laughed. She sat as Roxanne finished plating the meal. She set the steaming platter before her and held a knife and fork aloft.

'Veg first, okay? I'm not having your mum moaning at me.'

Ellie nodded and tucked into the broccoli. She'd had the vegetable before but it had never tasted like this. She was about to ask what she'd added to it but Roxanne spoke first.

'So, how are you feeling about everything now?'

Ellie considered her response. The anxiety she felt around her mother was gone. Sitting in pyjamas eating a delicious Sunday lunch with this glamorous woman taking such an interest in her was flattering. She couldn't remember a time she'd felt so relaxed.

'Happy,' she answered.

Roxanne smiled and nodded before spearing a roast potato.

'Listen, I've done something I hope you don't mind. After our chat earlier it seemed to me that tensions between you and your mum are at breaking point. Perhaps what you need is a bit of time apart.'

Ellie nodded her understanding.

'Sometimes it's all that's needed. It gives you a chance to miss each other a little bit.'

Ellie thought about that and it seemed like a good idea.

'But she doesn't know where—'

'It's okay. I've messaged three of your friends on Facebook and asked them to give your mum a call and let her know that you're safe. I explained what happened earlier and I've asked them to pass on my mobile number so your mum can ring me any time she wants to.'

'So, she knows?'

'Yes, sweetie. She knows you're safe, so you don't need to worry about that.' She shrugged and put down her knife and fork. 'So, the choice is yours. Your clothes will be ready in a bit and I'll put you in a taxi back home or you could chill here with me for a day or two, do some girly stuff, build a snowman and go back home feeling calmer and more objective about the whole thing.'

Ellie put down her knife and fork, after she'd cleared her plate. The temptation of the offer was too attractive to refuse. The idea of not having to face her mother for a few more days felt like Christmas morning. And as long as her mother knew she was safe and with an appropriate adult, Ellie could really see no reason to refuse.

'I'd love to stay if it's really no bother,' she said, remembering her manners.

''Course not, sweetie. I wouldn't have offered if I hadn't meant it.'

Roxanne took the plates, emptied her own leftovers into the bin and placed the dishes in the dishwasher.

'Okay, go find a DVD while I fix us a hot chocolate.'

Ellie stepped across the hallway and into the lounge. The DVD collection consisted mainly of chick flicks that were totally uncool but enjoyable nonetheless. She took out a few for a shortlist and was down to three by the time Roxanne entered the room with two steaming mugs.

'What have you got?'

Ellie held the three films aloft.

'It's got to be Bridget Jones,' Roxanne said, emphatically.

Ellie put the DVD into the player and took her place on the two-seater sofa.

The credits began to roll and out of the corner of her eye she saw Roxanne pick up her mobile phone and check it. A frown passed across her face as Ellie guessed she was probably wondering why she hadn't yet received a call from her mother.

And if she was honest she was beginning to wonder the same thing herself.

CHAPTER TWENTY

It was almost nine when Dawson parked up at the factory. Just as an articulated lorry was pulling out. He kept the engine running to wipe away the thickening snowflakes. Stacey was struggling to remember a day that it hadn't snowed.

'Looks like they made their deadline,' she observed, pushing open the car door.

'Not yet,' Dawson said, placing a hand on her arm.

'But I thought you wanted to speak to some of the girls,' she said, closing the door again.

'I do, but preferably without the Robertsons or Igor in the background.'

'You mean Nicolae, the foreman,' she said.

'Yeah, him. Didn't you get the feeling the bosses didn't really want us speaking to the girls?'

The lorry had just laboured around the corner and out of view.

'Well they weren't lying about getting that order out,' she said.

'I'm sure a couple of minutes wouldn't have hurt,' he replied, and she agreed with him.

Right now there was a baby in the care of foster parents who needed to be back with his mother. She doubted that a few minutes would have made the difference.

'Well, the bosses have obviously left for the night,' she said.

'How do you know?' he asked, looking towards the building.

'The silver-and-black Mercs parked here earlier have gone,' she observed.

He said nothing. Clearly he did not notice everything.

'So, we're waiting for them to leave work so you can try and speak to a couple privately?' she clarified.

'That's the idea, and it shouldn't be long now,' he said, as the showroom light went out.

He pulled the car further along the car park, nearer to the reception door.

'Come on,' he urged towards the building. 'You'd think they'd be spewing out of there like rats down a drainpipe,' he said.

It wasn't an analogy she liked but she too would have thought they'd be eager to leave the premises after what must have been an intensely long and gruelling shift.

Dawson's eyes were trained on the reception door.

'Come on,' he repeated, impatiently. 'They should have been coming out—'

'Kev, look,' she said, pointing to the rear-view mirror.

'What the…?'

A blue minibus had exited the gate. And it looked like it was carrying every single worker.

CHAPTER TWENTY-ONE

Kim hurtled along Tavistock Road frantically waving her right hand in the air. 'Maddie, Maddie, is that you?'

She felt every pair of eyes on her as she jogged along the pavement.

The young girl stood beside the open door of the car.

'Hang on, Maddie, it's me…'

Kim reached the door and slammed it shut. She grabbed the girl by the upper arms. Looking into the startled eyes of a frightened kid who looked no older than fifteen, Kim locked her gaze.

'Run, run now and don't stop.'

Kim turned her around and pushed her back along the strip.

The girl didn't hesitate. She turned and ran as the blue BMW sped up and rounded the corner out of sight.

Kim turned as the minder began to make chase. She threw herself into his path. He towered above her by a good four inches. He tried to dance around her but she danced along with him. He reached out and tried to swipe her out of the way. Kim grabbed his wrist and turned it. He screamed out in pain and fell to the ground. Kim followed and landed on top of him. He wrestled his arm free and tried to use it to push himself up. Kim managed to get a knee in his balls.

He groaned and tried to push her away.

'Bitch, get off me now,' he growled.

'Sorry, I thought I knew her,' Kim said, wrestling him back down.

'Bitch, I ain't kidding. Get the fuck off me now or you is gonna regret it.'

Kim moved to the side. 'Hey, you ran into me,' she said, standing up and dusting herself down.

The male looked past her but the young girl was long gone.

He shook his head. 'Fucking crazy bitch,' he said, walking past her.

Kim looked along the strip, searching for the woman who had given her the tip. A few faces smiled begrudgingly in her direction but Sal was already busy getting into a car at the other end of the street.

CHAPTER TWENTY-TWO

Andrei tried to ignore the shiver that vibrated through his body. They were becoming much more frequent and violent. It was like a rumble of thunder that began at his core and reverberated through every fragment of his body.

Each one left him more exhausted than the last.

At first he had tried to hunch his back against the biting wind, to form himself into a smaller being but his broken leg prevented him bringing up his knees. He had tried to turn his face away from the snow when it had turned to hailstones in the early hours of the morning. The pellets of ice had left the skin on his cheeks reddened and sore before falling onto his trousers and melting into the wet fabric sticking to his skin.

He couldn't count the hours he'd sat in the weeds. He knew that darkness had come and gone and snuck up on him again. He thought it was only once but could no longer be sure.

The snow had continued to fall heavily bringing a lonely stillness to the world. The distant hum of traffic at the bridge had died down a long time ago and had never returned. He could not hear life or movement anywhere.

He had wondered if the heavy snowfall had stopped the man from coming back for him. But he knew he was just fooling himself.

He had already tried to move along the bank twice and each three foot distance had exhausted him. He had tried to move away from the bridge as he knew he would never be able to get up the steep slope that led back to the road but trying to shuffle along without moving his leg had been futile.

And he knew he didn't have the energy to try again.

His hardest fight right now was exhaustion.

Oh, how he wanted to give into it and yet something stopped him. He had a sense that he was not being pulled towards sleep, that there was a finality just waiting to grab him as he closed his eyes.

Any hope of being saved had gone. He had not seen or heard a soul since he'd been dumped here and yet he still felt the need to hang on.

The pain was excruciating and yet somehow reassuring because it told him he was still alive. But his mind was playing tricks on him. He kept remembering a night in a lorry many years ago. He wanted to reach into the crook of his arms even though he knew there was no one there, sleeping beside him.

He could feel the pull of his eyes. Every muscle reached out towards the beckoning darkness. The pain in his broken leg made him groan out loud.

Suddenly the tears spilled out from his eyes. In a moment of clarity he realised that he was going to die.

Panic surged through his mind. He didn't want to die. There were things he needed to say, should have said, should have explained to the only person that mattered. He knew that moments of consciousness were now as precious as his only child.

The emotion gathered in his throat and it tasted like regret.

I don't want to leave you, my love, his mind screamed.

His last conscious thought was whispered into the breeze.

'Who will care for you now?'

CHAPTER TWENTY-THREE

It was eleven thirty when Kim opened her front door.

Following her scuffle with the minder and armed with a page full of registration numbers, Bryant had dropped her off at the station.

'Hey, you, come here,' she said, as Barney sashayed towards her. His black-and-white head was tipped slightly to the left as he rubbed against her. His tail thumped against the door frame.

'If I had a tail it would be wagging right now too,' she said, rubbing his thick fur all over. No matter what the day had held, Barney's welcome was enough to put a smile on her face.

She glanced towards the fireplace, as she always did, as though checking that the photo was still there. The two of them, her and Mikey, sitting side-on and turned forward to the camera. It was the last remaining copy of their only school photograph taken when they were six years old, their dark heads close together. She could almost feel the sensation of his hair against her cheek.

She remembered that she'd had to tickle him to make him smile for the camera but he'd not had a lot to smile about. When not at school they had both spent every waking moment trying to protect him from their mother whose paranoid schizophrenia had convinced her that he was the devil.

And two months after the photograph was taken the bitch had got her wish and Mikey had died of starvation in her arms.

And yet, this photograph didn't remind her of the bad times. It served to remind her that they had laughed as kids and had

had each other. It helped her recall how much she had loved him. It meant she would never forget the tarry blackness of his hair or the amber colour of his eyes or what his face had looked like in laughter.

It reminded her that he had lived.

She removed her jacket and put on a pot of coffee. Despite the time she knew it wouldn't be wasted.

She turned to the dog and patted her chest. 'Up,' she said.

His front paws landed gently and she felt between the pads. There was a slight dampness to the protruding fur which told her Charlie hadn't long delivered him back from an afternoon two doors down finished off with a gentle stroll around the block.

She grabbed his eager face in her hands and planted kisses on the top of his warm head. 'Wanna go again?' she asked.

His behind started to move from side to side making it unclear if the dog was wagging the tail or the tail wagging the dog.

'Okay, half a cup and we're off,' she said, pouring a small amount of coffee into a mug.

He sat and patiently watched her. She would swear that he understood.

She loved their late-night walks. There would be few people around right now, which suited them both perfectly. The inclement weather conditions didn't bother either of them and there was nothing to keep her here.

For the first time in years the only motorcycle in her garage was the Kawasaki Ninja that had been benched due to the snow. Her last project had been sold and the proceeds donated to the PDSA, so right now her garage floor was swept and tidy, the work surfaces were free of motorbike parts and every oily rag was folded neatly in a drawer. And she bloody well hated it.

She hoped the walk would deplete her remaining energy levels and help make her ready for bed. The normal process of sleep often eluded her.

Normal people lay down, closed their eyes and controlled their conscious minds for a short while. Lists would be made, chores would be identified, the day's events analysed and the following day organised. But then some magic would occur when the mind took control and offered its own thoughts, a delicious state of limbo where the sleeper was no longer the driver but the passenger being guided into unconsciousness by their own mind.

Kim's own journey from A to B could only be achieved once exhaustion was totally upon her. And the night's events were still spinning around her head.

Of course they hadn't been on Tavistock Road to interfere. There was a dead girl in the morgue who needed answers but how could she, in all good conscience, stand in the doorway taking registration numbers knowing that a young girl was being offered as a sacrificial lamb to a pervert who liked young girls? That the girl had been an unwilling party had been evident in her eyes.

Kai Lord was not a stupid man and it would not take long for him to put two and two together and make four. He would know it was her that had interfered with the transaction and probably cost him a lot of money.

She smiled to herself. Oh well, too bad. That was definitely not a fact that would keep her awake at night.

The smile was wiped from her face as she heard a sound at the front door. She tipped her head, listening for any follow-up noises. Nothing. She headed for the kitchen and took a carving knife from the drawer. She turned off the lounge light and edged towards the front door, placing Barney firmly behind her.

She stood in the darkness of the hall as she looked around the doorway but there was no shadow against the crescent-shaped piece of glass at the top level. The deadbolts were still engaged and the chain still bridged the door to the frame.

Kim placed the knife on the table and opened the front door. She looked to the ground. Ten minutes earlier her feet had been the only ones to have trodden the fresh snow. And now she could see clearly a second set of prints double trodden as they approached and then receded from her doorway.

She stepped out, pulled the door closed behind her and followed the prints to the end of the road, where they simply stopped.

So, her visitor had either grown wings and flown away or parked away from her house and then walked down.

Kim quickly assessed the surroundings. Only a handful of lights illuminated the quiet street and those were shrouded in heavy curtains to keep out the cold. The sound of a car pulling to the side of the road would hardly have produced spectators or inquisitive glances.

Kim rubbed her bare arms and trudged back to her home. She locked the door behind her and turned on the light.

And that was when she saw it.

A slip of paper had been posted through her letterbox and had fluttered to the ground.

She reached down and picked it up, turning it over. The paper simply stated a name. A frown rested on her face as she reached for Barney's lead.

If this was anything to do with the death of Kelly Rowe then someone linked to the investigation knew where she lived.

CHAPTER TWENTY-FOUR

'Okay, boys and girls, are we all sitting comfortably?' Kim asked, perching her bottom on the edge of the spare desk.

They all nodded in her direction.

She'd just had a call from the front desk, so by her reckoning she had approximately two minutes to come clean.

'Boss, there's something not right about the Robertsons's place. They've got the girls being ferried in and out on a—'

'Okay, Kev, just give me a minute to—'

'Owners wouldn't even let us have a word with a couple of the women to see if—'

'All right, Kev, I just want to share something—'

'Hey there, peeps,' said a voice from the door.

Kim groaned inside. He'd obviously made the stairs quicker than she'd thought.

All heads turned to the gangly male dressed in plain black trousers and an open-neck check shirt. The strap of a man-bag cut diagonally across his chest. The bandana holding back the fair curls was tie-dyed green.

'Guys, you remember Detective Sergeant Penn from West Mercia?'

Dawson and Bryant nodded suspiciously while Stacey simply frowned. She knew the name and she knew of his involvement in the Hate Crimes case that had almost cost her her life but they had never met.

'He's agreed to come on over to us for a little while to help out,' Kim said.

Secondments in the police normally fell into three categories: overseas deployment, mission deployment or under section 97 of the Police Act covering the need for specific expertise.

'I need someone to liaise with the teams out in the field gathering information on Kelly Rowe—'

'So, he's replacing me?' Dawson asked.

'And I want someone equally capable of data mining and—'

'So, he's replacing me?' Stacey asked.

Penn stood in the doorway, watching the exchange with amusement.

'And someone who knows the area well,' she said.

Penn had moved from Halesowen to West Hagley seven years earlier when he was twenty-three. When Woody had generously left the case of the abandoned child on their desks she had insisted that she needed an additional two officers. He had agreed on one and she had specifically requested the assistance of Austin Penn.

Bryant stood and strode towards him with his hand outstretched.

'Welcome to the team, Penn,' he said, pleasantly.

Bryant's act seemed to press the refresh button on common courtesy as both Dawson and Stacey rose to shake his hand.

'Where do you want me?' Penn asked, stepping into the room.

She removed her behind from the spare desk and pointed. She perched next to the coffee machine at the top of the office.

'Okay, Penn got his logins and access yesterday and started work remotely.' She nodded towards him. 'Anything to do with Kelly on the CCTV front?'

He grimaced as he removed his bag and set his coat on the back of the chair. 'No local authority cameras close by. I've checked three service stations in the immediate area that caught nothing and a timber yard that covers the footpath completely is not currently in working order.'

They all groaned.

'Want me to go any further out on that, boss? I'm at a radius of just under a mile.'

Kim appreciated that he would respect her authority so quickly. Travis was his real boss. She shook her head. There was no point. Anything caught further away from the crime scene would be useless.

'To recap from yesterday: we know that Kelly Rowe was one of Kai's girls.'

'Anything to connect him to her murder?' Dawson asked, quickly.

Oh, how she wished there was.

'Not yet,' she answered. 'Her mother knew nothing of Kelly's new career and thought she was working late nights at a bar. We found a pimp payment book which we now believe to be that of Kai Lord—'

'Jesus, for a first-timer she couldn't have got caught up with anyone worse,' Dawson said.

Kim continued. 'By the looks of it she got desperate for money and took a loan from him without fully understanding the repercussions. The interest rate was extortionate but she worked hard and was close to paying it off.'

'Always someone waiting to take advantage,' Stacey said.

Kim nodded. 'Oh yeah, but what I'm struggling with at the moment is an obvious link between Kelly and Kai Lord. I can't see where their paths would naturally cross. Before moving back in with her mother Kelly rented a converted flat in a decent street in Netherton neither close to Hollytree nor Tavistock Road. So, there had to be a broker that put them in touch with each other.'

'I'll dig a bit on that,' Penn offered.

'We also got a lead on a customer that works with kids and apparently he's a bit weird,' she said, emphasising the word *weird*. 'We're heading over to the community centre on Hollytree to see if anyone there knows him, and we collected registration numbers of potential punters and witnesses.'

'Not all we did last night, was it, guv?' Bryant asked, raising an eyebrow.

'There was an attempt from one of Kai's minions to hand over a girl to a customer who likes them young. Luckily, that transaction was thwarted,' she explained.

'What did you do, boss?' Dawson asked.

Why did he assume she had done anything at all?

Bryant grinned. 'Well, let's say I've been tackled on the rugby pitch with more finesse.'

'Hey,' she defended. 'We got the punter's registration number, didn't we?'

And for a full day's work yesterday that was all that she had. If they didn't make serious progress on the case today it wouldn't be just the press after her blood. Woody would be leading the pack.

'So, Kev, any progress on our child?'

'Our child, boss?' he asked with a lopsided smile.

She narrowed her eyes.

'Sorry. As I was saying earlier we tried to speak to the girls at Robertson's…'

Kim nodded. It was well known that they employed a high percentage of Romanian women. It's where she would have started.

'Bosses there wouldn't allow us even a few minutes. We went back later just as they were all being ferried out of there on a minibus.'

Kim frowned. 'You going back?'

Dawson nodded. 'We'll give it another try.'

'Okay, but if you have no luck, cast your net wider.'

He nodded his understanding.

Kim took a piece of paper from her pocket and handed it to Penn. He looked at it and read it aloud.

'Lauren Goddard.'

Kim shrugged in the face of everyone's puzzled expressions.

'I have no idea either but that note was hand delivered to my home late last night.'

Stacey's mouth dropped open. Kev shook his head and Bryant swore under his breath.

Kim held up her hands. 'It's fine, guys, honestly. Whoever left this thinks they're trying to help.'

'Still, though, boss,' Dawson said.

She waved away his concern and turned to the newest recruit. 'Penn, I know it's not much to go on but see what you can dig up?'

Penn nodded and began tapping away at his keyboard.

'Also, Penn, Bryant will pass you the registration numbers from last night. Can you start to get some names? Two are marked. Start with those.'

Bryant took the paper from his inside pocket and handed it across the office as two figures appeared in the doorway.

'You asked to see us, Marm?'

She cringed at the term but waved them in.

The older male stepped into the room but the younger male stood in the doorway. Both were dressed from head to toe in black. Combat trousers with black T-shirts and a standard issue stab vest. Instantly they reminded Kim of the two guys from *Law and Order*. The older officer looked weathered but friendly. The younger male was obscenely good-looking and well sculpted beneath the black.

The older male introduced himself as Sergeant Gerry Evans and his colleague as Constable Ian Skitt.

'Thanks for coming up, guys. Just wanted a word about Tavistock Road. That's your area, right?'

Kim looked from one to the other. PC Skitt stood in the doorway saying nothing and looking to the floor. She was struck by the fact that there were some officers that really made the uniform look good. She looked at the paunch on Sergeant Evans. And then there were some that really didn't.

Sergeant Evans put his hands inside his vest and rested them on his chest.

'It's part of our beat,' he said, using an old-fashioned term.

'Girls said anything to you about any new guys on the scene?'

Evans shook his head. 'Terrible business about Kelly Rowe. Kid only wanted to take care of her little 'un.'

'Was there any animosity out on the streets towards Kelly? Any enemies that you know of?'

He straightened and seemed to be trying to suck in his generous belly. 'Wouldn't have mattered with Kai Lord as her pimp: no one was gonna touch her.'

But they had, she thought to herself.

'Okay, guys. If you do hear anything, let us know, eh?'

'Will do, Marm,' Evans said, heading towards the door.

Kim had a sudden thought. 'Sergeant, does the name Lauren Goddard mean anything to you?'

Gerry Evans's eyes rolled up and to the left. Slowly he shook his head.

'Should it?'

'Not sure.'

She turned, fixing Skitt with a look. 'You?'

He shook his head and returned his gaze to the ground.

'Is she a prostitute?' Evans asked.

Kim shrugged. At this point she had no idea.

'I can ask around, if you like. See if the name means anything?'

'Yeah, if you would,' she said.

'Of course, you know that some girls use a—'

'Different name out on the street. Yes, I know.'

'Leave it with us, Marm,' he said, as the two of them left the office.

Kim felt an unease worm under her skin. Ian Skitt had not been able to meet her gaze once.

'Hey, Sergeant,' she called out. Evans's head reappeared.

'Is he okay?' she asked, nodding towards the door.

Evans lowered his voice. 'He's a bit strange, I suppose. He's not a mixer. Keeps himself to himself but he ain't a bad lad.'

'Okay, thanks, Sergeant.'

'You know,' he said, thoughtfully, 'there is somewhere you could try: that shelter on Pearson Street. It's a druggie drop-in centre but a lot of the girls pop in there for a warm cuppa, handful of condoms and stuff.'

Kim knew the one he was talking about.

'Okay, cheers,' she said as he nodded and disappeared from view.

His younger colleague had already left.

CHAPTER TWENTY-FIVE

'So, what do you think?' Stacey asked as soon as the boss had left the room. She had taken the new boy up to introduce him to Woody and Stacey was unsure how she felt about his presence.

He shrugged. 'Looks like one of us is fighting for their job,' he said, seriously. 'It's like a scene out of *Gladiator* and only one of us can survive.'

Her eyes widened. 'Kev, I ay gonna…'

'Oh, Stace, stop being so gullible,' he said, laughing.

In all honesty she wanted to hate the new guy. The team worked just fine without any additional help. She'd happily have covered both roles if the boss had asked but she knew he'd been instrumental in saving her life. Something she needed to address when she got the chance.

'So, how do we find out where that bloody minibus went?' Dawson asked, tapping his index finger on the mouse.

The previous night they had turned the car around and headed after the vehicle, but they'd been too late due to a juggernaut forcing them to stay on the trading estate as it took four attempts to negotiate the corner turn onto the main road.

'It could have gone anywhere,' Stacey said. 'And if I'm honest, Kev,' she offered quietly, 'I'm not too sure what following it would have achieved. So far no one has done anything wrong.'

He frowned at her across the desk as Penn slid back into the room and into his seat. He threw a lazy smile in their general direction before reaching down to his right.

'Is your gut not in overdrive at the minute?'

She shrugged as she watched Penn retrieve a set of headphones from his man-bag and put them over his ears.

'The Robertsons would not allow us to speak to their employees yesterday,' Dawson said.

'Because they were under pressure to dispatch a shipment,' she said, reasonably.

'We return to try and speak to them later and they are bundled onto a minibus and whisked away before we get a chance.'

'Waiting for the crime here, Kev,' she said. 'Firstly, no one died. There's no murder or indication of foul play. It's very likely an overwhelmed young mother who couldn't cope with a newborn. Hell, we doe even know if she is Romanian. That shawl coulda been picked up at any charity shop. Could have been a gift.'

'She's Romanian,' he said, quietly but definitely.

Stacey shook her head. 'And you're sure of this because?'

'Where were the baby's clothes from?'

'Matalan,' she answered.

'And the coat?'

'Primark,' she said.

Identifying the clothing had been one of the first jobs on their list.

'Any physical injuries noted?'

She shook her head, glancing towards Penn who had not looked their way once. She appreciated his unwillingness to try and insert himself into what they were discussing, although she suspected he couldn't hear their voices above the music in his ears.

'So the child was well cared for, not abused by someone on limited means,' Dawson said.

She nodded her agreement.

'Except the shawl doesn't fit.'

'Why not?'

'This baby was loved, Stace. His mother took very good care of him. Now picture that she's giving him up for good. In her mind she's never going to see him again. You can't leave a note because you don't want to be found. So, what's the only thing you can do?'

She got what he was trying to say. 'Give the child something personal,' she breathed.

He nodded. 'That's why I think the blanket is important,' he said, grabbing the car keys. 'So, let's get out and solve this thing.'

Stacey grabbed her satchel and followed him out of the door, following Dawson's lead and nodding towards Penn on the way out. She had almost reached the top of the stairs before she tapped Dawson on the shoulder.

'Give me a minute, will yer, Kev? I'll catch up.'

Dawson frowned, shrugged and headed down the stairs.

* * *

She walked back to the office and stood next to Penn's desk.

'Hi,' he said, raising one eyebrow.

'Could you…?' she said, pointing at the headphones.

'Sure,' he said, taking them off and placing them on the desk.

Stacey wasn't really sure what she wanted to say. She just knew she needed to say something. 'Listen, about the case… your involvement… putting together the invitation and…'

He waved away her words. 'Just doing my job, Stacey, and pleased it all came out well and we got you back safe and sound.'

There was a bright and breezy tone to his words that belied the seriousness of the situation. She knew it had been two months but the event was still pretty monumental in her thoughts. Clearly not so much in his.

He glanced towards the headphones. 'Are we done?' he asked. 'Only I need to get back…'

'Of course,' Stacey said, flummoxed.

Somehow she had expected a different kind of conversation between the two of them.

She shook it off and stepped out of the room. She hesitated and took three steps back. Despite his lack of emotional warmth towards her, she still didn't want to see him in hot water with the boss.

'Umm... Penn,' she said.

He turned his head to face her.

'Not sure the boss would approve of you listening to music during working hours,' she said, not unkindly.

He shook his head. 'No music,' he said, handing her the headphones.

All she heard was nothing.

'You wear silent headphones?'

He nodded, taking them from her.

'Why?' she asked, frowning.

He hesitated as though a memory passed through his mind but he shrugged it away. 'Just helps me focus, is all,' he said.

'Okay, cool,' Stacey said, as he put them back on and turned back to the computer.

Feeling as though she'd been dismissed, Stacey headed towards the stairs. She forced herself to remember that Penn was not a part of their team. He had his own team and they had merely borrowed him to help out. He would return to his own crew and she was unlikely to ever see him again.

* * *

She still had the feeling that there was much more to the bandana-wearing Penn than met the eye when she reached Dawson who was waiting at the bottom of the stairs.

'Everything okay?' he asked, as his phone rang. He frowned at the display.

'Dawson,' he answered, foregoing his usual greeting of 'yo' for people he knew.

His frown turned to surprise and then back to a frown. He mouthed the word 'Keats' to Stacey. The pathologist only called their boss, or Bryant at a push. But never either of them.

'Sorry, but what does that have to do with…' she heard him say.

His jaw slackened as he listened to the answer.

'Got it,' he said. 'We're on our way.'

'What the… where are we…'

'Looks like you were wrong earlier, Stace,' he said, with a tight smile.

She waited for his explanation.

'Looks like someone did die after all.'

CHAPTER TWENTY-SIX

'Go on, try it on,' Roxanne urged, as Ellie touched the shoulder of a denim jacket. A printed design of a butterfly decorated the back.

'I can't,' Ellie said, shaking her head. Even if her money had not been taken she would not have been able to purchase the item. Her mum would have said she had two perfectly good jackets in her wardrobe. That they were two years old and tight on her upper arms would have prompted an argument about her being an ungrateful child.

'Oh, go on,' Roxanne said, smiling. Her own arms were laden with jeans, jumpers and a couple of pairs of boots. 'It's just a bit of fun. Come on, I don't like going into the changing rooms alone and you can tell me how this lot looks.'

Ellie nodded her agreement. There was something surreal about her current situation. Shopping in Primark on a Monday morning was not something she would ever have done with her mother. All her friends had been trudging to and from school the last couple of months before exams started but Ellie couldn't even see the point any more. It was only leading her to a future she didn't want. By now her mother should know that she had not turned up for school and Ellie hoped she now realised that this was more than a tantrum.

Being with Roxanne was fun, forbidden and a little bit exciting. Roxanne was not like a motherly figure. She was much too young and pretty for that tag.

She was honest enough to admit that she was flattered by the attention she was receiving from this confident, glamorous woman. Roxanne seemed to enjoy her company and treated her like an adult. She listened to whatever Ellie had to say. She didn't roll her eyes or set her mouth in measured tolerance, and Ellie didn't feel that Roxanne was mentally compiling the weekly shopping list as she spoke.

Roxanne pulled back the curtain of one cubicle and sorted the clothes into two piles. An attendant appeared behind them.

'Is there anything I can help you with?'

'We're fine, thanks,' Roxanne said, pleasantly. 'Just having a little spend.'

'I'd like an older sister like you,' the attendant laughed.

Roxanne widened her eyes at Ellie, amused at the assumption. Before Ellie had a chance to correct the attendant. Roxanne pulled her close and ruffled her hair.

'She's worth it.'

The attendant smiled and walked away.

'Here, this is your pile,' Roxanne said, thrusting an armful of clothes towards her.

Ellie opened her mouth to protest but Roxanne had already closed the curtain behind her.

Ellie stepped into the next cubicle and removed her jeans. She pulled on the trousers which felt soft but crisp against her skin. She chose a pink T-shirt bearing an emblem of a spotted bow. Not appropriate for the current climate but that made it even more fun.

She was about to remove it when Roxanne called for her to come out.

Ellie pulled back the curtain and Roxanne clapped her hands with delight. 'Oh, you look adorable, turn round.'

Ellie chuckled, enjoying the pleasure on Roxanne's face. It was difficult not to get caught up in the woman's infectious excitement.

She changed the T-shirt and donned the jacket. She stepped out to Roxanne holding a pair of flat shoes with black bows. 'Here, try these.'

Ellie slipped them on and felt like a fourteen-year-old but the sensation of the new clothes against her skin was seductive.

'You look positively lovely,' Roxanne said, bunching her hair into a ponytail. Ellie saw her shake her head in the mirror from behind. 'Young girls are just too eager to grow up these days. Youth should be enjoyed not escaped,' she said, resting her hands on Ellie's shoulders.

'But you haven't changed clothes,' Ellie said to Roxanne's reflection.

Roxanne put a finger to her lips. 'All the jeans I chose are too tight. It must be the meals we've been eating.'

Ellie laughed.

Roxanne tapped her shoulders. 'Okay, so change, pass the clothes out and I'll put them back and then we must have a drink. Shopping is thirsty work.'

Ellie did as she was told and passed the clothing back out to her new friend.

As she put on her old clothes she had the feeling that she was playing truant from her real life. All her problems, her worries still existed but just not here. She knew she would have to face them some time but she wasn't ready to leave Roxanne. Not quite yet.

Ellie exited the dressing rooms and looked above the clothing racks for Roxanne's red head. She spied her near to the entrance.

As the figure came into view Ellie saw that she was holding a clutch of brown Primark bags.

Roxanne smiled and thrust them towards her. 'Happy birthday,' she said, smiling.

Ellie shook her head. 'But I can't. I mean it's not...'

'The presents are early. You'll be home by then, so I have to do it now.'

'No, Roxanne, honestly. I can't accept—'

'Ellie, please. I'd like to make you this gift. I feel terrible for what happened to you on Saturday. It wouldn't have happened if I hadn't asked you to come and meet me.' Roxanne held up her hands. 'It's the least I could do, so please just forget it. It wasn't a lot of money and any further argument is gonna offend me. Okay?'

Ellie closed her mouth. That was the last thing she wanted to do.

'Now, come on. I'm as dry as a bone. We need a drink.'

Roxanne headed towards Starbucks in the next mall.

'You get a table,' Roxanne instructed. 'Cappuccino or milk-shake?'

'Cappuccino,' Ellie answered, feeling quite sophisticated.

As Roxanne joined the queue, Ellie sat at one of the window seats. She sneaked a look in the bags to find that some packs of underwear and socks had been added also. Ellie wondered how she could ever repay this woman's kindness.

She glanced at Roxanne. Now at the head of the queue waiting for the drinks. Ellie watched as she reached into her handbag and removed her mobile phone and scrolled. She then tried to sneak the phone back into her handbag before handing a £5 note to the server.

Ellie felt emotion clog her throat.

Roxanne placed the drinks on the table and took the tray back to the counter.

Ellie waited until she was seated

'Roxanne, you don't have to do that, you know.'

Roxanne looked blank. 'What?'

'Check your phone secretly. You can't hide the fact that my mother hasn't called to check on me.'

Roxanne coloured and looked away.

'Look, there's probably a hundred reasons why.'

'Name one,' Ellie challenged. 'Give me one good reason why she hasn't even phoned to make sure I'm okay?'

Roxanne opened her mouth and then closed it again.

Ellie knew there was no answer, no reason, no excuse. She'd been out of the house for forty-eight hours and her own mother couldn't care less.

Roxanne took the phone from her handbag and held it out. 'Perhaps, you should give her a call and—'

'Thank you, Roxanne, but no,' Ellie said, shaking her head.

If that was the game her mother wanted to play she'd be damned if she'd call first.

CHAPTER TWENTY-SEVEN

Kim pulled up at the row of shops at the entrance to the Hollytree estate. She immediately thought that the term 'community centre' had been applied loosely to the old doctor's surgery. In her opinion the title was aspirational.

The lobby area was the size of a small elevator. The walls to the left and right of her held a collage of hand-written signs, some of which had been ripped or defaced with phallic symbols.

'Classy,' Bryant observed, as she pushed open a heavy glass door.

Kim entered into what she supposed would have been the surgery waiting room. A receptionist counter dominated the left-hand side of the room. On top was a sharps box and a bowl filled with packets of condoms. On the right-hand side of the room there were two doors for toilets. Both marked up with black marker pen. A small television sat in the corner but the picture rolled every three seconds. Behind the door was a metal urn with plastic cups and a jar of value coffee.

A lanky young man eyed them, pausing from the activity on his mobile phone. A tattoo emerged from beneath his shirt and crept up his neck. His eyes were alert and suspicious.

'Damn it,' they heard from a small room behind the reception.

'Hello,' Bryant called.

A second man appeared in the doorway. Kim guessed him to be around her own five nine height and in his late thirties. His hair was fair and slightly too long. A two-day stubble mottled his chin. He was dressed casually in sweatshirt and jeans.

His gaze narrowed. 'May I help you?'

'Is there somewhere we can talk?'

He nodded. 'Yeah, one of you can come back here.'

'One of us?' Bryant asked.

'Take a look, you'll see what I mean.'

Kim stepped behind the desk and looked in. The space was five feet wide by about six feet long. Attached to the wall was a two-feet wide stretch of cut-down kitchen counter. The area was littered with folders, paperwork and a dated computer with its guts all over the side. Two folding chairs filled the rest of the space.

Kim took one. The man took the other and Bryant propped up the doorway.

'Tim Price, how can I help?'

'We're detectives,' Bryant offered, taking out his ID.

'Yeah, I kinda got that,' he offered with a smile.

'Problem?' Kim asked, glancing towards the computer innards.

He nodded. 'Blue screen of death. The machine is seven years old and has less memory than a decent mobile phone.'

Kim assessed the components and shook her head. 'Yeah, it may be time to give it up and buy another.'

'Of course, officer, I'll just pluck a £1,000 from the money tree in the garden.'

Kim shrugged. 'Sometimes you gotta accept when something is broken.'

'And sometimes you gotta remember that you don't give up on something just because it's not perfect.'

'Fair enough,' she said, looking around. 'Is that what you do here, mend things that are broken?'

'No, we provide a place where poor sods can come and get a cup of coffee.'

'What type of "poor sods"?' she asked, repeating his description.

'Drug addicts, homeless people. Prostitutes come in for free condoms.'

It was clear to Kim that this facility was not council funded. There was no regulatory signage or evidence of health and safety considerations.

'You run this place?'

Tim shook his head. 'None of us run it.'

'Who is "us"?'

'Local citizens who believe charity begins at home. The centre opens for two days each week. We all donate half a day.'

'To do what?' she asked, incredulously. It was hard to believe that anything positive came out of this place.

'Offer a cup of coffee, a clean needle, condoms, the use of a computer…' He looked dolefully at the mess on the table. 'Sometimes. And primarily advice. Sometimes legal, sometimes housing, benefits, job opportunities, whatever we can.'

'Well, if charity begins at home, ask matey boy out there for the use of his benefits-funded touchscreen phone if he's done tweeting,' Bryant offered.

Kim shot her colleague a bemused look.

Tim stood and edged past Bryant.

'Hey, Len, pass the phone a second.'

Len stood and brought him the phone.

Tim stepped back into the room and scrolled along the open tabs. 'You'll see that every site he's activated is a jobs site, officer. Normally he would have sat patiently at the computer while it chuntered and limped from site to site but as you can see it's not available for use, right now.'

He handed the phone back to Len, who ambled away from the doorway.

Tim sat back down. 'Oh, and officer, the phone is mine. Now what can I help you with?'

Tim's voice had dropped a few degrees.

Kim was struck by the irony that for once it was Bryant who had pissed someone off instead of her.

'Listen, I'm sure my colleague didn't mean anything—'

'Of course he did. That man out there has served his time and for two years has fought against being drawn back to his old life. He has a young child for whom he is desperate to provide for legitimately. He gets turned away from every interview because of his appearance and still he comes in here whenever he can to try and stay legal.

'In the job that you do, is this not what you hope for? That people will learn from their mistakes and try to live a better life?'

'Okay, okay,' Bryant said, holding up his hands. 'I accept there may be the occasional exception.'

Tim appeared to calm as the redness of his neck receded.

'And I accept that you're probably right. But I happen to think each exception is worth the effort.'

A look passed between the two men. Kim felt a compromise had been reached. She understood completely Bryant's point of view. Their line of work didn't bring them into contact with many reformed characters.

'Tim, did Kelly Rowe come in here much?'

'She'd started to during the last couple of weeks. Never came to supper club but was here some Tuesdays and Thursdays to help out. I think she was kinda lonely.'

Kim thought about all the secrets Kelly had from her mother and wasn't all that surprised.

'What did she do here?' Bryant asked. It wasn't exactly a hive of activity.

'Letter writing. She was well educated and helped some of the others put together job applications. That's the frustrating part with a lot of these ladies, officer. They are by no means stupid women.'

He reached for a red ledger. 'This is the balance sheet over which I pored for two days because it wouldn't add up. It took Sal, one of the more experienced ladies, two minutes to find where I had transposed two figures three pages earlier. She showed me how to do page totals so that small mistakes didn't get compounded.'

'Sounds like Sal,' Kim said.

'You know her?'

'Oh yeah,' Kim said. She remembered when Sal had secured a part-time job doing a paper round and each week she would divide her earnings into used envelopes all marked with different headings.

Kim rued the day that the woman had discovered the comfort of alcohol.

'What do you know of Kelly's relationship with Kai Lord?'

'I know she was terrified of him.'

Kim knew that the relationship between pimp and prostitute was often abusive, often defined by violence, sometimes using psychological intimidation, manipulation, starvation, gang rape, confinement and implied violence towards family members.

'You know he is often referred to as Jofin?'

Kim didn't know that but it took her less than ten seconds to figure out why. His nickname was a convergence of two names adopted from America. A Jonas pimp was known for using violence and intimidation. A Finesse pimp was known for psychological trickery.

'Is there anything you know of that could have contributed to her murder?'

'There is one thing I heard the other day but it's only a rumour. I overheard a couple of the girls saying that Kelly had been planning to bounce.'

Kim had heard the term before. It was when a prostitute transferred to another pimp. The new pimp would buy the original debt and a 'moving tax' would be agreed between the two pimps.

'Any idea who she was planning on moving to?'

Tim shook his head. 'Like I said, it was just a snippet I overheard.'

Kim idly wondered if Kai Lord had found out about Kelly's intention. There were many transfers that occurred without incident but no pimp really wanted their pride damaged. Could the discovery of her intention have filled the man with such rage that he'd cut a dozen holes in her body?

'Anything else you can think of?' Kim asked.

He thought for a few minutes. 'Do you know something, officer? Kelly didn't fit. It's hard to label a prostitute a certain type because there are a hundred reasons why a woman might choose this profession but there was just something about her. Street life hadn't hardened her yet. She was kind, educated, helpful and compassionate. My understanding is that she was just trying to get herself out of a hole.'

'You hear anything about some weirdo around at the moment?'

'Can you be more specific?' he asked.

Kim shook her head. 'Apparently works with kids, or something.'

He nodded. 'I've heard about him. Girls don't mind him. Apparently he's quick,' he said meaningfully.

'Got a name?' she asked.

He shook his head.

Kim nodded her understanding and stood. She handed him a card. 'If you think of anything else or hear any rumours going around, give me a call.'

'Will do, officer.'

Kim stood and Bryant moved out of the doorway.

'Hey, that good kid of yours has done a runner with your phone,' Kim said.

Tim rolled his eyes. 'No, he's abiding by the rules and has gone outside for a smoke. Which is where I'm going now if the two of you have finished with me.'

Kim thanked him again as he picked up a pack of Marlboro Lights and a box of matches.

She followed him out of the poky office just as a familiar face with short, blonde curls appeared in the doorway.

Gemma took one look at her and scarpered.

'Just one more thing,' Kim said. 'Does the name Lauren Goddard mean anything to you?'

'Of course, everyone around here knew Lauren.'

'Why?' she asked, frowning at Bryant.

'Went by the name of Jazzy. She was the youngest girl on the strip.'

'Was?' Kim asked, as the feeling of dread began to rise.

He nodded. 'She committed suicide a few weeks ago.'

CHAPTER TWENTY-EIGHT

'You really think this has anything to do with our case?' Stacey asked, following her colleague down the slope onto the canal towpath. The icy ground was hard and unforgiving beneath her feet.

Keats had called the boss first who had directed him their way once she'd heard the words 'possibly Romanian'.

Dawson reached the bottom of the slope and turned, offering his hand to steady her. She waved it away.

Police officers in yellow jackets were visible as far as the eye could see on both sides of the canal. The bridge they'd used was only one of a hundred shortcuts to the waterway, used by walkers and cyclists.

Stacey spotted five white suits gathered around the diminutive figure of Keats.

An officer held out two pairs of blue slippers at the walkway cordon. They quickly put them on and headed towards the huddle.

Keats finished what he was saying to the photographer and turned their way.

'Dawson, Wood, meet our customer,' he said, pointing to an area of tall weeds.

The body of the man was half sitting and half lying in the brush. Remnants of the snow that had covered him still glistened from his clothing.

'Is that how he was found?' Stacey asked. The positioning looked staged to her.

Keats nodded.

'He looks asleep,' she noted, fighting the urge to reach down and shake his arm.

'That may have been the issue,' Keats said.

'You think he's homeless?' Stacey asked.

Keats shrugged. 'We've had two so far this month, one in Dudley and one in Stourbridge.'

'I'm guessing we've got no cause of death yet,' Dawson observed.

Keats shook his head. 'Nothing obvious right now. No stab wounds or clear signs of trauma or violence.'

Stacey could feel Dawson's waning interest. The signs were pointing towards a homeless male who had fallen asleep and frozen to death. Unlike her colleague, Stacey couldn't help her mind wandering to the reasons the man was homeless, the reasons why he'd fallen asleep beside the canal.

'You said something about a notebook,' Dawson said.

Keats nodded and leaned down to retrieve a clear evidence bag holding a small notebook.

Dawson took it from him and examined the A6 leather pad. The fabric was old and worn. An elastic band was looped around it vertically.

'May we take it?' Stacey asked. On first inspection there appeared to be no suspicious circumstances surrounding the male's death.

Keats shook his head. 'Forensics will need to check it for fingerprints first to try and identify the male and we don't need to make their job any harder by adding more fingertips.'

'And you think the contents of the book are Romanian?' Stacey asked.

'Indeed I do,' he answered.

'You speak Romanian?' Dawson asked doubtfully.

'Not at all, Sergeant. It says Romania on the second page in. Kind of gave it away.'

Stacey found herself smiling at the pathologist's nature. She knew her boss had experienced run-ins with the man at almost every crime scene they'd shared but she also knew her boss respected this man immensely.

'Any idea how long?' Stacey asked innocently as Dawson shook his head.

'Oh, constable, constable,' Keats said, pursing his lips. 'As this is your first time I shall only maul you gently in response to that question.'

'Hang on,' Dawson protested. 'Why the special...'

'When a body has been frozen,' Keats offered, ignoring her colleague. 'There is no way for bacteria to grow or for insects to attack. These being reasonably accurate indicators of time of death.

'In this situation cells are frozen in place and prevented from decaying. The temperature arrests the process of decomposition.'

'Thank you,' she said, politely.

'I shall look for other clues once I have him back at the morgue.'

'Err... Keats that's not really how you spoke to me the first time I asked you for an estimated time of death,' Dawson said, sulkily.

Keats growled. 'You people expect the broken watch method every time even though you know it doesn't work that way and is not a reliable—'

'Of course it is,' Dawson interrupted.

Stacey instantly felt her colleague had made a mistake.

Keats regarded Dawson for ten long seconds before deciding to offer the benefit of his wisdom.

'Sergeant, one of my practical tests during training involved a staged crime scene in a living room. It was a violent affair with blood spatter, a broken, smashed clock and livor mortis. To pass, I had to estimate time of death to within an hour.'

'A bit easy,' Dawson offered.

'Apparently so for my colleagues who tried to make the physical data match the time on the clock.'

'Reasonable assumption. It's a powerful clue,' he said.

Keats nodded. 'If it fits the clues from the body.'

'So, what did you do?' Stacey asked.

'I discounted it altogether, my dear,' he answered pleasantly.

'Why?'

'Because I had no knowledge as to whether the clock had been working before the crime. My expertise lies in deducing clues from the body not a timepiece.'

Stacey got it. Some clues were helpful and some were not. The key was identifying which was which.

'Just one more question,' Dawson said. 'Why did she get a nice explanation and you all but ripped my throat out?'

'Because she's prettier than you,' he said, smiling. He turned her way.

'My apologies if that is not strictly PC in this day and age and no offence intended.'

'None taken,' Stacey said.

'So, when might we get copies of the contents?' Dawson asked, nodding towards the book.

'They'll be with you later today,' Keats answered.

They both thanked him and headed back to the car.

* * *

'So, what do you think?' Stacey asked, as Dawson put the key into the ignition. 'Connected to our abandoned child or not?'

Dawson shrugged. 'Could just be a coincidence as I'm really not seeing the connection between the death of a homeless man and an abandoned baby even if they are both Romanian,' he said, forcing the car into a line of traffic.

'Where are we going?' Stacey asked.

'Back to the station; there's more to learn about that place.'

Stacey realised he meant Robertson's. She wasn't sure if his fixation on the factory was born of a hunch or because obstacles had been placed in his path. He had wanted to interview the girls and he'd been told no.

And she had come to realise that Dawson didn't like being told no.

CHAPTER TWENTY-NINE

'What the hell has a suicide got to do with our case? How is Lauren Goddard related to Kelly Rowe, and who wants us to think she is?' Bryant asked.

Kim shook her head, staring out of the passenger window, her eyes scouring the street.

'What does our anonymous tipster hope to gain by bringing us a bloody suicide?' he said, exasperated.

'Dunno, Bryant, unless they know something we don't.'

'Then they might have bloody well said so,' he said. 'Rather than just—'

'Pull over,' Kim said, sharply.

Bryant aimed the car into the pavement and stopped.

Kim jumped out and ran three paces.

'Hey, you up to your old tricks again?' she asked, grabbing Gemma by the shoulder and turning her around.

'Oi,' Gemma snarled before realising who it was.

Kim had to admit that the kid dressed like no other prostitute she had ever known. Her denim jacket was too thin and her trainers had tell-tale dark patches along the sides where they were taking on water.

'You trying to find punters at this time of day?'

Gemma looked to the left, to the right and, realising there was no escape, she faced Kim head-on. 'There's sometimes packs of biscuits on the counter in there but what's it to you?'

'Oh, I always take special interest in anyone who tries to kill me,' Kim snapped. 'Especially the ones that prove me wrong.'

'Fuck off,' Gemma said. The right-hand side of her mouth lifted in a puppy snarl.

'What do you know about a girl named Lauren Goddard?'

'Who?' she asked, wrinkling up her face.

Kim remembered her nickname. 'Jazzy.'

'The one that topped herself?'

Kim nodded.

Gemma shrugged. 'Just a kid, really,' she said. 'Sixteen, I think.'

Kim wondered if Gemma realised just how little the two-year age difference between them was.

'Didn't know her well but she was busy as fuck, if you know what I mean,' she said.

'Because of her age?'

Gemma nodded and attempted to step to the side.

Kim stood in her way. 'What about this weirdo who works with kids?'

'Rapid Rodge?' Gemma clarified.

Kim remembered what Tim had said about being quick. 'Sounds right. What's his story?'

'Comes quick, goes quick, easy money. Nobody minds him. Pays well considering...'

'Considering what?' Kim asked

Gemma scrunched up her face. 'You paying me for this time or what?'

'That'll be "or what" or I could arrest you for attempted murder. That'd give us plenty of time to talk.'

Gemma changed her expression to bored. 'You woulda done it by now. I ain't stupid.'

Kim left that hanging.

'Considering what?' she repeated.

'It's a hand job. Thirty quid for giving him a wank. Not even a blowie, just a—'

'Okay,' Kim said. She got the picture. 'Is that why you think he's weird?'

Gemma nodded.

'So, what about Kelly Rowe, you know her well?'

'Well enough. She was all right. She had brains.'

'How do you know?' Kim asked. Gemma wasn't on the streets full time. Just when she couldn't con someone into giving her a meal.

'Helped me out with a letter to the council when they tried to take my mum's house while she was banged up.'

'So, you're still out here doing this, even though one of your mates…'

'Hey, she wasn't a fucking mate. There ain't no mates out here. You know it's every pro for themselves.'

'Not that I give a shit but can't you get something to eat…'

'You gonna cook me a meal?' Gemma asked.

'Yeah, tried that and look where it got me,' Kim said.

Silence fell between them.

Gemma pushed her hands deep into her pockets. 'That guy… that night… Shane…'

'Don't you dare,' Kim thundered. 'Don't you bloody dare to pretend you give one shit for that lad.'

She turned and began to move away, wondering if there would ever be a time when the memory of his blood-soaked body in her lap would not cause her physical pain.

Shane had been one of Alex's early victims. A survivor of systematic sexual abuse by his uncle, he had been naively duped by Alex's promises to rid him of the self-loathing that had shaped his whole life. Instead of keeping her promise, she had broken him completely until his only option had been death. And he'd chosen to do that in her home, in her arms, on her kitchen floor, but not before he had tried to protect her from Gemma.

She didn't talk about Shane with anyone and she certainly wouldn't do it with this vicious kid who had been the catalyst for the whole thing.

She was almost at the car when she heard Gemma shout behind her.

'Hey, how'd I prove you wrong?' she asked.

Kim turned and faced her. 'By doing someone else's dirty work, Gemma. I really thought you were made of stronger stuff than that.'

Kim was surprised to see the frisson of hurt that flashed in her eyes.

Good, now who the hell was Rapid Rodge?

CHAPTER THIRTY

Dawson watched as Stacey stole right back under her cloak of familiarity. Sitting in the corner pounding away at the keys. Searching for information was right back in her comfort zone.

Penn had been heading out just as they'd arrived mumbling something about having a lead on Kelly Rowe's last customer.

Stacey glanced up and met his gaze.

'Stop watching me,' she said.

'Just checking you're hard at it,' he joked.

'I'm fine, Kev, now just leave me alone.'

He sat back in his chair. 'So, Stace, how do you know when enough therapy is enough?' he asked. He had refused all offers of help back when he'd been badly beaten but his situation had been nothing compared to Stacey's.

She drew her eyes back to the screen. 'I just know,' she said, honestly.

'Shouldn't the professional decide when you're done?' he pushed.

'Kev, fuck off. It ay your business, so—'

'All right, I'll quit bugging you if you just answer this one question.'

Stacey thought for a moment. 'Okay, first few weeks I was grateful for the help. I didn't fight him. I talked and I talked and then I talked some more and then I got to the point where I just didn't want to talk about it any more. It happened, I lived and it's over.'

Dawson understood her words but still wasn't sure.

'The thing is, Stace, if it was a physical injury the doctor would say you were healed, that your bones had mended and you were fit and well. How is that different with a therapist?'

'For you, Kev, that's not a bad question. But let me ask you something. What helps events like this become a part of the past?'

'Time,' he answered.

Stacey shook her head. 'Not so much. It's events, it's actual things happening. Did you ever go on a day trip as a kid?'

'Of course.'

'And when you got home at night it felt like days since you'd left the house?'

'Yeah, but…'

'It wasn't because of the time that had passed, it was because of how much you'd done, what you'd managed to fit into that time. Between my sessions, events would occur and push the incident back into my past and then I'd have to go and talk about it all over again.' She looked at him earnestly. 'I need it to be over, Kev,' she said.

'Are you still scared?' he asked, gently.

'Sometimes, just now and again but more therapy isn't going to make that go away.'

'Okay, I'll quit bugging you now.'

'Good, you should worry about your own problems. How is your missus by the way?'

'Pissed off,' he admitted.

Stacey pulled a face. 'What you been doing?'

'You automatically assume I've done something wrong.'

She thought for a minute. 'Yeah.'

He shrugged. 'Just been getting home a bit late, that's all.'

She regarded him seriously. 'Well, maybe you should stop doing whatever it is you're doing that's making you late home.'

For a moment he wondered if Stacey knew exactly what he was doing after work. He dismissed the thought. No, she couldn't know.

'Hey, Stace, maybe you could give her a call. Tell her I've been hanging out with you,' he said, raising one eyebrow.

'Feck off, Kev. You're big enough to look after yourself.'

'Fair enough,' he said, with a half-smile. 'So, what you got?'

She had been digging into the family and the business, and he had been looking for information on the foreman, Nicolae.

'So, Janette Robertson was born in 1967 and raised on Hollytree,' Stacey said. 'We're talking back in the seventies so it wasn't gang-controlled like it is now. Still not the nicest place to live,' she said. 'But our Janette wasn't going to let that stop her. She did a paper round six days a week, left school with decent grades, went to college for two years and then on to uni to finish her business degree.'

'Is that where she met her husband?'

Stacey shook her head. 'A couple of years later. It wasn't a long courtship and they married in 1993.'

Dawson tried to quell his boredom. 'All very interesting but—'

'It gets better. They started their knock-off handbag business from the garden shed. Focussed on car boots. Eventually moved to a tiny unit in Brierley Hill in '99. Moved to current premises in 2006. Got raided six years ago, as you know. Anyway, hubby ran off with the Russian maid four years ago taking the majority of the joint account with him.'

'Bloody hell, Stace,' he said, checking his watch. 'Not bad for an hour's work.'

She grinned. 'I've showed you mine now you show me yours.'

'Well, I've not really got a lot to…'

Stacey punched the air showing her triumph. This was her arena and she would be victorious.

'Don't worry, Kev, I'm sure—'

She stopped speaking as his phone rang.

He mouthed 'Keats' and put it on loudspeaker.

'Sergeant, the copies of the notebook are ready when you're passing, which I suggest should be reasonably soon.'

'Everything okay?' Dawson asked, frowning.

'There are some things I would like you to see. Our friend here has much more to say than I thought.'

CHAPTER THIRTY-ONE

Ellie folded the last item of clothing neatly on the chair beside the bed. The wardrobe was right in front of her but something stopped her from accepting that level of permanence. Although only a couple of days she felt she had been here with Roxanne for much longer.

The emotion gathered in her throat when she thought of her own room back at home, her own wardrobe full of her own possessions. Her clothes and trainers strewn around the room, some just inches from the place they were meant to be. And how magically a couple of times each week the items would somehow find their way home.

Sometimes she felt an overwhelming sense of homesickness and the next moment she felt a burning rage at her mother for not calling to check on her.

How could her mother be so cold?

How was her mother simply carrying on life without her? Almost as though she had never existed. One minute she wanted to confront her and ask when she had stopped caring at all. The next she wanted to ring and tell her mother she was never coming home. Sometimes she thought about her mother's flat refusal to entertain her dreams of becoming a mechanic and reasoned that maybe teaching her a lesson was not such a bad thing.

And then, just once or twice, when the house had made unfamiliar noises, she had experienced a slow sick feeling in the pit of her stomach. An ache for her own room which had led her right back to visions of her mother, and the cycle would start all over again.

Ellie really had no wish to leave Roxanne. She could feel a bond forming between them and she knew that whatever happened the two of them would be friends for life.

But a part of her sought answers from her mother so she could let it go, resolve it in her mind. Perhaps then she could come back.

Ellie thought about Roxanne. The woman hadn't bargained on getting lumbered with a teenager for days. She had been wonderful and patient but Ellie felt sure that Roxanne had put her own life on hold, not least because of what had happened as soon as she'd arrived.

As Ellie headed downstairs she felt relieved. She knew what she had to do. It was time to let Roxanne get on with her life and it was time for her to confront her mother.

Ellie ventured into the kitchen. The beginnings of a home-made lasagne were littered on the work surface. Two mugs waited by the kettle to be filled.

She felt an ache in her throat. Somehow in a couple of days a routine had developed between them. Ellie wanted nothing more than to just forget all her problems and stay within the uncomplicated safety of Roxanne's home. She had to release the rage at her mother and then she would be able to move on with her life.

She checked the lounge. The carpet was vacuumed and the cushions fluffed but no Roxanne.

She headed back upstairs and stood beside Roxanne's bedroom door. She heard a small sob from inside the room.

'Roxanne,' Ellie called.

A brief hesitation. 'Yeah, yeah, I'll be out in a minute.'

Ellie heard the thickness in her voice and knew immediately that Roxanne was not okay.

She opened the door gently. Roxanne sat on the floor at the foot of her double bed beside a drawer that slid from beneath. Her head was down and her shoulders trembled. Ellie crossed the distance between them and sat beside her.

'Roxanne, what is it, what's wrong?'

She shook her head, and grabbed for a tissue tucked into her sleeve.

'It's nothing, honestly, I'm fine.' She raised her head. The rims of her eyes were raw, her eyes sad. Despite her words Ellie could see that Roxanne's lower lip still trembled with emotion.

'Roxanne, please tell me what's wrong.'

'Just memories, sweetie,' Roxanne said, raising her gaze and staring at the wall.

Ellie looked down into the drawer.

Photographs were scattered face down. One was face up. Ellie reached for it. A young girl in her early teens with long silky blonde hair bobbed her tongue out at the camera. Her eyes were alight with mischievousness.

'Who is this?' Ellie asked.

'My sister,' Roxanne said as she dabbed at her eyes.

'I remember that day; we were at Stourport. Just a few miles down the road but we were so excited. It felt like holiday to us. There was a fun fair; the sun was shining. It could have been a hundred miles away.'

Roxanne reached across and took the photo. She touched the face of the child. 'We were so close. I loved her so much.'

Ellie watched as Roxanne's tears fell onto the polaroid.

Ellie didn't want to ask the next question and she was saved the trouble.

'She died,' Roxanne said, quietly.

Ellie felt her throat thicken. She had never had siblings but the deep hurt she felt in Roxanne touched her. She reached across and took Roxanne's hand.

'I'm so sorry,' she said, hearing her own emotion.

Roxanne lifted her head. Her cheeks were wet with tears. She squeezed Ellie's hand and smiled. 'You remind me of her so much. I think that's why we bonded so quickly. I feel like I've known you for ever.'

Ellie felt the tears stinging her eyes as she squeezed Roxanne's hand in response. She felt the same way.

Roxanne swallowed bravely. 'Look, I know you have to leave but I've just enjoyed having you here.'

Ellie nodded and leaned across and hugged Roxanne's slim frame. She blinked away the tears.

'How about I go and make us a nice cup of tea?'

Roxanne nodded and took a deep breath.

As she headed down the stairs, Ellie knew she could not leave Roxanne quite yet. Her friend needed her.

So, for now, her mother would just have to wait.

CHAPTER THIRTY-TWO

'Got a minute, sir?' Kim asked, popping her head around the door.

Woody looked up from his desk and peered at her over his glasses.

'Come in, Stone.'

She sat on the opposite side of the desk and pulled her chair forward. Most people would have pulled back from the desk a little. Woody did not.

Kim reached for the stress ball he always kept nearby and handed it to him.

'Here, sir, you might need this.'

He took it from her and placed it back. 'Already been used today, thanks, Stone. Now what do you want?'

'An exhumation, sir.'

'Connected to this current case?'

'I honestly have no idea.'

He frowned and glanced towards the stress ball but stopped himself from reaching for it.

'Then I'd like an explanation for your request.'

'Sir, Kelly Rowe was murdered by multiple stab wounds. She was working as a prostitute secretly while living with her mother and her young child. Kelly was under the protection of Kai Lord, if you can call it that, but there's a rumour she was planning to bounce.'

He needed no explanation. He knew the term just as well as she did.

'All very interesting and so far nothing that would not be contained in your daily briefing to me.'

'I'm still troubled by the link from Kai Lord to Kelly in the first place but I'll keep working on that.'

'Do you think Lord would kill one of his own girls?'

Kim shrugged. 'I don't know. He's not a stupid man and, whichever way you look at it, Kelly's death means a loss of income for the scumbag but if he heard about her intention, I'm not sure how much his pride is worth.'

Woody nodded his understanding. Kai Lord was one man they would both like to put behind bars but all past efforts had failed miserably.

'Stone, will your reason for an exhumation request arrive any time before my retirement?'

'Sir, an anonymous note was put through my letterbox late last night. It simply stated a name: Lauren Goddard, also known as Jazzy, a young prostitute who committed suicide by throwing herself from the top of a tower block two weeks ago, on Christmas Day.'

He waited for more. 'And?'

Kim shrugged. 'That's all I have, sir. At this point I can see no connection between the two women but the one thing I can't get away from is that someone wants me to find out more about either the life or death of this kid. I'm working on the former and I know that finding out more about her death was a bit of a long shot, but…'

'Look, Stone, you know the process involved for exhuming a body. You've not really come close to justifying probable cause.'

Kim knew that but it had been worth a try. And she wasn't done trying yet.

She took a breath. 'Sir, the note came through my letterbox so someone is quite clear that they want me to find out all there is to know about this young girl. She was sixteen years old,' she added, aiming for his paternal instinct.

'Sorry, Stone. This is not going to happen.'

She sighed heavily and stood. 'I just couldn't help feeling that maybe Lauren Goddard had something to tell us.'

'That's as it may be, Stone, but a request from the police based on that evidence would be laughed out of court. Not only would we be refused but we would look ridiculous even trying.'

As she had learned to listen to every word that came out of her boss's mouth, a smile itched at her lips.

'Absolutely, sir. I completely understand,' she said, heading towards the door.

'Not so fast, Stone,' he said.

She groaned inwardly. She sensed she was about to learn the reason for the use of the stress ball.

She turned.

He waved a piece of paper at her.

'From Kai Lord's solicitor. A complaint about his client being harassed while he was having breakfast.' He put on his glasses and read. 'Oh, and a mention of a dry cleaning charge coming our way.'

She shrugged. Letters like that formed the bulk of her Personnel file.

'You know how clumsy I can be, sir,' she said.

'Well, curb your clumsiness, Stone, and stop bothering the man while he eats. Pick your battles. Got it?'

Kim sighed heavily allowing her aggravation to be noted. Kai Lord knew what he was doing. Every interaction would now be met with claims of harassment and bringing him in for formal questioning would be an uphill battle.

He was trying to tie her hands behind her back and put himself outside the law.

And as Woody well knew, she did not like being handcuffed one little bit.

CHAPTER THIRTY-THREE

Stacey took a breath before following her colleague into the morgue. Her one and only previous visit had been an unforgettable experience. The body had been a fifty-nine-year-old man who had been found following his failure to return to his caretaking job after the school summer holidays. He had collapsed in the living room of his flat after suffering a fatal heart attack. The sun had passed over his body approximately twelve times in the July heat, burning through the lounge window, warming his dead flesh over and over again. The buzzing of the flies had been heard from outside his front door. The community of maggots, larvae and flies that had taken over his body had sickened her to the core.

She had almost gagged at the smell of gases from bacterial decay as the Y incision had been cut into the flesh. And the nightmare got worse when her eyes rested on the tools.

Somehow she had imagined that the instruments used to pry, saw and excavate the secrets from the human body were different to what you'd find in a hardware store. She'd expected them to be more gentle, refined, less intrusive, more respectful. The image of a bone saw had stayed with her for days.

Not only had she been forced to keep her face impassive beneath Dawson's prying gaze but had felt the need to pretend the experience had not affected her at all to avoid her colleague's mirth.

But today she was prepared.

'What you got for us, Keats?' Dawson asked, pleasantly.

She was pleased to see that the metal dishes were empty and the tools were out of sight. She suspected the man had been returned to the cooler.

Keats stepped back to the desk in the corner and reached for a sheaf of papers.

'The contents of the booklet,' he said.

Dawson took a quick look and passed them her way. They held little interest for him while they were in no position to action them.

Dawson waited patiently as Keats picked up a clipboard and leafed back a couple of pages.

'Physical description is little more than you already know. Caucasian male, height five feet four inches, slight build, light brown hair, no tattoos or other distinguishing features and my experience would tell me that he was not homeless.'

Stacey frowned. She thought it had been a safe assumption. No one had come forward to report him missing.

As though reading the doubt in her eyes, Keats continued.

'His hair is tidily if not expertly cut; he does not carry the odour of someone held together by dirt and stale sweat. There is no evidence of alcohol dependency and his toenails are clean.'

Stacey recalled the pathologist's words about putting all of the clues together.

'His last meal appears to have been some kind of pork, rice and cabbage concoction.'

'Okay,' Dawson said.

'Popular with Romanians,' Keats offered. 'A dish called *sarmale*,' he said.

'Okay,' Dawson repeated.

It was not difficult for Stacey to read the signs of her colleague's boredom.

'That's not why I called you here,' Keats said.

'Righty ho,' Dawson said, obviously not wanting to push the man into non-cooperation.

'This man did indeed die of hypothermia but I'd like you to see these.'

Keats stepped towards two wall-mounted light boards and switched them on. He placed an X-ray on each board.

Stacey looked from one to the other and gasped.

'His left leg,' Keats said, pointing to the first image. 'And his right leg,' he clarified, pointing to the second.

'What the hell?' Dawson asked.

Almost every bone in the right leg appeared to be broken.

'Twelve fractures from the tip of his toes to his knee. Nothing above.'

'The pain…' Stacey breathed.

'Would have been excruciating,' Keats agreed. 'He would have had no use in that leg at all.'

'Blood loss?' Dawson asked.

Keats shook his head. 'Very little blood loss, Sergeant.'

'Car accident?' Dawson asked, echoing Stacey's thoughts. She too could imagine a vehicle ploughing into his leg and causing this level of damage.

Keats shook his head. 'I don't think so. This is not consistent with victims of RTA incidents, in my experience.'

Stacey tried to picture any other type of impact to cause this level of damage.

'Crushing?' she asked.

Keats nodded. 'That would be my guess, and there's something else,' he said, returning to the clipboard.

'This man has ninety-six different injury sites around his body including his face, skull, arms, leg, torso and behind.'

'"Ninety-six"?' Stacey repeated, for clarification.

'Some possibly twenty years old,' he said. 'I've examined a cage fighter with less injuries than this poor fellow.'

'How did he get so many?' Dawson asked, horrified.

'It's my guess that this male was regularly and systematically beaten over quite a number of years.'

'Poor soul,' Stacey breathed, shaking her head. How could someone do this to another human being? She had the sudden image of this man cowed and frightened, trying to fend off blows. Each punch and kick demeaning him even more, grinding him down so that over time he probably lost the will to fight back.

'Keats,' Dawson asked, frowning. 'I assume I'm right in thinking that our guy could not have got down to the canal on his own.'

'That is correct,' Keats answered.

Stacey met Dawson's gaze as the final horror dawned on her.

Although not murdered, their victim had been taken to the canal and left there to die.

CHAPTER THIRTY-FOUR

'I bloody hate this place,' Bryant said as they pulled onto Hollytree. 'It's where hope goes to die.'

Kim silently agreed with him and tried to avoid looking into the grey faces of people they passed by. Every expression was filled with despair, suspicion, muted rage or hopelessness. She'd always had the impression that people on Hollytree had given up. That they had accepted that this was as good as it got. There were no aspirations to get out, ambitions to improve, energy or initiative.

Kim understood Bryant's depression. This case was bringing them to Hollytree too often.

He stopped the car at a fenced refuse area to the side of a maisonette block. Kim tried not to inhale the stench from the line of council bins with their lids forced open by overflowing rubbish.

'It's the end one on the ground floor,' Bryant said.

Kim approached the door and shook her head at the cardboard piece where a pane of glass should have been.

She heard a peal of laughter from the open kitchen window and a man's voice shouting something unintelligible as he headed towards the door.

The door opened on a man sporting shorts and a football shirt that did not meet the waistband of the shorts, exposing a portly, milk-white stomach.

'What?' he answered with the tiny end of a roll-up clutched between his fingers.

'Mr Goddard?' Kim asked, although she didn't think there was one.

He guffawed as he wiped his index finger beneath his nostrils.

'Not bloody likely. I'm Ken, and you are?'

'Police officers,' Bryant said, showing his ID.

Kim thrust her hands into her trouser pockets. She would not shake that hand if her life depended on it.

'May we speak to Margaret?'

Again with the loud laughter from the kitchen.

'Maggie, c'mere,' he called.

The woman who appeared was reed thin and sickly looking. The smile died in her eyes.

'What you want?'

'To talk to you, if you have a moment,' Bryant said, pleasantly, aware that they needed something from this woman.

She nudged her head inside and stepped away from the door.

A staircase up to the second level rose up just a few feet from the front door of a dark, unlit hallway. Margaret Goddard stepped into the kitchen which was first door on the right.

Ken took himself to the furthest point of the small room, grabbing a can of cider as he passed the two-seater table just inside the door. A few more six-packs and a couple of bottles of spirits appeared to have been recently unloaded.

'Sorry if we're disturbing a party,' Kim offered.

Bryant shot her a warning glance. The woman's daughter had been dead for a whole fourteen days.

Ken smiled widely. 'Nah, it's benefits day,' he said, cheerfully.

Kim kept her irritation in check. These two were a walking stereotype for every Channel 5 documentary she'd seen on *Benefits Britain* and yet Kim knew there were families that used the system properly.

'We're here about Lauren,' Bryant said, taking a seat.

Kim remained standing in the doorway.

'What about her?' Maggie asked suspiciously.

'It's about her death,' he offered, gently.

'What about it?' she asked, wrinkling up her nose.

Kim detected no deep swallow or rush of emotion reddening the eyes.

'We think there are questions to be answered,' he continued, although the gentle consideration for her feelings had left his voice.

'Such as? She topped herself. Simple.'

Kim wondered if she had ever witnessed a mother so devoid of emotion when talking about such a recent death.

'Only buried her a week ago; why weren't you asking your questions then?'

'Information has recently come to light,' he offered.

'You mean that tart being murdered the other—'

'Her name was Kelly Rowe,' Bryant snapped.

She shrugged, oblivious to Bryant's change in tone. She held out her right hand towards Ken who seemed to know what she was requesting and placed a pack of smokes and a disposable lighter in her palm.

'So, what's that got to do with Lauren?'

'The timeliness of her death when considered alongside recent...'

'I still don't get... oh, hang on, you think she didn't commit suicide. You think she was murdered?'

Finally, her eyes began to widen.

Bryant didn't confirm or deny. 'As I said we have questions about her death.'

There was a sharp cackle from her lips like the one they'd heard from outside. 'Well, it ain't like you're gonna be able to ask her, now, is it?'

She realised she was the only one laughing and stopped suddenly.

'So, what the fuck you doing here?' she asked, suspiciously.

'There may be evidence on her body that was overlooked during the initial—'

'Shit, you want to dig her up?' she asked, aghast.

'Awww… gross,' Ken said, from the corner.

Kim was pleased that they had finally said something to disgust the pair.

'We would like to ask your permission to exhume—'

'Fuck off,' she said, finally lighting a cigarette.

'Mrs Goddard, we need your permission before we approach—'

'No bloody chance,' she said, shaking her head, vehemently.

Kim could feel the irritations at the woman's manner. Pity she hadn't been quite so protective of her daughter when she was alive. Her thoughts led her to a suspicion that was almost too twisted to consider. But consider it, she must.

'You're not working tonight, Mrs Goddard?' Kim asked.

'Nah, retired, I did. A while ago now.'

Maggie Goddard lived on Hollytree. Kai Lord controlled Hollytree. His employees didn't just retire.

The sickening truth of this woman's ruthlessness hit her with force.

'You exchanged places with your daughter, didn't you? You offered her to Kai instead of you. Just so you could get out,' she spat.

Ken made a noise from the corner. 'Nah, she didn't. That would be sick,' he said.

Strangely, of the two of them, only Ken looked disgusted at the accusation.

Maggie Goddard just stared at her.

'You did that to your own child so you could get out,' Kim said, with disgust. 'And how was Lord ever going to refuse that trade, eh?'

'She's the only one they left me with so I had to make use—'

'The only what?' Ken asked, stepping forward.

'Kid,' she screamed as though it was obvious.

'You had more than her?' he asked, staring her down.

'Two boys and a girl,' she said, as though she couldn't be bothered to recall their names.

Kim looked at her and then nodded towards her boyfriend. 'Go on, tell him you did it, because he still doesn't quite believe you.'

The woman didn't remove her gaze from Kim's face. 'Well, I did it to feed her for all them years, what was the harm?'

'Fuck this,' said Ken, stepping towards the table. He grabbed an armful of cans and headed towards the kitchen door. He stopped when he reached Kim.

He turned. 'You're disgusting, woman,' he said, before spitting right at her.

Kim stepped aside for him to pass as Maggie Goddard shouted after him while grabbing a tea towel and wiping at the white spittle in her hair. Pity the guy was leaving just when he was starting to grow on her.

Kim moved forward and took the prepared paperwork from her pocket and laid it on the table.

Bryant produced a pen.

'Margaret, you gave her fuck all else as a mother. The least you can give her is this.'

The woman eyed her with pure hatred for a moment before grabbing the pen and signing her name.

Kim put the paperwork back in her pocket and paused at the door. There was so much she wanted to say to this foul, repulsive woman who had done the unthinkable to her own flesh and blood. But there were no words that would penetrate the layer of disinterest of the piece of shit cracking open another can of cider.

She turned and left the kitchen.

Her colleague slammed the door behind him.

'Bryant, I just simply have no words for that excuse for a mother in there.'

He offered no response and she could see the tension in his jaw.

Kim opened her mouth to distract him just as her mobile phone sounded.

'Hey, Penn,' she answered.

'Got a result on one of those registration numbers, boss,'

She put the phone on speaker. 'Go on.'

'You're gonna love this. The white Astra is registered to an owner in Gornal, a Mrs Beverley Greaves.'

Kim glanced at Bryant whose surprised reaction mirrored her own.

'Thanks, Penn,' she said, ending the call.

'So, what was this woman doing crawling along Tavistock Road on a Saturday night?' he asked.

'Dunno, partner, but I think we should head over to her address and find out.'

CHAPTER THIRTY-FIVE

'Kev, what's the point of coming here again?' Stacey asked, as he pulled up outside Robertson's.

'There's a reason these people don't want us talking to these workers. I don't believe their story about that urgent order and that minibus thing gives me the creeps. You ever known that before?'

Stacey wanted to offer a balanced, reasonable response to his suspicion but she had none. Seeing those women being ferried en-masse away from the factory had reminded her of a programme she had once seen on the American facility of Area 51, where workers were bussed in and out and allowed no contact with anyone.

'Where are you going?' Stacey asked, as he walked away from the main entrance.

'Just want to check something,' he replied, cryptically.

She followed him past the showroom to the end of the building. The high metal gates were closed but not locked. She followed Dawson's gaze to a single back door partially obscured by towers of wooden pallets and a metal trolley.

'What are you looking for?' she asked.

He ignored her for a moment and then smiled in her direction. 'Aha,' he said. 'As I thought.'

He started pulling back the metal gate handle.

'Kev, this is trespass,' she said. 'And there's a camera up there.'

He shrugged. 'Not actively monitored, I'm guessing.'

'Kev, we can't—'

'Stace, there are times out in the field when you have to ask yourself one question and one question only.'

'Which is?'

'What would the boss do?'

Stacey immediately knew the answer to that one and followed him through.

'I still don't know what the hell…'

'Look at the floor,' he said, pointing towards the blue door.

She saw nothing except a smattering of cigarette ends.

'Aah, got it,' she said.

Clearly where the staff came for a fag break.

'So, we just gonna hang around here until…' Her words trailed away as the blue door opened.

A slight woman in a red overall stepped out and froze. Two other women barged into her and forced her forward. Panic filled all of their eyes as they looked from Dawson to her and back again.

'It's okay,' Stacey said, holding up her hands and smiling. 'We're not here to hurt you or get you into any trouble. We just want to talk. Do you speak English?'

Two of the women shook their heads but the slight woman nodded slowly, caution shining from her eyes. She still held the blue door open and could bolt back in at any second. The door was key coded and they would have no chance of following her.

'You shouldn't be here,' she whispered as the other two ladies moved away and lit cigarettes from cupped hands. They whispered and stared before moving away even further.

'Can we just ask you a couple of questions, while you have your smoke? And then we'll go,' Stacey said.

The woman began to close the door slowly behind her. Stacey guessed her to be early twenties. Her hair was dark brown; a long, untidy bob with a blunt fringe that was falling over her eyes.

'What's your name?' Stacey asked.

'Cristina,' she answered, quietly.

'Cristina, are you Romanian?' Stacey asked, realising Dawson had taken a step back.

Cristina nodded.

'Are all the girls in the factory Romanian?'

Again she nodded but Stacey was concerned to see that the fear hadn't yet left her face.

'I promise you, we're not here to cause you any trouble,' Stacey assured her.

The young woman offered her a tremulous half-smile.

'Is everything okay in there?' she asked, nodding towards the door.

'Yes, yes, is good place to work,' she offered automatically, taking a draw on the cigarette.

'Only, we tried to speak to you the other day but the minibus left…'

'Nicolae takes us home,' she said, nodding.

'And where is home?' Stacey asked.

'Brockmoor,' she said, quickly. 'We… I live in Brockmoor.'

'Cristina, do they treat you okay?' Stacey asked.

The girl's fingers were red raw and blistered on the ends. Cristina followed her gaze to her fingertips.

'I am new. Skin is hardening to the fabric.'

Stacey felt her heart plummet slightly. It was unlikely she'd be familiar enough with the other girls to know if any of them had recently had a baby but she had to try anyway.

'Cristina, do you know of any of your colleagues who has had a baby in the last few months?'

She frowned and shook her head, and Stacey realised they were only a moment away from the end of that cigarette.

'Are you sure? It could be very important. If you could just think about it…'

'I'm so sorry but I do not know these ladies. I am new here. I wish I could help…' she said, throwing the cigarette on the floor.

Stacey had a sudden thought.

'Maybe you can,' she said, removing the pages from Keats from her satchel. 'This book has come to our attention. Is this written in Romanian?'

Cristina took a quick look at it and nodded before turning back towards the door.

'I'm sorry but I have to—'

'Cristina, would you be able to help us translate this? Your English is very good and it might assist us.'

She shook her head.

'Please, and then I promise we'll leave you alone. Would you take a look at it for us?' Stacey asked separating the two sets of photocopies.

She sighed and took the pages from Stacey's hand. She keyed the entrance code into the number pad.

'Cristina, how will we contact…'

'Here, again, tomorrow,' she said, disappearing inside the door. The other two women slunk in behind her.

* * *

'Good job, Stace,' Dawson said as they headed back towards the gate.

'For what?' she asked.

'Finally opening your mouth,' he said.

'And good job to you too,' she said.

'For what?' he asked, confused.

'Finally learning to keep yours shut.'

CHAPTER THIRTY-SIX

'Bryant, slow the fuck down,' Kim cried as her left-hand side crashed against the passenger door.

'What?' he snapped.

'Nothing, I'm sure my shoulder will pop right back into its socket once you turn left again.'

'Of all the heartless bitches I've ever had the misfortune to—'

'Watch that van,' she said, monitoring vehicles exiting the side streets more closely than he was.

Bryant hit the brakes. Hard.

'Pull over,' she demanded.

'With pleasure,' he growled, stopping in front of a small tobacconist.

She followed his gaze. 'Oh no you don't,' she said.

'Oh yes I bloody do,' he said, taking off his seatbelt. 'I'm buying a pack of twenty and smoking the whole damn lot.'

She grabbed his arm. 'Oi, talk,' she ordered.

'I've never wanted a cigarette more than I do right now,' he said, trying to shake his arm free.

'Because of that foul woman?'

He grunted.

'You're gonna let a vile, repulsive, sad excuse for a woman give you a reason to start killing yourself again?'

'I'm just so bloody angry…'

'Absolutely you're angry,' she said, loosening her grip on his jacket. At least he was talking now. 'I wanted to wring her neck.

When matey boy Ken spat on her I wanted to haul him back and insist he do it again.'

'How could a mother do that to her own daughter?' he asked, gripping the steering wheel with whitened knuckles. 'To knowingly offer her up to Kai Lord for any kind of punter to use her and… Jesus, I can't even finish the sentence.'

'That's not a mother, Bryant. It's a woman who gave birth to a child. There's a bloody big difference.'

He sighed, heavily.

'Guv, I try to keep the faith; I swear to God I try to remember that most people are decent and good. Just some days the balance of what we see ain't in my favour.'

'Yes, it is,' she said, simply.

He shook his head.

'That guy, Tim, volunteers at the community centre off his own back because he believes in human nature. An ex-convict named Len uses that place to try and stay out of trouble. Even Ken ended up surprising us.'

He turned to look at her. 'You're advising me on positivity?'

'Oh, the irony,' she observed.

She allowed him a moment of silence.

'You okay to drive sensibly now?' she asked.

'And the irony continues,' he said, smartly.

'You know, it's a good job Woody pairs you with me so I can keep you calm,' she said, seriously.

Bryant's sudden laughter filled the car as he pulled out and joined the queue of traffic.

* * *

Eventually he turned into a side street that would retain the snow long after it had disappeared everywhere else. The car slid to a halt in front of a row of terraces. The front bumper almost kissed the rear of a white Peugeot.

'You wanna lead or shall I?' Bryant asked.

'You,' Kim answered. She wanted to use all her senses to see what this woman had been doing kerb crawling the night before.

Bryant knocked the front door. It was answered by a woman in her early forties. Her eyes were dark yet filled with hope, until her gaze moved between the two of them.

The colour began to drain from her face.

Bryant held out his card and introduced them.

The woman's eyes rolled in her head right before she fell to the ground.

CHAPTER THIRTY-SEVEN

'I'm gonna ring the Home Office,' Dawson said, tapping his fingers on the steering wheel.

The Home Office controlled immigration and passports amongst Immigration Enforcement, Border Force, HM Passport Office and UK Visas and Immigration. Immigration Enforcement was set up in April 2012 to prevent abuse, track immigration offenders and increase compliance with immigration law. They carried out some six thousand raids per year based on intel from approximately fifty thousand allegations from the public.

'For what?' Stacey asked.

'I want them to do a raid on the factory.'

'Hey, I know, instead of inventing a crime why don't we deal with one we've already got?'

'I'm gonna call 'em,' he insisted.

'Or we could go and check for CCTV footage of our guy close to the canal towpath.'

'Yeah, and with no estimated time of death what day month or year should we start?'

'Bloody hell, Kev. Use your brain. What day did we have that last bad snowstorm?' she asked.

'Friday night.'

'And when was he found?'

'Monday morning, this morning.'

'You really think he'd have lain there undiscovered if he hadn't been covered in snow?'

'So, you think it happened Friday night?'

Stacey nodded. 'He'd have been spotted otherwise. I went to bed it was a light flurry. I woke up and there was a three-foot snowdrift up my front door. You just want to get into Robertson's because someone told you that you can't.'

'Did you see how frightened she was?' he asked, staring out of the window. 'She didn't want to talk to us for a minute longer than necessary in case she got caught.'

'Kev, get off it,' she said.

He shook his head and took out his phone.

'Nah, they've got those girls working there illegally. I know it. If we can get Immigration Enforcement to pay them a visit we could get their addresses, speak to their neighbours. I'm telling you, Stace, someone in that building knows something about that child.'

'So, how are you gonna get it raided?'

He shrugged. 'Anonymous tip.'

Stacey knew that the majority of raids on business premises were carried out on the back of anonymous tips. But she wasn't sure how it would help them if they weren't involved.

Dawson's fingernails returned to the wheel.

She sighed heavily, as she took out her phone.

'What are you doing?' Dawson asked, as she scrolled through her contact list.

She reached D and hit on the name Devon. She put the phone on the dashboard and put it on loudspeaker.

'Hey, babe,' came the female response.

'Hi Dev,' Stacey said, quickly. 'I'm here with my colleague. You got a minute?'

'So, now's not a good time to ask why you never called me after our one night of steaming hot—'

'Dev,' Stacey cried, feeling the colour flood into her cheeks. For once she was pleased her caramel skin hid it from view.

'Please, continue,' Kev shouted with wide eyes.

'Just kidding,' Devon said, with a throaty laugh. 'Wishful thinking on my part,' she added.

It had been one date, two drinks and definitely no sex.

'What can I do for you, babe?'

'We've got a factory full of Romanian girls. Not sure if they're legal or not,' Stacey said, refusing to echo Dawson's suspicions on the back of no evidence.

'And?'

'Truthfully, I think someone in there is hiding something.'

'Come on, babe, you know we need more than that,' Devon said. 'You know the process. We get an allegation, field officers hit the streets and put together an intel pack. Then we make a decision on a raid, appoint an OIC, make a plan and get a warrant from the Magistrate's…'

'Yeah, right,' Stacey said, affably.

'Okay,' Devon admitted. 'We sometimes skip that last bit but we do have a process to go through. We can't just storm into premises and round up every employee. We have to know who or what we're looking for and target only those individuals.'

'You're kidding?' Dawson called across the car.

'Nope,' she answered. 'We can legally question other people who arouse our suspicion once we're in but we gotta go in for a reason.

'In some cases we can get consent on the door from the employers but they aren't normally that cooperative,' she said.

'Why not?' Stacey asked. Surely employers would want to weed out illegal workers.

'Twenty grand fine per worker,' Devon answered.

Dawson whistled.

'And we have a body,' Stacey said.

'Linked to the factory?' Devon asked doubtfully.

'No,' she said honestly. They could barely link him to being Romanian.

Dawson appeared to have lost interest and was tapping away on the steering wheel again.

'Any suggestions?' she asked.

Devon sighed heavily. 'Offer to take me out for a drink and then ask me again.'

The smirk on her colleague's face mirrored the smile threatening her own.

'Okay, I'll buy you a drink,' Stacey said, trying to keep the chuckle out of her voice. 'Now what?'

'I'll put some feelers out on the street.'

'You'll get some field intel?'

'Hey, hey, hey, slow down. What I'm gonna do is so far below field intel it's in another country. Girl, for that I'd want much more than a gin and tonic.'

'Okay, okay, anything you can do to help,' Stacey said, smiling. 'And I'll give you a call,' she said, hanging up.

'Spunky. I like her,' Dawson said, tapping something into his phone.

'Like I give a shit about that,' Stacey said, shaking her head.

'Okey-dokey, let's try this one,' he said, pressing the call button.

Like her, he put the phone on loudspeaker.

'Hello,' grumbled a deep low voice.

'Is that Romy's in Ambelcote?'

'Yes, if you want table we no do booking,' stated the thick accented male.

Stacey typed in 'Romy's Amblecote': A mixture of English and Romanian cuisine.

'Do you offer takeaway?' Dawson asked.

'Yes, five to eleven,'

Stacey assumed he meant from five until eleven.

'You sell *sarmale*?' Dawson asked.

'Yes,' the man said as though it was a no-brainer.

Stacey smiled at her colleague. It was as thin as rice paper but it was a lead nonetheless.

CHAPTER THIRTY-EIGHT

'Jeez, Bryant, what is it with you today?' Kim asked as she knelt beside the woman.

Bryant joined her on the opposite side. He grabbed a jacket from the hooks behind the door and placed it under the woman's head.

'Must be my animal magnetism, guv,' he said.

'Yeah, that'll be it,' Kim said, as the woman began to moan.

'Mrs Greaves, it's okay. You're safe,' Kim said, reassuringly. She thought it best not to mention again that they were police officers.

The woman opened her eyes. It took a second for her to focus.

'It's all right, Mrs Greaves. You just fainted. Are you hurt at all?'

The woman shook her head as she began to return to the present. And as she did her eyes filled with fear. Her hand clutched Kim's. Her grip was ice cold.

'Is she dead?' The words were barely more than a whisper.

Kim looked to Bryant who shook his head.

'Is who dead, Mrs Greaves?'

The woman forced herself to a sitting position, shaking her head.

'My daughter, of course. Eleanor Greaves. Ellie…'

'Mrs Greaves, I'm really sorry but we have no idea what you're talking about.'

Kim watched the relief turn to frustration, as she helped the woman to her feet. With her legs now cleared from the doorway

Bryant closed the front door. Mrs Greaves was a little unsteady but she held onto the bureau against the wall.

'Then why are you here?' she asked. 'Are you finally going to help me look for her?'

'If we just step inside, Bryant will make some tea—'

'I don't want bloody tea, officer. I want someone to help me find my daughter.'

She turned around and walked into a lounge on the right. Kim followed. Although small, the room was tastefully decorated in neutral colours.

'How old is your daughter, Mrs Greaves?'

'Sixteen, which is why you lot couldn't give a damn when I reported her missing last night.'

Kim understood the woman's frustrations but a sixteen-year-old not returning home at the weekend was not a high-priority case.

But the dates slotted into place in her head.

'So, you've been out looking yourself?' Kim asked.

'Well, of course I have. No one else is going to help me.'

'Her father?'

'Has never been in the picture and if Ellie could find him she'd have done a much better job than the CSA.'

'Could she have found him?' Kim asked, gently. Teenagers could be secretive creatures.

The woman shook her head. 'She didn't even know his name. She's never been interested.'

'So what happened between the two of you?' Kim asked, glancing at Bryant.

If Mrs Greaves had been able to hear the silent conversation, Kim reasoned, it would have gone something like:

'Take out your notebook.'

'This isn't our case.'

'Just do it.'

Bryant opened his book at the next blank page.

'She left yesterday morning. Said she was going to Caitlin's house and she'd be back for tea. That normally means around six so I left it a couple of hours thinking she'd just met up with more friends. I tried her mobile at about nine and it kept going straight to voicemail.'

'What did Caitlin say?'

'That they'd had no plans to do anything together and she'd spent the day at her grandmother's in Enville.'

'Does Ellie have a boyfriend?'

Mrs Greaves shook her head. 'Not that I know of. She hasn't mentioned any particular boy to me and I hadn't noticed any change in her behaviour. No extra effort in her appearance or coyness, although Caitlin did say she thought Ellie had been talking to someone new on Facebook, but she checked Ellie's list of friends and there's no one on there that Caitlin doesn't know.'

'Is there anything missing from her room?'

She shook her head. 'Nothing that I can see. All her clothes are still here and her make-up case. Only her purse, phone and backpack are gone. That's why I couldn't understand why the officer was so unhelpful. I knew she hadn't run away.'

Kim nodded sympathetically. And now she had to ask the most painful question of all. The one that would have kept this woman awake for every hour since.

'Had you recently argued?'

'Officer, she's sixteen. It was almost an hourly occurrence.'

And wouldn't this woman just give everything she had to be arguing with her child right now?

'About anything in particular?'

'Pretty much everything but the biggest issue between us is college.'

Mrs Greaves stared off into the distance, reliving every one of those arguments.

'Was there anything she said, anything at all that seemed strange or out of character?' Kim asked. People often gave themselves away during arguments when they were not censoring every thought before it came out of their mouth.

'She'd started saying she was beginning to see the bigger picture. When I asked her what she meant she just huffed and walked away as if I was proving her point for her.'

Kim knew there was little she could do here to help. There was no evidence of foul play. The girl was a resourceful sixteen-year-old. She had taken whatever money she had, her phone and she'd made a new friend that she'd kept secret.

Kim knew that her presence on Tavistock Road had simply been a mother trying to track down her child and, although unwittingly, they had raised the woman's hopes that her daughter had returned and then made her think her daughter was dead.

'Do you have a recent photo?' Kim asked.

Bryant coughed and Kim ignored him. She knew the procedure. She could offer this woman no false hope that a team could be dedicated to her runaway daughter but she clearly had no one to turn to.

She reached for her handbag and took out a picture. It showed a blonde girl with pale skin and no make-up smiling into the camera. She looked younger than her sixteen years.

'That was taken at Christmas when I gave her a new phone. I left it until last. She was so excited.'

Kim took the photo. 'Look, Mrs Greaves, I can't make any promises but I'll hand this out to the neighbourhood team and ask them to keep a look out. It's the best I can do,' she said, as she felt her phone vibrate in her pocket. She ignored it.

The woman nodded her understanding and offered the ghost of a smile.

It wasn't much but Kim hoped the woman didn't feel quite so alone.

Mrs Greaves followed them to the door. Kim offered her a card. 'If she turns up hungry and sorry, just give me a quick call.'

'Thank you, officer. Thank you so much,' the woman said, as Kim's phone began to vibrate again.

'Bloody hell,' Kim said, taking it out. People who rang her in quick succession annoyed the hell out of her. If she was in a position to answer it she would.

Two missed calls from Keats.

She leaned against the car and waited. If he'd called twice, she could guarantee he was about to try again.

'Stone,' she answered, the second his name appeared.

'About damn time,' he snapped.

Her antennae reacted instantly to his mild curse. Keats rarely cursed at all.

She stood. 'What is it?' she asked, already fearing his response.

'I'll give you one good guess.'

'Shit,' she said, looking to Bryant.

His eyes demanded a response.

'Looks like we've got another.'

CHAPTER THIRTY-NINE

Cristina lay on the top bunk and stared at the naked yellow light casting a sickly glow around the small room, highlighting the starkness of her surroundings.

She closed her eyes as the gentle sobbing reached her from the bunk bed opposite. Natalya reached out and touched the wall close to her thin pillow. Cristina knew that she was touching a photo of her two young daughters back in Romania, and on the end of those fingers was a kiss.

After a few minutes the gentle crying turned to a soft snore. Even the deepest sadness could not fight exhaustion.

Normally, Cristina would be close behind, following Natalya to the place of peace, the relief from the emotion, the fear, the loneliness. Sleep was what they all craved at the end of the day.

But not tonight. Cristina was wide awake.

She took the sheaf of papers from beneath her pillow and began to read the first entry dated nineteen years earlier.

Her brain switched easily between Romanian and English as she began to make notes. She had been taught well.

* * *

Today we arrived at Calais two weeks after leaving home. We ate the last of the food while we waited on an upturned wooden box.

The fear turned my stomach despite the miles we'd travelled. Romania still felt so close while we waited. The terror that we would be stopped and returned would not leave me until we crossed the water.

A man named Ralph found us as darkness fell and you nestled in my arms.

He gave me a piece of paper and ushered us to a row of tall lorries. A man stepped out of the shadows. An envelope changed hands. The curtain of the lorry opened and the man pointed.

We climbed in and over the plastic-covered boxes. We found a corner and huddled. I pulled you close and you slept. The loud hum of the engine beneath us lulled you and your breathing changed.

The lorry stopped and started before finally staying still. I prayed and I cried as you slept peacefully beside me.

I knew we were on the sea. The secret darkness around us both comforted and scared me.

No one could find us here.

Surely we were invisible to the world in this tiny darkened corner of the lorry. Suddenly I wanted to stay there for ever.

For just a few hours I felt relief. The doubts of what I'd done swirled around in my head but I tried to bury them with hope. We were going to a land with work, with food, with opportunity. We were going to be somewhere safe.

As the lorry began to move again you stirred.

You looked to me with a mixture of hope, fear and trust.

I pulled you closer and held you tight.

Your faith humbled me to tears. I knew that we would be fine as long as we had each other.

* * *

Cristina put the pencil to the side and wiped away the tears that were streaming down her face.

CHAPTER FORTY

Kim pulled up at the cordon which stretched across the road and restricted access to a car wash on one side and the entrance to a small playground on the other.

The building itself was a dated, single-storey brick structure with a doorway at each end. One marked 'Ladies' and one marked 'Gents'.

'Bloody classy,' Kim muttered approaching the public conveniences at the end of Brierley Hill High Street.

No badges were required. The guarding officer was a constable they knew well. He lifted the tape and they ducked underneath.

'What do we know?' Kim asked.

'Further update identifies her as Donna Hill.'

'Oh Jesus,' Kim sighed. Although the girl had barely spoken the other night Kim did remember the trembling that had nothing to do with the temperature.

Kim spotted a foot as she stepped into the entrance of the Ladies. Kim didn't care who the girl was, or what she'd done. To meet her end here filled her with a mixture of revulsion and sadness.

Keats looked up from his kneeling position and opened his mouth to speak. Kim was in no mood for any wisecracks and cut him short.

'Not here and not now,' she said, stepping around the pathologist.

The body lay as though it had fallen or slid to the ground. The knees were bent and she lay partly on her side. Her high heels remained firmly attached to her feet. Her bare legs did not appear bruised and her skirt, although short, was in position around her thighs. The yellow T-shirt had been dyed crimson from the blood. The lightweight jacket was thin and had offered no protection against the temperature.

'Two stab wounds to the back and one to the front.'

'To the back?' Kim asked. The assailant had followed her into the toilets.

Keats nodded. 'Small amount of blood loss but the third wound was the fatal one.'

'Any sign of sexual assault?' Kim asked Keats.

'I haven't moved her yet. Waited for you good folks to arrive. No obvious signs at this point.'

Kim studied the face in detail as the photographer took the last few shots. The pink eye shadow was smudged on the left-hand side. The poor skin condition was beginning to fight through the layers of foundation and concealer. Her lips were free of make-up.

'Definitely need to find out who her last client was,' Kim said, as Bryant appeared beside her. 'Because it wasn't long afterwards. She's made no effort to re-apply her make-up so either she didn't have time or she was done for the night and on her way home.'

Bryant made a note.

'Guv, she was found by that lady over there. She's a long-distance lorry driver. Took a wrong turn after driving most of the night and parked up quickly to use the toilet. Norwegian, I think, but speaks reasonably good English.'

'Anything suspicious about her?'

At this point everyone was a suspect.

Bryant shook his head. 'Not that I can see. Her consignment notes confirm that she's heading for Norton and took a wrong turn off the Stourbridge ring road. Couldn't find anywhere to turn her rig around.'

'That's lorry to you and me,' Keats said to her.

'And she's still whiter than the snow she's sitting on. Got her details in case we need her later but the FOA is taking a detailed statement.'

Kim nodded her understanding. The first officer attending appeared to have done a good job of securing the scene and witnesses.

Kim stepped back, away from the technicians, and surveyed the scene for a second. The woman had been attacked from behind as she'd entered the public conveniences. Her gut told her that meant something but she had no clue what.

Bryant joined her as Keats gently turned the victim onto her back.

'Definitely not moved,' he said, pointing to the purple staining of her skin.

Lividity had pooled down her entire right side. Kim had seen it many times before. Upon death the blood in the body travels to the lowest point and stains like a birthmark.

Keats gently moved aside her clothing looking for signs of sexual assault.

'Nothing obvious around her thighs or breast area, Inspector.'

'Approximate time?' she asked.

Keats took out the rectal probe.

Kim really didn't feel the need to watch any more.

She reached down and dislodged the gold lamé handbag. Bryant opened an evidence bag ready as she carefully clicked the clasp. Inside she saw clutches of cash, a supermarket brand lipstick, a compact with powder, a selection of condoms and a house key.

She very carefully lifted out the clutch of notes closest to the top of the bag. The roll was thicker than the other one.

She opened it up and counted it.

She frowned at Bryant.

'It's £40 and it's all in £5 notes.'

CHAPTER FORTY-ONE

'Okay, boys and girls, where are we?' Kim asked.

'Board updated, boss,' Penn offered.

Kim had already noted that the wipe board had been cut in half and Donna's details now headed the right-hand side.

'Okay, let's crack on. I don't want to divide that board again. What else you got, Penn?'

'Exhumation Licence for Lauren Goddard has been sent to Environmental Health who are currently drawing straws to see who attends. Funeral Directors are confirmed and the crematorium is on standby awaiting the exact time.'

Kim nodded. If she was honest she did wonder what the exhumation would reveal but if there was something untoward surrounding this girl's death it might just shake the murderer out of the woodwork. At the very least the person responsible would know that her death had not been forgotten.

'Anything more on the link from Kelly Rowe to Kai Lord?' she asked, sticking with Penn.

It still bothered her that there was no clear trail from the young mother to the gang leader. How the hell had their paths crossed?

He shook his head. 'Spoke to a neighbour of hers named Roxanne Shaw who confirmed everything we already know about her. Nice girl, no boyfriend and lived quietly with her daughter. Neighbour had no clue she was a prostitute until she saw it on the news.'

Damn Kelly Rowe for being so good at keeping secrets.

'Registration numbers?' she asked.

'Still tracking that BMW, boss, but I might have something good for you in a minute,' he said, looking at his screen.

'Kev?' she said, glancing across the room.

'Currently trying to identify Romanian links to our victim at the canal,' he said.

'And those injuries?' she asked. Keats had sent the post-mortem report to her email.

He shook his head. 'Horrific,' he answered.

'Recent or historic ones?'

'Both,' he answered. 'His leg looked like a three-storey building had fallen on it and there was little of his body that had escaped injury over the years. Six broken ribs, a fractured collarbone, small breaks around his head, eye, temple and nose probably from being punched.'

'How about his hands?' Kim asked.

Dawson frowned, thoughtfully. 'Not too much damage, actually,' he said.

She decided to let that just filter into his brain. It would fertilise a cell eventually.

'So he could still work?' Stacey said.

Kim shrugged. Okay it had fertilised the wrong brain but as a team they were working well and following up leads and clues effectively.

'Any fresh leads on the child?' she asked.

'We're gonna try the factory again,' Stacey offered, tentatively.

'Was that a question or a statement?' Kim asked, narrowing her gaze at the constable.

'Statement,' she answered.

'Good idea,' she agreed.

The folks at Robertson's had been given enough leeway and the story about the minibus had touched something on the back of her neck too.

A tentative shadow appeared at the doorway.

'Marm, may I?'

'Come in, Sergeant Evans.'

As he entered he glanced sideways at the board. He swallowed. 'It's true then?'

Kim nodded. 'Donna Hill was murdered late last night.'

The sergeant shook his head. 'She wasn't a bad kid, though some would disagree.'

Kim looked after him. 'Where's happy chappy today?'

'Called in sick. Stomach bug or something. I had a message you wanted to see me.'

'That was me,' Bryant said, standing.

He retrieved a clutch of papers from the printer and passed them across.

'Can you hand these out to a few of your guys. Her name is Ellie Greaves and she's been missing since Sunday night.'

Sergeant Evans took a good look at the picture.

'This isn't an official missing person's case,' Kim clarified. 'She is sixteen years of age and has most likely taken a breather for a couple of days but if you guys could just keep an eye out for her we'd be grateful.' She nodded towards Penn. 'We have her phone number and will be trying to get in touch with her as well.'

He nodded. 'Of course, Marm.'

He turned to leave and took another look at the board. His shoulders slumped a little and he shook his head again.

Kim understood. The 'beat boys', as Dawson called them, spent a lot of time out on the streets. They liaised with local businesses and were the primary face of the police force. Their designated areas were like extensions of their own homes. It was their patch; their area of protection.

These girls would have been more than a name on a board. The beat officers would know their backgrounds, about their kids, their lives. Deaths on the beat were taken very personally.

'Thank you, Sergeant,' she said as he disappeared from sight.

'Yes, got it,' Penn cried.

'I hope it's not catching,' Stacey quipped.

'The Toyota from the other night, boss,' Penn continued.

'I thought we'd eliminated that from our enquiries,' Kim said. The registered owner was a seventy-nine-year-old male with severe physical disabilities.

'Couldn't understand why our registered owner would be out at that time of night, so I ran a search again yesterday, and another hit came up – for the AutoTrader website – and there it was for sale, a month ago. Tried to ring Mr Bingham but he doesn't hear so well. Went to see him and he confirmed he'd sold the car but couldn't remember the name of the man who'd bought it.'

'Any description?'

He smiled ruefully. 'Average height, average build, mousy hair but he was wearing a green Puffa jacket.'

'Get an urgent bolo out on that guy,' Dawson said, shaking his head.

Yeah, and be on the lookout for alert for that description would have three-figure sightings within the hour.

'Cash sale?' she asked.

Penn nodded. 'I asked about the registration slip, which he'd only got round to posting a few days ago. Been waiting for it to register on the DVLA.'

'And?'

'The Toyota now belongs to a local guy named Roger Barton.'

Kim glanced at Bryant. 'Rapid Rodge,' they said, together.

Dawson and Stacey looked at each other while Penn continued to look at the screen.

'Not sure if this means anything, but a Google search names him as a local Scout leader.'

Kim remembered everything they'd learned so far.

'Normal entrance fee to a Cub Scouts meeting anyone?'

'Probably a fiver,' Dawson said with a shrug.

'That's what I thought and this is beginning to make a lot more sense,' she said, launching herself from the table.

'Get your coat, Bryant. Looks like we might have found Kelly and Donna's last client.'

CHAPTER FORTY-TWO

Stacey tightened the woollen scarf at her neck as Dawson parked the car. Her feet crunched onto grey sludge that had re-frozen overnight at temperatures of minus two. The chirpy weather presenter had promised a high of three degrees above freezing by 11 a.m. Stacey wasn't holding her breath.

She closed the car door and looked at him across the bonnet. 'Kev, this is such a long shot we'll need a bloody trebuchet to get—'

'A what?' he said, opening the door to the café.

'It's a weapon that uses a swinging arm to… oh, never mind,' she said, following him inside.

She wasn't sure anyone here was going to be able to help them identify their victim.

The warmth of the sparsely populated café charmed her instantly. The furnishings were simple wooden tables and chairs that had their fair share of war wounds but the corners of the tiled floor looked clean. Two food hygiene posters were displayed beneath a chalkboard listing specials. The deli-style counter was tastefully arranged and contained a mixture of soups, smoked sausages, and baked potatoes with different fillings.

Stacey felt her stomach growl in response to the delicious smoky aroma that wafted towards her.

'Vasile?' Dawson asked of a rounded man in his mid-fifties. His white T-shirt was crisp and clean.

He nodded.

'Is there somewhere we can talk?'

'Mariana,' he called, as the remaining customers left the building.

Looking around, Stacey realised there was no longer the need for privacy. The café had emptied. Two half-eaten plates of food had been left. Neither herself nor Dawson had taken out their identification or introduced themselves as police officers which made her wonder how they had so quickly been pegged as officials.

A woman in her late teens appeared. Her face was thin and pale with dark circles around her wary eyes. She rubbed flour-covered hands on her apron.

'Pa?' she asked.

'Mind the shop for a minute,' he instructed, indicating they should follow him out back.

Once beyond the café the space opened up into a roomy, stainless steel endowed kitchen area. Rows of foil trays were arranged along the longest surface of the kitchen.

'How can I help you?' he asked, in that rumbling deep voice they'd heard the day before.

'You told us on the phone that you serve *sarmale*?' Dawson asked.

He nodded. 'Of course.'

'Is it a popular dish?' Stacey asked, hoping it was a rare choice and only one man had asked for it in the last few weeks.

'Very popular. Romanian staple,' he answered. 'Maybe twenty to thirty portions each day.'

Stacey felt her heart sink.

Dawson took out his phone. He scrolled for a minute and held it out.

'Do you know this man? Has he been in here?'

Vasile looked and frowned with distaste. 'Is this man dead?'

Dawson nodded, and Vasile looked again.

He began to shake his head. 'I don't think…'

'Take another look,' Dawson said, handing him the phone. 'Are you sure he wasn't in here late last week, maybe Friday?'

He looked again but shook his head more definitely this time. 'I don't know this man,' he said.

And neither did anyone else, Stacey thought. So far no one had reported him missing.

'Sir, his immigration status is not important to us…'

'Not to me either,' he answered. 'My daughter and I are legal residents here in—'

'That's fine,' Dawson said. 'We're not here to question your legal status. We just need to identify this man and find out what happened to him.'

'I understand but I do not know him.'

Dawson nodded his acceptance. 'I appreciate that you must see many people in and out of here each day. You can't possibly know or recognise every one of them.'

'I know all of my customers,' he said defensively.

She understood Dawson's little test. He appeared to be telling the truth.

'Is there another café like this close by?' Dawson asked. 'Catering to the Romanian community.'

'Nearest I know is in Wolverhampton,' he said.

Dawson put his phone back into his pocket.

'Well, thank you for your time,' he said, just as Stacey had a sudden thought.

'Is that *sarmale*?' she asked, pointing to the food being prepared into the foil trays.

He nodded.

'For the shop?' she asked, looking to the full containers ready and waiting.

'No. This is being prepared for one of our corporate orders.'

Stacey felt a jolt of excitement in her stomach.

'Can you tell us who?' she asked.

'It's for Robertson's Handbags. We deliver there every Thursday.'

CHAPTER FORTY-THREE

'Pull over here, Bryant,' Kim said, suddenly.

'Guv…' he warned.

'What?' she asked, innocently.

'We appear to be uncomfortably close to the café that a certain person favours for his breakfast.'

'Really? I hadn't noticed,' she said, taking another look at the front window. 'I'm just deciding if I fancy a bit of toast before we chat to Roger Barton. I mean, what are the chances Kai Lord would be at the exact same place at the exact same time?'

'You know you can't go in there and without any direct proof you can't bring him in…'

'Oooh, looks like I am hungry after all,' she said, opening the passenger door.

'Oh, shit,' Bryant said, as Kai Lord stepped out of the café.

'Good to see the death of another one of your colleagues hasn't affected your appetite,' Kim said, standing directly in his path.

A slight flare of the nostrils demonstrated just how pleased he was to see her.

'You're not supposed to be here,' he snarled.

She looked around him. 'Aww, come on, I let you finish your bacon and eggs in peace, didn't I?' she taunted.

He stepped around her. She turned and walked by his side.

Bryant was opening the driver's door. She shook her head in his direction. This was just the two of them.

'Not gonna look good on your appraisal, is it?' Kim asked, matching him stride for stride. 'Losing two employees in a few days. You're a shit pimp, eh?'

'Fuck off,' he said, increasing his stride.

She kept pace.

'Unless you just don't give a shit because you're the one doing them in.'

He said nothing as he turned the corner and headed towards the gold Range Rover parked in a disabled spot.

Kim was disappointed to see it had not been ticketed. She stepped ahead of him and leaned against the driver's door preventing him from touching the handle without touching her first.

'Get the fuck away…'

'What are you trying to hide, Kai?' she asked, suspiciously. 'I never had you pegged for any murders but your actions are making me think I was wrong to write you off as nothing more than a pathetic low life living off the sweat and misery of other people.'

'I didn't fucking kill—'

'Yeah, that's what I was thinking. You don't have the bollocks to kill anyone. You can terrify one of your troops into taking the rap for a manslaughter charge that would have looked better on you. You can order your minions to beat up a copper four on one and you can handle cowed and frightened women who are desperate, but actual murder. Not even close…'

'Are you trying to fucking bait—?'

'Except, I'm the only one that thinks so, Kai. The rest of my team reckon you're a nasty enough bastard to have killed Kelly and Donna for some petty kind of reason, and I think you're too pathetic. So who is right – them or me?'

'Move away from the fucking car,' he growled.

Oh, how he wanted to push her to the side and get into the car, and how she wished he would. She'd have him cuffed and on his way to the station before he had a chance to press the button on his key fob.

She folded her arms and leaned against the metal.

'And it's not enough that two girls you're responsible for are dead but another transaction didn't quite go to plan, did it?' she asked, smiling.

He shrugged. 'Easy come, easy go, innit? Plenty more—'

'Isn't it just sooooo annoying when obstacles get in the way of you just doing your job? It's turning into a bit of a shit week for both of us.'

'What da fuck you want?'

Her best aim was for him to put his hands on her and give her a reason to haul him in for questioning. The two-foot distance between them told her that was unlikely.

'Cut the gangster speak with me, Kai. We both know you were no hood kid before your parents died and left you two hundred grand, which you spent in just under three years. It might work with your flunkies on Hollytree but not with me.'

His body moved towards her at the mention of his parents but his self-control was as impeccable as his designer clothing.

Did he not think she would take the time to find out everything she could about her enemies? Kai's father had built a property portfolio of rental accommodation specialising in houses of multiple occupancy in university towns before his death in a freak storm while on holiday in Indonesia. Neither of Kai's parents had survived the collapse of a three-storey hotel, and Kai had liquidated all the brick and mortar assets within six months of their deaths.

'Officer, you better state your business before my solicitor—'

'I want you to be aware that I know you're into something more than cheap drugs and prostitution. I don't know what it is but when I find out I am gonna make sure you go away for a bloody long time,' she said, stepping away from the car.

Woody would not take a second letter from his solicitor with the same level of understanding.

'I'm an entrepreneur, officer. Always gotta try new things,' he said cockily, getting into the car. 'Some you win, some you lose but one thing's for sure…'

A van rumbled past as he said his final words and Kim couldn't quite make out what he'd said.

But to her it had sounded like – 'not everyone is exactly what they seem'.

CHAPTER FORTY-FOUR

Dawson was in no mood to be appeased quite so easily this time. Fatigue always manifested itself as impatience for him. He'd had another late night made even later with the hour-long argument and the two-hour silence that had followed.

He made no small talk or even friendly eye contact with Melody as they waited for Mr Robertson to appear in reception.

Forget Damascus, he thought. Every road was currently leading back to this rip-off bag factory.

'Officers, how may I help?' Steven said appearing behind the young receptionist.

'Mr Robertson, we'd like to speak to you about a few things. Is there somewhere…?'

'Of course, follow me,' he said, heading past them out of the door. They followed him into the showroom.

'My mother is in a meeting with prospective clients at the moment.'

He led them to a small table at the back of the showroom.

As he followed, Dawson couldn't help but glance over the selection of goods being displayed. He could visualise his fiancée carrying any one of them. If this was cheap shit, it was impressive cheap shit. Although, not impressive enough to get him out of the current doghouse he'd landed himself in.

'Please sit,' Steven said, pushing the keyboard away and leaning his arms on the table.

'Mr Robertson, is it correct that you place a regular order with Vasile's Café for *sarmale*?' he asked.

The man frowned and then smiled as though it was a trick question. Clearly not what he'd thought was going to be asked.

'Umm… yes, it's a very popular Romanian dish and once a week we order it in for the girls,' he said. 'They work very hard, officer.'

'I don't doubt it,' Dawson answered tightly. 'You said "girls". Don't the men get to eat it?'

'You mean man?' Mr Robertson asked, ignoring Dawson's tone. 'Our only male employee is Nicolae and of course he can have as much as he wants. I use the term "girls" only because the majority of our staff are female.' He paused. 'That's not sexist,' he defended. 'But we can only choose from the people who apply.'

'And how do the women apply to work here?' Stacey asked.

'Nicolae brings in CVs and we choose whom to interview.'

'So, you have no other men working here at all?' Dawson clarified.

Mr Robertson shook his head.

'I think I'd like to know exactly why you're here, officers. I'm not sure how us treating our employees to lunch once a week can have any bearing at all on any case you're working.'

Dawson felt the nudge of Stacey's leg beneath the table.

His hostility was born of frustration at the lead going nowhere. He took out his phone, and once again scrolled to the photo.

'Sir, do you know this man?' he asked.

Mr Robertson frowned at the picture. His lips formed into a thin line of distaste.

'Oh my goodness. Is he dead?'

Dawson wished they had a picture that hadn't come from the morgue.

'I'm afraid so,' he said. 'Do you know him?'

Mr Robertson shook his head. 'Is there a reason why you'd think I would?'

Dawson was not prepared to admit they were here simply because the man had *sarmale* in his stomach.

'I'm really sorry, officer,' Mr Robertson said, glancing at his watch. 'But I don't think there's anything else I can offer.'

'Is there a chance we could speak with some of your employees?' Stacey asked pleasantly. 'Perhaps one of them might know this man.'

Dawson admired his colleague for trying but suspected he knew the answer.

'Of course, officer. You can speak to them all if you'd like.'

Dawson hid his surprise. Not the response they'd been expecting.

Steven Robertson laughed. 'I'm sorry if I've disappointed you but these girls are not our prisoners. We have nothing to hide.'

'Thank you for your cooperation, Mr Robertson,' Stacey said.

'Not at all, officer. All you had to do was ask.'

CHAPTER FORTY-FIVE

Ellie stepped out of the shower and listened keenly, sure that she could hear voices from downstairs. Probably Roxanne singing along to the radio again. Anything from Pink and the woman couldn't help herself.

Ellie had resolved that today she would definitely call her mother. She knew it would probably end in an argument. Her anger at her mother's total lack of concern was bubbling away beneath the mature high ground she had chosen to take. If this was how her mother wanted it to be then that was fine by her but she needed to hear it properly before she moved on.

And she would just as stubbornly refuse to acknowledge that there had been moments over the last few days when she had missed the sound of her mother humming to old eighties tunes as she pottered around in the kitchen. Or that she had missed their good-natured bickering over the bathroom first thing in the morning.

If that was her mum's game then she could play it too.

Ellie combed her hair and headed down the stairs. For lunch they were cooking Mexican together. And afterwards she would call her mother.

* * *

Ellie stopped dead in her tracks at the sight of a huge black man sitting at the kitchen table. His entire wardrobe was as dark as his skin, except for a glistening gold watch on his wrist.

Roxanne turned from the counter as the kettle boiled. Her face looked drawn and pensive. The smile was forced.

'Ellie, I'd like you to meet a friend of mine. This is Kai Lord.'

Ellie forced a smile and nodded towards the male. She caught his gaze as it travelled over her body from head to toe. His smile made her a little uncomfortable. It was not the benign type offered on greeting someone for the first time. There was an element of pleasure, satisfaction. The way you viewed something you'd made, or acquired, a possession.

'Pleased to meet you, Ellie,' he said, offering his hand.

He remained seated, which meant she had to walk towards him or risk offence and she would not be so rude to a friend of Roxanne's no matter how creepy he was.

His grip was firm, his skin warm. He held her hand for a second too long. He squeezed, she winced, he smiled.

Ellie felt the anxiety build in her stomach. She did not like this man one little bit.

She backed away towards the door. 'I'll umm leave you to it...'

'Sit, please,' Kai said, pleasantly.

She hesitated and looked to Roxanne but was met with the back of her head.

Ellie sat.

Roxanne turned and placed a mug of hot chocolate before her and a cup of green liquid before her friend. She looked at neither of them.

Kai sat forward and moved his drink to the side. He rested his elbows on the table, linked his fingers and rested his chin on his hands.

'You probably don't know this, Ellie, but Roxanne is not only a friend to me, she is an employee, and a very good one at that.'

Ellie felt her mouth begin to dry. This was not general conversation. The words he spoke were measured and meant solely for her. She looked towards him but could not meet his eyes. There was something scary that lived there. Ellie instantly wondered if she'd done something to get Roxanne into trouble. Perhaps she had taken too much of her time and her work had suffered. Perhaps this man was here to tell her she had to leave. She didn't even know what Roxanne did to earn a living.

'I'm sorry if I—'

'Don't be sorry, although it is good to hear that you understand my predicament.'

Ellie looked from him to Roxanne but her friend had still not turned. Her apology had been a polite response to his inference. Her stomach began to turn at the feeling she had done something wrong.

He slid a small red book towards her.

'That is a record of what you owe me. Please take a look.'

She felt a nervous heat rush to her face as she looked to her friend. There was a tension growing in the room that she didn't understand. 'Roxanne, what is going—?'

'Look at the book, Ellie,' Roxanne said, without turning. It was a cool, hard voice that she didn't recognise.

'R-Roxanne…' she tried again. Damn her stutter for giving away her fear.

There was no response from her friend.

Real fear began to course through her veins. She reached for the book. The inside cover held her name and Sunday's date. Ellie leafed through the pages which listed every meal she'd eaten, every drink she'd consumed. There was an entry for petrol, for clothes and even for utilities consumed over a two-day period. The final entry was for Roxanne's time valued at £500 alone. The grand total was just under a thousand pounds.

Ellie shook her head. 'But I d-don't. I mean… I c-can't… Roxanne is my f-friend.'

'Do you dispute any expense listed?'

Ellie shook her head numbly. No, it was definitely all there. Every single penny.

This had to be some kind of a joke. Any second now Roxanne would turn around and laugh at her expense, at how she'd been taken in and they would all laugh together. And Ellie would not reveal how frightened she had been.

She looked up from the book. Nobody was laughing.

'Roxanne… w-what's going on. I th-thought the clothes were a g-gift,' she said to Roxanne's back.

There was no reply.

The man continued. 'If you are able to access that money right now and reimburse me in full I will drop you off at the end of your road with your new clothes and this will have been a pleasant little holiday and nothing more. If not, we have ourselves a little problem.'

'I don't h-h-have that kind of money,' Ellie spluttered. Her meagre savings account held less than two hundred pounds.

'Oh, that's a shame. We appear to have a predicament. This is not money I can afford to lose. What do you propose to do about it?'

Ellie heard the control in his tone. This conversation was following an agenda. She felt she was reading from a script that had already been written.

'Perhaps my m-mother could…'

'I suspect your mother does not have access to that kind of money but as a last resort, perhaps. Although, it's hardly fair to burden your mother with a debt incurred by you, is it?'

Ellie had the sudden urge to run away. The man's low, controlled voice was more frightening than if he'd been screaming at her. She realised she was nearest to the kitchen door. She wondered how quickly she could turn and get out of the house.

Kai Lord smiled at her as he placed a key onto the table. 'Not an option. You see, Ellie, I can't possibly allow you to leave until we have reached some kind of agreement.'

Ellie swallowed, realising now that her only objective was to leave the house. She had to get out. However angry her mother was at her she would know what to do.

'I can g-get a job. I can make p-payments. I'll sign anything you w-want.'

He tipped his head to the side and smiled at her indulgently.

'I like your thinking, Ellie, but you're sixteen years of age with no qualifications. Minimum wage won't even cover the weekly interest payment, which incidentally starts now.'

Ellie wondered what exactly she needed to say to get out of this house. There was still a small part of her that hoped this was some kind of joke, but that hope was dying every second Roxanne didn't turn around. She shook her head, bewildered. 'I'm sorry, b-but I really don't know what to o-offer.'

His smile was slow but full. It chilled her blood. 'Then it's a pretty good job I do.'

CHAPTER FORTY-SIX

'You wanna lead?' Kim asked, as Bryant pulled up outside a mid-terrace just outside Lye.

'Of course,' he answered.

She had asked Bryant to lead because she wanted ample opportunity to observe the man who was potentially the last person to see both Kelly Rowe and Donna Hill alive.

'Well, there's the Toyota so at least we know he's home,' Bryant offered, knocking the door.

It opened to reveal a man whose head was level with the door frame. His width left very little wiggle room either.

Their witness description from the Toyota seller of average everything was not even close to accurate. A few inches in both directions put this man distinctly outside the range of average. She had to wonder who old Mr Bingham was spending time with.

'Roger Barton?' Bryant asked.

His face was instantly creased into concern.

'Yes, but who…'

His words trailed away as he inspected the warrant card, proffered by Bryant.

He stepped aside. 'Please, come in.'

Kim almost balked as she looked inside. A very narrow walkway led all the way to the back of the house. On either side were magazines, books and newspapers piled precariously high.

She travelled slowly through the paper valley into a room that she couldn't name but had one usable armchair. The place was bursting with plastic bags, bin liners, bicycle parts and old pet cages. It was like someone had taken a trip to the rubbish dump and brought it all here.

'Sorry for the mess,' Roger Barton said, arriving at the only available patch of carpet space.

His apology was out of place and was more suited to a house that hadn't been vacuumed or polished before the arrival of an unexpected visitor, or a house littered with kids' toys. It was an apology that hinted that the occupant had been caught off guard not that they were a seasoned hoarder.

Kim tried to ignore the aroma of stale food that met her nostrils. God only knew what was growing mould beneath the layers of newspapers but it was more than a few escaped crumbs.

The area immediately surrounding the single armchair was organised and clear. If the man owned a television she had yet to spot it.

'Bloody hell,' Bryant said, tripping over something behind her.

Kim had no idea about the state of the other rooms and she had no wish to find out.

'Sir, we need to establish your activities for Saturday night,' Bryant said, finally arriving alongside her.

The three of them now stood in a small space in the middle of the room.

His face was instantly alarmed. 'May I ask why?'

Close up Kim was surprised to find that the man was clean-shaven and smelled reasonably fresh.

'If you could just tell us where you were we'll be on our way.' Bryant's voice was firm but pleasant.

'Officer, I insist that you tell me what exactly is going on.'

Although not invited to do so, Kim took a seat in the armchair and instantly regretted it. At the lower level the piles of stuff towered above her. How did he live like this?

She stood back up.

'Mr Barton, it is in connection with a murder we're investigating.'
Any trace of colour left his face.

His nails were short and clean and, Kim noted, slightly effeminate for a man of his size.

'But who? What…'

'Mr Barton, your car was identified as being in the general area of the incident and we would like to exclude you from our enquiries. So, if you could just tell us where you were Saturday night, we'll be on our way.'

'Of course. I spent the morning grocery shopping. Had a spot of lunch, took a drive up to Clent and then stopped at a scrapyard in Halesowen.'

Bryant had taken out his notebook.

Kim noted that Roger Barton had blinked four times. 'And then I came home and read a book.'

The man was overcompensating. He had offered the entire day's activities when they'd asked for much less. And pretty much none of it could be corroborated.

Kim couldn't keep track of the blinks that had given away the dishonesty of that last sentence.

'Mr Barton, shall we try that answer again?' she asked.

'It's the truth.'

'Sir, can you confirm you are the local Scout leader for Lye and Stourbridge?' Bryant asked.

'I am,' he answered, somewhat proudly.

'And does that include taking care of the finances for the weekly sessions?'

He nodded but didn't speak.

'And how does that work?' Bryant asked.

'I take the money from the parents and then raise a cheque and pay it into the account.'

'So you keep the £5 admission charge from the parents?' Bryant clarified.

'Yes, but there's nothing—'

'Of course, Mr Barton, I was implying no such thing. The cash is yours to spend as you please.'

'Yes, yes, exactly,' he said, frowning.

'And does that include paying prostitutes for sex?'

His face suffused with colour.

'I don't… I'm not sure…'

'Please don't take us for fools, Mr Barton. We took down your registration number on Sunday night, driving along Tavistock Road. You are known to many of the girls that work from that patch,' Bryant said.

'I w-went for a drive… just…'

'Mr Barton, did you meet with Kelly Rowe on Saturday night?' Kim asked.

He shook his head vehemently.

'Did you meet with a young prostitute named Donna Hill last night?' she continued.

'You must have heard of their deaths,' Bryant interjected. 'Why did you not come forward?'

He rubbed at his head. 'I wasn't there those nights. I have nothing—'

'Do you seek out any girls in particular?' Bryant asked.

He looked her way and shook his head. 'They're all very nice…'

'So, you could have had dealings with both of them?' Bryant asked.

The man was shaking his head from side to side. 'I told you, I wasn't there those—'

'The £5 notes in their handbags would tend to disagree,' Bryant pushed.

Realisation began to dawn in his eyes. The questions about the Scouts and his financial arrangements.

His head stopped shaking as the final traces of colour left his face. 'Officer, I think I'd like to speak to my lawyer.'

Yes, Kim thought. That was beginning to look like a very good idea.

CHAPTER FORTY-SEVEN

Ellie tried to swallow down her fear. She had the feeling they were getting close to the place they'd been travelling towards all along, that nothing she could have said would have changed whatever was to come next.

'It is lucky for you that I have a way for you to pay me back. You're not the first, you see. You craved your independence, sought a way to speed your journey to adulthood and you have succeeded. This is your debt and your responsibility. You got exactly what you wanted.'

Ellie could not deny that there was some truth in his words.

'You have been successful in escaping the clutches of your mother. She is no longer in charge of your decisions and this next one you will make yourself.'

Ellie held her breath. There was a mesmerising quality to his voice that, although it filled her with fear, she felt compelled to listen to.

'You are here, alone, with no money, no family, no friends and no safety net yet you have the one thing that will set you free.'

Ellie frowned.

He raised one eyebrow and looked her up and down. 'You have your body.'

For a few seconds, Ellie was confused. She thought about her hands, arms, legs, feet and as she thought about the bits in between her fear turned to abject horror. The bile rose in her throat and she fought to swallow it down.

'You can't m-mean… prostitution?'

'Such an outdated word but, yes, that's exactly what I mean.'

Ellie shook her head vehemently. 'No, no, I can't do that,' she cried, backing away from him.

The thought of strange men touching her body made her throw up in her mouth.

'Then offer me an alternative,' he said, sipping the green liquid.

Ellie had the feeling they were playing some kind of cat-and-mouse game, and that he was enjoying the game immensely.

'Roxanne…' she whispered, looking to her friend.

Roxanne still didn't turn but Ellie saw the tensing of her shoulders.

'Roxanne…' she called again, more urgently.

Ellie suddenly understood that Roxanne was just as trapped as she was.

'So, little one, do we finally understand each other?'

Ellie shook her head. 'I c-can't… really I can't,' she said, weakly.

He sighed heavily and shook his head. 'You seem like a very smart young lady. I had hoped we could settle this like adults. I ask you one last time to reconsider.'

Ellie shook her head slowly. She couldn't do it. What was the worst he could do?

He reached for something beside the kitchen chair and stood.

Ellie's eyes travelled down his arm to his right hand. Clutched between his fingers was some kind of wire contraption that looked like metal coat hangers entwined together.

He moved towards her and reached over to turn up the volume on the radio.

'I didn't want to resort to this but you have left me no choice.'

Ellie knew she could not move. Every bone in her body was trembling. She couldn't tear her eyes away from the weapon in his hand.

He advanced towards her, and Ellie tried to push back the chair but the bones in her feet had dissolved into her flesh. She watched as he drew closer and raised the weapon. The breath in her body stilled, her heart beat wildly in her chest, as the weapon whipped down.

Roxanne cried out in pain as the metal struck her lower back.

Ellie screamed as Kai raised the weapon and thrashed it against Roxanne's thighs.

A second muted cry escaped from her lips as her legs buckled and she fell to the ground.

'Stop,' Ellie cried.

Kai ignored her and lifted Roxanne from the floor by her hair.

Ellie watched in horror as he thrashed the object at her knees. Again, her legs buckled but her body could not fall because of his grip on her hair.

'Stop, p-please stop,' Ellie begged.

'There are always consequences for your actions, little one, and they may not always be for you.'

He dropped the metal contraption to the floor and used his free hand to punch Roxanne in the face. Her bottom lip exploded and blood spurted down her chin.

Ellie prayed to wake up from this nightmare but knew that the scene before her was very real.

'Would you care to reconsider before I damage this pretty little face for ever?'

'Leave her alone,' Ellie cried, finally pushing herself to her feet.

Kai still held Roxanne by the hair. He shook her head like a rag doll.

'Stay back or she's going to get it worse.'

Ellie could see that Roxanne was trying to get a hold of her own hair but the shaking meant she couldn't get a grip.

Kai threw her to the ground and kicked her in the stomach. Roxanne began to cough and Ellie could see blood spatters all over the floor.

Ellie felt the tears stinging her eyes.

Kai continued to kick Roxanne in the stomach and then in the back.

Ellie sobbed uncontrollably as Roxanne groaned from the floor.

'Stop, please, just stop it,' Ellie cried, wiping away the tears from her cheeks.

'You know how to make it stop for your new best friend, little one.'

Ellie turned away as he landed another blow to the back of the head. Roxanne's cheek was covered in blood from the ground as she rolled around trying to escape.

She was moaning unintelligibly. Kai retrieved the metal weapon and stood above Roxanne, a leg either side of her inert body. He raised his arm in the air but Ellie could bear it no longer.

'No, s-stop, don't. I'll do it. I'll do whatever you w-want but please just stop.'

Kai lowered his arm and placed the weapon on the table.

Ellie dropped to the ground and tried to cradle Roxanne's head in her hands.

Suddenly Ellie felt herself being lifted back to her feet by her hair. Her scalp stung.

Kai stepped over Roxanne's inert form on the floor and dragged her to the kitchen door. He opened the door to the cellar and pushed her inside. She stumbled down the steps and landed in a heap.

She looked up to see his figure standing in the doorway.

'I thought you'd see it my way, eventually.'

The door closed and the world went dark.

CHAPTER FORTY-EIGHT

Kim tapped her foot impatiently as the landlord opened the door to Donna's flat.

As he stepped aside she realised that the word flat was purely aspirational for the entire space that was no bigger than her garage and kitchen combined.

Bryant thanked the man who happily headed back down the stairs.

She guessed he was thinking that he would be able to re-let it straight away and make a few quid from the money Donna had already paid for the rest of the month, not to mention any security deposit.

She would allow Bryant the pleasure of suitably advising him that wasn't the case once they were done.

From the doorway the single room held a drop-down double bed in the corner. Half of the bed was covered in clothes and doubled up as storage leaving just the left-hand side free for her to crawl into each night. Above the bed were two shelves lodged into the corner. The left-hand side of the room held a two-seater sofa that faced a dark wooden drawer unit with a space that would have accommodated a small television if she'd had one.

Kim guessed that anything of value was long gone, having been sold to support her drug habit.

Mounds of clothing littered the space with a pile of dirty underwear in the corner beside the sofa. Kim opened the top drawer of the dresser. It was full of odds and ends: manicure set, charger cable, loose change and drug paraphernalia. Kim spotted a mirror and razor to chop powdered cocaine, a syringe, spoon, tourniquet and a broken meth pipe at the back.

She closed the drawer and stepped into the kitchen as Bryant approached the bedroom area.

Kim was struck by the order of the small space. Only two narrow work surfaces were present above a fridge and a freezer. A plain silver kettle and tea canisters took up the area next to the sink. A spice rack and a blender sat next to one of Jamie Oliver's early cook books. She opened the top drawer to find the cutlery organised and segmented, unlike the one in the dresser. The second drawer housed giant plastic spoons, a masher and other utensils that Kim did not recognise. The third and biggest drawer was full of pots and pans and a slow cooker, a measuring cup and a set of old-fashioned weighing scales. The surfaces although old were clean and shiny. A small bin in the corner held squares of kitchen roll. The dated taps had been wiped clear of smears and watermarks. The two top cupboards were sparse but ordered with a few tins and half a loaf of bread.

She heard Bryant sigh and glanced across. He had picked up a couple of garments from the bed. In his left hand was a short black skirt and in the other a yellow spaghetti-strapped vest top.

'Not a bloody cardigan or jumper in sight,' he said.

Kim turned back to the kitchen. At some stage this girl had enjoyed cooking and if she didn't do it any more she had still not let go of the tools and equipment.

'Hey, guv, look at this,' Bryant said, quietly.

Kim took three steps and joined him next to Donna's bed. He pointed to the shelf above the small collection of comical pottery pigs. 'Pride and bloody Prejudice,' he said, nodding towards one of the books. 'Can't believe this poor girl was still searching for happily ever after.'

'Or salvation,' Kim said, nodding towards the other book which appeared to be a second-hand bible.

'A contradiction, eh?' Bryant asked.

Kim shook her head. 'Just a person, Bryant. Full of likes and dislikes, fears and hopes. I'm still waiting to meet the stereotype.'

She reached for the well-thumbed paperback and leafed through it. A single photo fell out and fluttered to the ground.

Kim reached down and turned it over. She frowned as she took a closer look. It was a girl in her early teens sitting in front of a blue sky. Her hair was mousy but well cut around the plump, attractive face.

'That's not Donna,' Bryant said, shaking his head.

'I think it is,' she said, taking in the warm, genuine smile and the friendly hazel eyes that stared right down the lens of the camera. She'd seen those eyes staring up at the sky, lifeless.

Kim felt the stab of sadness. This girl was vibrant, hopeful. There was an anticipation of life radiating from her. Suddenly Kim felt the burden of Donna's death on her shoulders. While Donna had been alive those dreams could have been realised and now they were gone for good.

Kim went to put the photo back in the book and then paused as something else on the photo caught her attention.

Donna was wearing a green school blazer with a sewn motif on the pocket. She squinted to be sure of what she was seeing.

She pointed.

'Jesus, Bryant, will you take a look at that?'

CHAPTER FORTY-NINE

Kai watched Roxanne struggle to her feet.

'For fuck's sake, Kai, you could have gone a little easier,' she said, wiping at her bottom lip.

He shrugged and took a sip of green tea. It was still warm.

'She's a stubborn one. Stronger than she looks.'

Roxanne nodded her agreement.

'But quite attached to you, I feel.'

Roxanne shrugged

'As long as those feelings are not reciprocated.'

He caught her gaze. There was a deadness in her expression. A complete lack of emotion that brought a genuine smile to his face.

'Of course not.'

He looked deep into the eyes that bore no evidence of a soul within. He believed her.

They made a good team, the two of them, and she had proven her loyalty to him repeatedly. She had come to work for him voluntarily when he'd taken command of Hollytree. And he had been amused by her arrogance when she stated they would be business partners in two years.

Four months later she had become the girl who earned most and complained least. Two months after that she had successfully proven to him that two of his girls had been keeping back money. The two slags had been dealt with, and Roxanne had become his 'Top Girl'.

Roxanne had quickly proven invaluable. She kept his records, kept him updated on law activity and took responsibility for recruiting prostitutes. It had been her idea to diversify into procurement of young girls.

He had tested her numerous times by leaving money lying about or purposely transferring too much money into her account each month. She had never let him down and, although their little fight scene had been perfected for effect, a few well-placed blows ensured she remembered who was in charge, at all times.

The sullen look on her face told him she'd got the message loud and clear.

He finished his drink and stood. 'I'll be back to get her tomorrow.'

'I thought you were putting her out on the strip?' Roxanne asked, wrapping blocks of ice in a tea towel.

'She's going to be trouble. I can feel it. I'm going to change the plan.'

Understanding began to dawn in her eyes.

'The mess-up on Sunday night?'

He nodded. 'That bitch copper got in the way. We owe our client a girl.'

'And she was terrified you were putting her out on the strip,' Roxanne observed, with a smile.

He laughed. 'Oh, how she'll wish I had,' he said, cheerfully.

Where she was going was a one-way trip.

CHAPTER FIFTY

'I'm going to have to ask you to do it here,' Steven Robertson said, showing them into a break room. A row of lockers lined one wall, pausing for a sink unit. On the shorter wall was a small workspace with a kettle and tea-making canisters. Beneath which sat a narrow fridge. A round table with three chairs dominated the centre of the room.

Stacey was sure they could have been housed somewhere better than the tea room but she supposed he didn't really want prospective clients asking difficult questions.

'Are all the girls fluent in English, Mr Robertson?' Stacey asked, casting Dawson a sideways glance.

He shook his head and then seemed to have a thought.

'I'll have Cristina come in with you. She's new and doesn't know the others too well but she'll be able to assist with the language barrier.'

'Thank you,' she said.

'Is there anything else I can get you?' he asked politely.

They both shook their heads.

'Okay, I'll get the first girl sent in.'

'Good thinking, Stace,' Dawson said, once the door had closed behind him.

'Yeah, still not sure why he's suddenly being so helpful,' she admitted.

'One of two reasons,' Dawson said, stifling a yawn. 'Either he has nothing to hide or he's incredibly confident we won't find what he has to hide.'

'Do you think he does know our victim?' Stacey asked.

'I don't think so,' he answered. 'I didn't get that impression when he looked at the photo. And it was a bit thin to be honest. So, it's back onto the Romanian eateries tomorrow,' he said, as a soft tap sounded on the door.

'Come in,' Stacey called.

Cristina's head appeared around the door.

Stacey beckoned her in.

She hesitated then entered.

'How are you?' Stacey asked with a smile. The woman seemed consistently nervous.

'I am well, thank you.'

'Did you have a chance to look at those pages for us?' Dawson asked.

She nodded, took some folded pages from her overall pocket and passed them her way. She looked back to the closed door as though waiting for someone to come in and berate her. Stacey quickly put the pages into her satchel, and thanked her.

'Did Mr Robertson explain why we need you?' Dawson asked, gently.

She nodded. 'You want to ask the ladies some questions and you want me to translate.'

Dawson nodded and once again took out his phone.

'We've already asked you about the baby, but would you mind taking a look at this photo for us?'

Cristina stepped forward.

'Do you know this man?'

Cristina stared at the photo for ten seconds before shaking her head.

'N-no, I don't know him, I'm sorry.'

'Cristina, are you sure?' Stacey asked.

The girl nodded and looked back at the phone. 'He looks dead,' she breathed.

Dawson removed the photo from the screen.

'Cristina, is everything…'

Stacey stopped speaking as a knock sounded on the door.

Cristina took two steps back to the corner of the room as Dawson shouted 'enter'.

A thin sliver of a woman entered. Her back appeared to be slightly hunched and she looked a few years older than Cristina.

'This is Natalya,' Cristina said, as the woman slid into the spare seat. She turned and looked to Cristina for some kind of reassurance.

'Can you please tell her that she's done nothing wrong and isn't in any kind of trouble?'

Cristina relayed the message, and Natalya turned to face them. None of the tension had left her face.

'Cristina, would you please explain what we told you about the baby left at the police station?' Stacey asked.

Although they also had a dead body to identify, Stacey didn't want to show the anxious woman the picture immediately. Seeing photos of corpses tended to hinder your focus.

Stacey watched as horror filled the woman's face, followed by a slight reddening of the eyes. Eventually a shake of the head.

'She doesn't know anyone,' Cristina said.

'Does she know anyone that has recently had a baby?'

Cristina asked. The woman hesitated before launching into an angry tirade. The words shot out of her mouth. And just as suddenly stopped as she turned away from Cristina.

'She says no,' Cristina said.

'Seems like she said a whole lot more than that,' Dawson observed.

'She also asked if you morons were going to ask her everything twice but I didn't think that was relevant.'

Stacey forced down the sudden smile that came to her lips. There was an element of relief that they had found someone with an ounce of spirit.

'Natalya, could you look at this photograph and tell us if you recognise this man?'

Dawson pushed the phone towards her once Cristina had finished speaking.

She took one look and shook her head. Her eyes had barely glanced at the screen.

'Please take another look,' Dawson said, willing to risk the woman's wrath again.

Her face tightened but she looked back at the phone. She looked right at them and shook her head.

'Natalya, is everything okay? Are you scared of anyone?' Stacey asked.

Cristina translated her response.

'She says she is not scared. She is happy here and the Robertsons are a good people.'

Stacey found the detailed response odd but let it pass.

Her gaze met Dawson's and a message passed between them. They were getting nothing more from Natalya.

'Okay, Cristina,' Stacey said. 'We're ready for the next.'

* * *

Two hours and five interviews later Stacey found herself with no more information than when they'd walked in.

Cristina took the opportunity to hold up her cigarettes and lighter.

'May I?'

'Of course,' Stacey said, and then turned to Dawson. 'I could do with a bathroom break myself.'

He nodded and she knew his frustration matched her own.

It was the same response from every woman.

No, they knew nothing about a baby.

No, they didn't recognise the man.

They were happy to be here and the Robertsons were good people.

They were no longer asking about the factory but were getting that answer anyway.

Stacey headed back to the toilets she'd passed earlier. She paused and then carried on walking. The next corner along the corridor led to the shop floor.

Stacey took a look at all the heads bent while their hands and feet worked in unison at the sewing machines.

A woman they hadn't yet spoken to appeared to exit a tiny office in the corner of the factory beneath the mezzanine. She started heading across the factory floor towards her. Clearly she was next.

Stacey watched in fascination as another woman was summoned to the poky room in the corner.

Stacey turned on her heel and left.

'Well, this is a complete waste of time,' she said, closing the door to the break room behind her.

'Keep the faith, Stace. It only takes one.'

'Never gonna happen, Kev,' Stacey said, reaching for her satchel. 'Because every one of these girls has been coached.'

CHAPTER FIFTY-ONE

'Where the bloody hell is he?' Kim asked, ending another attempt to call Penn.

She was eager to pass on what she'd learned about Donna Hill.

'Give the kid a break. You've got him running here, there and everywhere. I'm sure the seven missed calls will demonstrate how urgently you want to speak to him and he'll ring you back when he can.'

'Stacey would have—'

'Don't even,' he warned. 'You put Stacey out in the field and brought Penn in, why?'

'Because it was the right thing to do,' she replied.

'Exactly but you've got that poor Penn kid on the phones, out in the field, mining data. To be fair, Stacey never had to—'

'Oh shut up,' she snapped, maturely.

He chuckled, knowing she had no answer. 'So, is Roger Barton fizzing about in your gut?' he asked, as he negotiated the narrow Drive Thru at McDonald's.

'I'm not sure "fizzing" is the right word. I'm pretty sure he's lying to us about something but he handed the car over without a warrant so he must be pretty sure we're not going to find anything to link him to either Kelly or Donna,' she said, as Bryant spoke into a silver machine. He enunciated every word as though speaking to a foreign exchange student. The cheery voice repeated his order and instructed him to move onto the next window.

'Or feels he'll be able to explain it away because they were both known to him. And he'd have a point. There's every chance we might find some evidence of either one of them having been in his car.'

Yeah, she knew that. The request had been more to gauge his reaction to it. After a private phone call to his lawyer he'd agreed it could be collected for forensic examination. They had waited over an hour for the techs to turn up and take it away.

'We could have brought him in for questioning on what we had?' Bryant observed.

Except they'd already shown him all they had, which was the £5 notes and his knowledge of both victims.

'I want something more before we question him again,' she said, as Bryant took his brown paper bag and placed it on the dashboard.

He eased into a space that faced onto the road.

'Not good for you,' she said, shaking her head.

'I'm sure this is healthier than not eating at all,' he rebuked, opening the paper bag.

'May I?' she asked.

He nodded. She reached into the bag, took out the large order of fries, wound down her window and dropped them in the bin.

'Jesus, guv…'

'Your wife and cholesterol level will thank me,' she said, wiping her hands on a napkin.

He took out the burger. 'Permission to eat the rest of my lunch, guv?'

'Granted,' she said, removing the lid from her drink.

He took a bite, chewed and then turned towards her.

'Guv, I've just got one question I need answered before we move on?'

'Go on.'

'Can't I file a grievance against you?'

'For what?' she asked, fighting a smile.

'Throwing away my chips.'

She shook her head. 'Not really. Comes under my duty of care.'

He lifted the burger to his mouth and then threw it back into the bag, shaking his head.

'Weird how your disapproval has a direct line to my taste buds.'

She laughed out loud. 'We'll pick up something your missus would approve of in a bit. Now you check in with Dawson and Stace while I give Penn another call.'

He threw the bag into the bin and took out his phone.

Penn answered on the second ring. 'Boss, I was just about to give you a call,' he said as a greeting.

'I should think so after all my messages,' she said, 'but let me go first. Get back to digging on Donna Hill. Found a photo in her flat. Looks like she attended Heathcrest Academy over in—'

'The private school in Harvington?'

'That's the one,' she said.

He whistled on the other end of the phone. 'You wouldn't have thought that, would you?'

No she certainly wouldn't. Suddenly she remembered what Kai Lord had said about not everyone being what they seemed. Had he been talking about Donna?

'I'll get digging once I've updated you. I missed your calls 'cos I was on the phone,' he explained. 'I spent a couple of hours trying to track this bloody BMW through company records and I was getting nowhere,' he said. The BMW was the car that had pulled up alongside the young girl; the car that Kim had scared away.

'So I turned into angry dad,' he continued.

'Into what?'

'I called the Head Office of the pharmaceutical company shouting and screaming that one of their cars had just cut me up on the motorway and caused me to crash. I threatened them with criminal action and a civil case for my whiplash injury and the trauma to my child.'

'Your child?' Kim chuckled.

'Hey, boss, don't laugh. Rupert was very upset by it all. Anyway I demanded the name of the driver so that I could pursue a case against the individual.'

'And?'

'The rest was easy.'

'Penn, tell me you got me an address.'

'Well, err, yeah,' he said, as though it was a no-brainer.

'His name is Jeremy Templeton. The house is rented and a very nice house it is too.'

She listened to the address and ended the call.

'Come on, Bryant,' she said, interrupting his call. 'Your salad is going to have to wait.'

This was a man she was dying to meet.

Oh yes, her stomach was fizzing now.

CHAPTER FIFTY-TWO

'What does he do again?' Bryant asked.

'Regional Manager for a pharmaceutical company. Covers anything south of Wakefield.'

'Pays well, then,' Bryant said, crunching up the gravel drive. He took care to avoid ice-filled potholes that would not have troubled the tyres of a four-by-four.

The property was a converted barn on the outskirts of the affluent Kinver.

'How much?' Bryant asked.

'Around two thousand a month,' Kim guessed.

Bryant whistled. 'Can you imagine shelling out that each month just for rent?'

Kim shook her head. It was an amount of money that was way above their pay scales combined.

'And just for one person, too,' she said, spying the BMW that had crawled past them the other night.

The door was opened by a man close to Kim's own height. There was a new iPhone clamped to his ear, and he held up one finger to ask them to wait. He turned his back but not before Kim saw the frown that drew his fair eyebrows together.

Bryant's expression mirrored her own surprise.

His plain black trousers reflected the price tag that was evident in the impeccable tailoring. The expensive clothing, while smart and professional, did nothing to hide the athletic build beneath.

'Maria, I've already told you, I haven't been on the motorway this morning, I've been working from home.'

Kim coughed lightly.

'Look, I've got to go but I'll see you in a couple of days, okay.'

Kim heard the change in his tone on the last few words.

The softening and the hint of promise in his voice told her Jeremy Templeton was sleeping with Maria, and she'd be willing to bet Maria wasn't his wife. His smile was manufactured but disarming all the same. She could imagine there was a queue of women lining up around the corner to sleep with him.

'Mr Templeton,' she said, stepping forward. 'My name is Detective Inspector Stone and this is my colleague, Detective Sergeant Bryant. May we come in?'

If Bryant felt any surprise at the softness of her tone he didn't show it.

Templeton's eyes met hers and held for a second. Interest flickered as he stood aside. 'Of course.'

'First door to your left,' he said, as she came to a halt in the hallway.

Kim stepped into one of the most spectacular rooms she had ever seen. Brown leather sofas dotted around a wood-burning fire. A plush neutral carpet removed the starkness from the pine floor and added warmth. Roof beams drew the eye to an upper level gallery fronted by a glass balustrade.

'Thank you for seeing us, Mr Templeton. We won't take up much of your time. You are clearly very busy,' she said, indicating the open laptop and the paperwork scattered on the sofa nearest to the fire.

'I have no idea why you're here,' he said, tipping his head. 'Unless it's about some kind of misunderstanding regarding an incident on the motorway…'

'No, that's not why we're here,' she said, looking around. 'A lovely home you have,' she added.

'Thank you, Inspector, but it's not mine. It's rented by my employers. I use it to visit my local branches around the Midlands.' He caught her eye. 'I'm normally here one week out of every month.'

Kim heard the invitation in his voice and noticed that he had not looked at Bryant once. She allowed a small smile to lift her lips but lowered her eyes to the ground.

'That's good to know, Mr Templeton,' she offered, as he sat and closed the laptop. The view between them was now unobstructed.

'Jeremy, please,' he replied with a lopsided grin. His handsome face was like a vehicle that he knew how to drive. There was a sex appeal about him that was undeniable and it was coming at her in waves.

'Thank you, Jeremy. Your vehicle has come up in an investigation we're conducting, so if we could just ask you a couple of questions I'm sure we can resolve our business.'

'Please, go ahead,' he said, leaning forward and resting his elbows on his knees.

His cuff rose up slightly displaying a Bvlgari watch. Like the rest of him it was expensively tasteful. This man would never wear a Rolex.

'Can you tell me what day you arrived this week?'

Kim had dropped all reference to 'we'. There were only the two of them in this conversation.

'Yes, officer, I arrived around Sunday lunchtime. My first meeting was in Oldbury on Monday morning at seven o'clock.'

'So you had no meetings on Sunday?'

He thought for a moment. 'No, I was here working, preparing for the early meeting.'

'And for dinner?'

He shrugged. 'I probably threw something together.' He tipped his head slightly. 'It's not much fun preparing elaborate meals for one,' he said, asking a question.

'I know exactly what you mean,' she said, answering it.

'And you didn't leave the house again?' she continued.

Kim allowed their gaze to hold for a second too long. 'You're sure that's what you did on Sunday night?'

'I'm sure, officer.'

She frowned slightly. 'There must be some mistake, Jeremy. Your vehicle was seen driving through Tavistock Road at around nine o'clock.'

'Aah, occasionally, the gardener, Eddie, borrows the car.' He rolled his eyes up and to the left. 'Wait a minute, of course, he asked to borrow the car to collect his daughter from the cinema. Yes, that was Sunday night. I remember now. The snow was quite bad and he has a front-wheel drive.'

Kim smiled and nodded. She pushed herself forward to a standing position. 'That explains it, Jeremy. You've been most helpful and I'm sorry for having disturbed you.'

Surprised by her movement, Bryant got up from the third couch. She turned quickly, practically bumping into Jeremy Templeton. They almost banged heads. He reached out and steadied her. She chuckled.

'Oops, sorry about that,' she said.

'It's no trouble at all,' he said, as his hands slid down her upper arms.

'So, if you could just give us Eddie's phone number to clear this away I shouldn't need to bother you again. Well, not for this anyway.'

'Of course,' he said reaching for his wallet.

He stopped as the wallet snapped open. He tapped the side of his head and again offered the disarming smile.

'Oh my, what is wrong with me, Inspector? You have me all of a fluster. I seem to be getting my days mixed up. Of course, it was Monday night that Eddie borrowed the car.

'I remember now. I did leave the house again on Sunday. I'd had a recommendation about a casino in the local area and decided to go out and try it.' Again with the smile. 'Being on the road so often can get quite lonely.'

'A casino in Brierley Hill?'

'Like I said, I don't really know the area.'

Kim got to the front door and turned.

'Well thank you for your time, Jeremy, you've been very helpful.'

His eyes caught her gaze and held. His sexuality was overpowering.

He held out his hand. 'It's been a pleasure, Inspector.'

She looked into his eyes and then down at his hand, which she ignored. The face of the young girl, child, that had been three inches away from getting into that car flashed into her mind. This man did not need to pay for sex. He could and probably would get that anywhere. What he liked was sex with young girls.

'And I can assure you that the pleasure is all yours, Mr Templeton.'

His hand dropped to his side as she met his gaze again but this time she did nothing to hide her true feelings.

'You disgust me, sir. My skin recoils at the very idea of shaking your hand. I am happy, for now, to rule you out of a murder investigation because you do not possess the bollocks for it.

'You prefer to have sex with little girls, and you sicken me beyond comprehension, you disgusting piece of shit. And yes, it was me that spoiled your plans on Sunday night.'

She stepped forward, invading his personal space.

'But I'll make you a promise right now, Mr Templeton: you touch another one of those young girls and you'll find yourself dealing with someone your own size.'

She pushed him in the chest, hard. 'Do we understand each other, Mr Templeton?'

He made no response but Kim felt she'd made her point.

Bryant followed her to the car. She turned as Jeremy Templeton closed the front door.

And she was sure his face held the hint of a smile.

CHAPTER FIFTY-THREE

'What are the odds,' Dawson asked, as they pulled their seatbelts on, 'that every single one of them would say the exact same thing.'

'Pretty high if they've been fed their answers and they're too scared to deviate from the script,' Stacey answered.

They had continued with their questioning and had spoken to one cowed woman after another. No amount of prompting would loosen their tongues.

'Bloody productive day,' he said, starting the engine.

Darkness had fallen, although they hadn't seen it in the airless, windowless room.

'Hang on a minute,' Stacey said, placing a hand on his arm. 'Perhaps they'd be more comfortable talking to us at home, away from the business.'

The metal gates opened and the minibus appeared.

He turned to her with a smile. 'Follow it?'

Stacey nodded. 'They have to be dropped off somewhere. We'll nab the first one to get off the bus and see if we can get anything.'

He waited until the vehicle had turned away from them before starting the engine and hitting the lights.

A Ford Escort van had pulled behind it as it waited to exit the trading estate and enter the traffic on the main road.

'So, what's your gut saying now, Stace?' he asked, as he kept pace with the traffic. He was interested if her instinct was on a par with his own.

She thought for a minute. 'It's thin, Kev. Everything we've got is thin. We have no absolute confirmation our baby is Romanian. We're going on a tip from Tracy Frost. We ay got no *sarmale* in his stomach. We're trying to tie a plate of food to a respectable business which appears to have done nothing wrong. Our guy had horrific injuries including a recently crushed right leg. We ay got no idea how it happened and have no one here who even recognises him.'

When she put it all together like that he had to wonder what the hell they were doing following this bloody vehicle.

The Escort van disappeared putting them directly behind the minibus.

'Thanks for the facts, Stace, but I could have got that from the board back at the nick. Tell me what your gut says.'

'That there's something not right in that place. Even I feel bloody anxious when I step in there and I've got nothing to be afraid of.'

He nodded at her answer which mirrored his own feelings. 'There's a tension around the place. It might have nothing to do with our case but they're bloody well hiding something.'

'I mean, even this gives me the creeps,' Stacey said, as the minibus turned off the main road. 'Why the hell has no one been dropped off yet?'

'Yeah, I know what you mean,' Dawson agreed as he eased off, allowing some space to develop between the two vehicles.

The minibus turned into a narrow residential street choked by cars parked on either side. It stopped in the middle of the road, blocking the street. From their view behind, Dawson watched as the factory workers stepped out of the vehicle and entered the terraced house in silent single file.

'Look at them. They're not even speaking. Just filing in like little lambs,' he said. But that wasn't what appeared to have caught Stacey's attention.

He followed her gaze. At least three of the women were carrying small foil packages.

'You seeing that?'

'Yep,' he said, as his brain followed the same train of thought as hers.

'The *sarmale* in the stomach of our victim. It could have come from bloody leftovers.'

CHAPTER FIFTY-FOUR

'Jesus, guv, I thought I was going to have to hose you two down in there.'

Kim's skin crawled at the thought of being anywhere near Templeton.

'Seriously, though, it was quite disturbing watching you flirt with him.'

Kim laughed without humour. 'That wasn't me flirting, Bryant. That was me fulfilling his expectation of how he feels every woman he meets will respond. It's called distraction and without it he would have had us on a waiting list to meet with his lawyer to answer any questions. His opinion of women is so low he had to think he could fool me into believing everything he said. If not, my first mention of Sunday night would have got us on a fast track to the front door and I wouldn't have found out what I have.'

'Which is?'

'That he is not our killer.'

'How can you be so sure?'

'His gratification appears to be in having some kind of power over young girls. He is many things, none of which I'd say in front of your tender ears but he prefers to leave his victims breathing.'

Bryant was silent for a minute. 'Do you think he'll heed your warning?'

Now that was another question entirely. If she'd had anything at all to charge him with she would have chanced it in a heartbeat, even if it just got him off the streets for a while but she had nothing, no complainant, no witness. And she suspected that his lawyer was of equal quality as the rest of his possessions.

The memory of the lazy smile on his face as he had turned away was still in her mind. She wasn't aware of having given him anything to smile about.

'Where to now, guv?' Bryant asked.

Kim checked her watch. It was almost six and the exhumation had been confirmed for 11 p.m.

'Drop me at home so I can catch up with my boy and then I'll meet you at the crem later on.'

She chose not to mention where she was really planning to go.

CHAPTER FIFTY-FIVE

'I mean it, Kev. No smart remarks or trying to matchmake. She's here to give us advice,' Stacey reiterated.

Dawson rolled his eyes as he took a sip of his tonic water.

'Jesus, relax, Stace. Can't a guy have a little fun?'

'No,' she said, flatly, looking to the door through the crowds. A pub quiz was due to start in half an hour.

'She's here,' Stacey said, seeing the dyed blonde tight curls of the immigration officer above the melee of quiz-goers.

'Fuck me, Stace,' Dawson said, spluttering out his drink. 'How'd you let that one get away?'

She wondered that herself as the long-legged figure strode towards them. The tight jeans accentuated her slim figure and the white V-neck T-shirt contrasted with the ebony skin. People looked as she walked by and Stacey knew why. Devon Reed exuded sexuality and made no apology for it.

'This is not the drink you promised to take me for, by the way,' Devon said, sitting on the third stool.

Stacey chuckled and immediately remembered what it was like to be in Devon's company.

'Hey, if she won't take you, I will,' Dawson said, offering her a charming smile.

Her eyes lit up with amusement. 'You do get that your charm is completely wasted on me, right?'

Dawson smiled back. 'You were worth a shot?'

'I appreciate the attempt,' she said.

'Ahem,' Stacey interjected just in case they'd forgotten she was sitting there.

Devon turned her way and met her gaze. 'Looking good, babe,' she said.

Stacey easily remembered how that soft, low voice could do things to her insides. Stacey looked away.

'So, how can I help you guys?'

Thankfully Dawson took over the conversation and gave her the background on the abandoned baby and the dead man at the canal. It offered Stacey the opportunity to recover her equilibrium. She couldn't stop her eyes from travelling to the graceful hands as Devon knitted her fingers together beneath her chin. Or the delicate wrists sporting only a thin silver chain. She pushed away the thoughts that were dancing all over her concentration.

She took a breath and joined the conversation as Devon opened her mouth.

'It's not beyond the realms of possibility that your guy is Romanian. We recently found forty Romanians living in a house in Lye. We have twenty-seven suspected slavery victims including women and young children.'

'Bloody hell,' Dawson said.

Devon nodded. 'Many travelled here illegally in the late eighties, early nineties. And we're not talking uneducated low lifers who just want to sponge off the system.'

'Why those particular years?' Stacey asked.

'Because Romania was a real shit place to be. You remember the Ceausescus?'

'Weren't they executed?' Dawson asked.

Devon nodded. 'Yes, and one of the charges was "Genocide by starvation",' she explained. 'Romania's foreign debt had increased from $3 billion to $10 billion between 1977 and '81. Ceausescu imposed austerity measures to pay the total back by '89. He managed it but in doing so impoverished the population and exhausted the economy. The revolution came in December of '89.'

'So the conditions here don't even compare to back home?' Dawson asked.

Devon shook her head. 'By their standards a mattress and a roof is bordering on palatial. We raided a farm in Worcestershire last year. Not a patch of floor without a makeshift bed.'

'Jesus,' Dawson said, shaking his head.

'Just last month we rescued a sixteen-year-old girl brought to Britain who had not seen daylight for seven years.'

'How is this happening?' he asked.

'People are smuggled into the country and forced into organised crime gangs. Slavery, drugs, money laundering, guns, loan sharking and prostitution. Some are just dumped on the street when work dries up, or even killed.'

'But we have laws,' Stacey said.

'We do indeed. We have the Modern Slavery Act passed just a couple of years ago. Compared to bonded labour, forced migrant labour is far easier to—'

'Back up,' Dawson said. 'What's the difference?'

'Forced migrant labour is when documents are seized and individuals work under the threat of violence, and undocumented immigrants are taken advantage of.

'Bonded labour differs from forced labour and human trafficking because the person consciously pledges to work as repayment. Debt bondage only applies to the ones who have no hope of ever paying it back.'

'Until the person dies?' Stacey asked.

Devon shook her head. 'Not necessarily.'

'How so?'

'Okay, let's imagine an illegal immigrant pays £5,000 to get passage into the country. That's his original debt but over the course of one week he will incur further debt for food, lodging, transportation and clothing that will far exceed whatever paltry pay he's receiving from his employers.'

'So, the debt never gets reduced?'

'Nope, it grows exponentially each year.'

Stacey felt the rage building within her at the injustice of the no-win situation.

'But how does that not end with death?' she asked.

'Because the debt will be transferred to any surviving family member.'

Stacey shook her head. It seemed hopeless.

Devon caught her look. 'The GLA does what it can but it's not enough.'

'The GLA?' Dawson asked.

'Gangmaster Licencing Authority. They do their best to protect vulnerable workers and victims of modern slavery but, like every other government agency, there ain't enough folks to go around.'

'We hear yer,' Stacey said.

'And what about Robertson's?' Dawson asked.

'Clean as a whistle,' Devon answered. 'Not even a hint of impropriety,' she said, looking troubled.

'What's wrong with that?' Stacey asked.

'Too clean for my liking. Not one complaint, not even anonymous. Given that they only seem to employ Romanian staff I've had more calls about the chippy just round the corner.'

'So what can we do?' Stacey asked, feeling the hopelessness settle all around her.

Devon leaned forward and rested her chin on her interlaced fingers. Her slow smile was intense and defiant.

'You can come with me when I go raid that place in the morning.'

CHAPTER FIFTY-SIX

Kim stepped out of the car and into a hive of activity.

Groups congregated outside the door in different states of attire. The working girls stood to the left already dressed for action. Donna had been murdered less than twenty-four hours earlier and the three days since Kelly's death on Saturday night had rendered her pretty much forgotten. She wondered how many other people set off to work under the threat of a vicious murderer being their next customer.

Kim caught a glimpse of the tattooed man she'd seen the previous day. He moved to the side to reveal a shorter female holding a baby.

All conversation stopped as she approached the front door and every gaze fell on the queue jumper. The door was open and a battered Tensa barrier was stretched across the opening. An A4 piece of paper hung from the ribbon stating, 'Open at 8'. Kim noted that the queue potentially held thieves, muggers, shoplifters and others with questionable morals. And yet nobody broke the food line.

Kim stepped around the barrier to find Tim at the front of the reception counter with his back to her. A middle-aged couple fussed behind the desk removing cardboard lids from oversized metal containers.

'Something smells good,' she said, approaching the desk.

Tim turned towards her. His face tried to make a smile but didn't quite manage it.

'Officer, how can I help?'

Kim stood to the side. 'You're a little busy at the moment. I can wait.'

He stacked paper plates and plastic cutlery at the far end of the desk. The woman ripped a roll of kitchen towel into individual squares to serve as napkins.

'Looks good,' Kim said, getting a smile from the woman towel ripper.

Tim stood back. 'We have meatballs from Gino's, chicken chow mein from Golden Star and our Nando's contribution should be here any second.'

He checked his watch. It was five past the hour.

'Martha, I don't think we can wait any longer. Anyone wanting chicken will have to wait.'

Tim stepped past her and unhooked the cordon.

'Come get it, folks,' he said as people filed in in single line and headed to the paper plates.

Tim came to stand beside her, away from the line.

'All donations from locals?' she asked.

'Mainly,' he said, but offered no more.

She glanced around the room. Her eyes rested on Len. His girlfriend sat on the banquette that lined the wall with the child on her lap. Kim guessed the girl to be about 18 months old. Her cheeks were rosy and her eyes bright and inquisitive. Kim was surprised they were sitting alone. Folks normally interacted with toddlers.

Len stood before the two of them, feeding small pieces of meatball to the child while the mother tried to hold onto the wriggler and take the occasional bite of food herself.

'Does no one like them or something?' she asked. She watched as Len wiped at his daughter's dribble. He put the tissue in his pocket.

Tim shook his head. 'It's not really that. They are HIV positive. Including the child.'

'Oh, Jesus,' Kim said, continuing to watch the small isolated family.

'It's not what you think. It was given to him in prison. I'm sure you can guess how. He didn't know. He passed it onto Wendy and then Wendy passed it to their child during pregnancy. They didn't know until it was picked up on the child during routine health checks.'

Kim shook her head sadly. That kid had not asked for it and, although it would mean nothing to her now, it certainly would when she was older. One thing that had arrived early was the stigma and isolation.

'Look, I've just gotta go and sort the drinks out,' Tim said.

'No problem,' she replied.

Kim found herself moving towards the insular little family.

'Hey, you were here yesterday,' she said, standing beside Len.

He eyed her suspiciously 'Yeah, you too.'

He used the edge of the fork to cut off another small piece of meatball, and fed it to his daughter.

He turned again. 'I know who you are. You're that cop on a bike.'

'That's not really the correct term,' she said. She knew the phrase and it included a farm animal.

At the mention of her job, alarm had registered on the face of the woman grappling the child.

Kim smiled at her. 'Don't worry, I'm not here for him.'

The girl smiled back tentatively.

'So, you got one of those Ninjas?'

Kim nodded.

'Nice bike,' he said, appreciatively.

'Oh yeah,' she agreed.

The child squirmed as the woman tried to spoon a forkful of chow mein into her own mouth. It landed on the child's shoulder. Len's own plate was on the banquette the other side of his girlfriend. Baby came first.

Kim pulled up a loose chair, sat, and held out her hands.

'Pass her to me while you eat your food.'

The girl's face creased with concern. She looked to Len.

'Look, it's nice of you to offer but...'

'It's fine, now just pass her to me while you eat your food.'

Len's girlfriend tentatively moved the child forward.

Kim took her and felt the solidness of the toddler. This kid did not miss many meals. She placed the child on her knee facing outwards so she could still see her parents. She repeated the rocking of the knee that the mother had been doing.

Len sat beside his girlfriend and both reached for their paper plates.

'So, you still managing to go straight?' Kim asked.

He nodded. 'Wouldn't be here if I was still robbing houses. We'd have money and wouldn't be treated like lepers to get a free meal.'

'So, what changed you?' Kim asked. She looked down. 'This one?'

He looked at his daughter and smiled. His face instantly lost its air of intimidation. He shook his head.

'She keeps me focussed but it was something that happened on the inside.'

Courtesy of Tim's explanation Kim knew more about what had happened to him in prison than she cared to.

He looked to his girlfriend then back at her.

'I had a visitor, one day. Little old guy came shuffling in with a stick. He owned a small bungalow in Norton. One of the last places I'd done before going inside. He didn't rant and rave. He wasn't even rude. He only wanted to know I wasn't ever going to come back again after I got out.'

He lowered his eyes and stared into his food. 'He told me his elderly wife was a nervous wreck. That she couldn't eat or sleep and she cried at any kind of noise. He just wanted to be able to reassure her that they were safe.'

'You really thought burglary was a victimless crime?'

He nodded but still didn't look up. 'To me, all I was doing was taking stuff, possessions that were probably insured anyway and, honestly, I didn't much care if they weren't. But once I'd robbed a place it meant nothing to me. I forgot about it. I never realised that I was leaving such fear behind. I've never been violent in my life and never had any intention of hurting anybody.'

Kim could see the regret in his eyes.

'The picture of that old lady petrified every single day because of me, well, it killed me.'

'What did you do?'

'Wrote her a letter. Afterwards, I wrote a lot of letters but that day I wrote one just for that old lady. I also told him what attracted me to his property in the first place so he could try and make sure it didn't happen again.'

Kim was moved by the genuine emotion she heard in his voice.

Finally, he looked at her. 'The worst thing is that when he left he offered me his hand. The guy offered me his fucking hand.'

Kim saw the redness that had appeared around his eyes.

'He tries really hard,' Wendy offered, touching his leg tenderly.

Kim had no doubt. This man wanted to work but with his record and appearance his prospects for full-time employment were not looking good.

The child on her lap gurgled.

'How much do you want to work?'

He looked at his daughter. 'A lot.'

'But what are you prepared to do?'

'Anything.'

'Then that's your answer.'

The child began to squirm and Wendy reached over to take her back.

His expression was puzzled.

'Do you know what, Len, everyone has jobs that need doing that they either just can't find the time or don't really wanna do.'

'But I'm not qualified to—'

'Do you know how to mow a lawn, shift rubbish? Start small, mow a lawn for free and do a good job, you'll get customers. Knock doors, wear a polo neck, talk to people, put cards in supermarkets, shop windows. What you have is yourself. You're young and healthy and keen. You have no car but you have your legs and a whole lot of time.'

Interest lit his eyes. She took out a business card and handed it to him.

'Go on, I'll be your first client. What do you know about bikes?'

He nodded. 'A bit.'

'Okay, I'm looking to find a frame, just a frame, for a Norton Commando '68. I'm happy to pay up to five hundred quid for it but I just don't have the time to go looking. You do the legwork and find the cheapest you can and you get to keep the change. And then you get a reference from a pig on a bike.'

Len looked from her to his girlfriend and back again.

'You serious?'

She nodded. 'This ain't charity, Len. I've told you what I want and the rest is up to you.'

The constant rejections from interviews had knocked the stuffing out of him, and Kim had no doubt about his sincerity or his motivation but his demeanour had been defeated and no one would even consider offering him a job. Given a purpose, his back would straighten, his eyes would brighten and he'd be out and about speaking to people and who knew what that could lead to.

'Officer, I don't know what to say.'

'Then, don't,' she said, standing.

She offered him her hand. 'We got a deal?'

He took her hand and shook it. His mouth opened to speak but a small cheer around the room stopped him.

A tray of Nando's chicken and chips had just entered the room attached to the hands of Police Constable Ian Skitt.

CHAPTER FIFTY-SEVEN

Cristina went upstairs, away from the air of stress and anxiety that had attached itself to the skin of her colleagues.

She used the bottom bunk to help her climb onto the top. Without the space to sit up straight, she immediately lay on her side.

She was not surprised when a figure appeared in the doorway. The anger she felt towards Natalya seeped into her face.

'Cristina… *imi pare rau pentru ce am facut.*'

Cristina ignored her apology. There was no point being sorry for her outburst now. Thank goodness neither of the police officers had spoken a word of Romanian.

'Do you have any idea what you could have done?' Cristina accused.

Natalya coloured and nodded.

Cristina acknowledged her apology and turned towards the wall and pulled the coarse blanket up over her legs. There was no heating on the upper level of the house. The warmth from the hot needles of water during her five-minute timed shower had long since been stripped from her skin.

She reached underneath her pillow and took out the pyjamas wrapped around the notebooks and pencil and took up where she had left off.

* * *

We were released from the lorry early the next day. We were in England.

A tall, bald man confirmed my name at a motorway service station and pointed to a white transit van. We opened the door and climbed in. The stench of body odour was foul but we huddled together in a corner. Sixteen more souls crammed into the space and not one single word was spoken. Two more men got into the van before it began to move.

Every mile it travelled away from the coast reassured me we were not being followed. I pictured us heading into the heart of the country. Distance meant safety. I wanted to hope for the future. For our life together in this new country. The fear of Romania still hung to my clothes but it was becoming easier to breathe.

I knew that I had taken a gamble. That you might never forgive me for the decisions I'd made but we could not have stayed in Romania.

The van continued its journey through the night and the doors were opened at dawn. The light hurt your eyes after so many hours of darkness.

I hoped this would be the last stop. That we would have the flat and the job I'd been promised. A place for us to call home. I knew it wouldn't be a palace but as long as we were together, I could manage with anything.

The van had stopped behind a supermarket. We were all told to get out and stand in a line. Three men stood and appraised us, one smoked a big fat cigar. He pointed first. The man he pointed to was pulled out of the line. The second man pointed and that man was pulled out. And then the third, smaller man, did the same.

Every person was removed from the line until it was only us left and the man with the thick cigar.

He sighed heavily and then nodded to the driver of the van. He pushed me towards the furthest group away.

The four men retreated to the back of the van while everyone waited silently.

I tried to listen to the hushed conversation but could only make out the occasional word.

Were they deciding who was to live where, who was to have which job?

I wished they had spoken to us, to find out our skills. I could have told them. I was a qualified dentist, that I had lost my business but not my qualifications. Maybe Ralph had passed this along.

The men reappeared with good humour. The van driver patted his back pocket and got back into the van.

The cigar man appraised us with a smile.

Encouraged, I stepped forward and asked: 'Are you taking us to our new home now?'

He laughed but no one else joined in.

I tried again.

'Please can you tell me what's happening?'

Cristina felt the rage growing inside her. With a trembling hand she translated the response.

'Of course, fella. You've just been sold. Now you belong to me.'

CHAPTER FIFTY-EIGHT

Kim stepped to the side as Skitt passed her with the steaming food. He placed it on the reception desk and bodies surged towards him. Kim could just about see his dark hair above the crowd.

'Oi, shouldn't you be out trying to catch a fucking psycho?'

Kim turned to find the owner of the hostility. Her eyes travelled down to a diminutive female with a shock of electric blue hair and a ring through her left nostril.

'Excuse me,' Kim said, fighting back her amusement.

'Just asking why yo ay out catching the fucker that did Donna.' She bobbed her head along with the street talk and looked Kim up and down. Her intimidating stare fell short, literally.

'And yow doe look like yow need a free meal so what yow doin 'ere?'

'What are you doing here?' Kim countered.

'Havin' me tay.'

'Then what?'

'Gooin to work,' she said. More attitude and more ghetto.

'So, despite the fact there's a killer out there and your mate Donna died last night you're right back out there?'

'I gorra fucking eat.'

Kim glanced pointedly at the plate of chicken. 'Well, looks like that's covered for tonight but you're still going out there?'

'It's your fucking job to protect—'

'If you couldn't give a shit about your own well-being, why should I?'

Kim leaned in closer. 'Now, you're a long way from the ghetto so just bugger off and eat your chicken.'

Kim stepped away from the girl who called her a foul name before moving towards the doorway.

The crowds had moved away from the reception desk. Kim cast her eye around the room trying to locate the dark head of the police constable. She spied Tim ducking into the small office behind the desk. She followed.

'Hey, Tim, did you see where that copper went?'

Tim placed a couple of receipts under a paperweight. 'He's gone. He normally hangs around for an hour or so but he's got some pressing business.'

Kim leaned up against the wall. 'How long has he been coming here?'

Tim shrugged. 'Couple of months. He talks to the girls, they trust him.'

'Last I heard, Nando's wasn't in the habit of giving away free food every week.'

Tim met her gaze. 'He says they do and I'm not gonna argue.'

Kim heard the rumble of voices reduce to a murmur.

Martha appeared at the doorway.

'It's all gone, Tim. I'll start packing away.'

'Thanks, Martha. Did Sal come in yet?'

Martha shook her head. 'Didn't see her.'

'Sal comes here?' Kim asked, surprised.

'Every week. She doesn't always eat but she normally comes in for a cuppa.'

Sal wasn't the one that Kim had come here to find but the fact she hadn't turned up set alarm bells off in her head. She rushed outside, surprised to see how quickly the place had emptied now that the food was gone. The kid who had given her a mouthful was leaning against a bus stand with a triumphant look on her face. She was a kid with a secret.

Kim felt the hairs on the back of her neck raise as she sprinted across the road.

'Where's Sal?'

There was no surprise at her question and just a shrug in response.

'Where is she?' Kim growled, stepping closer.

The girl swallowed but met her gaze. 'I saw what she did the other night. Tipped yow off when that girl come down the street. Yow ran into the minder 'cos of her signal, day yer?'

Kim grabbed her T-shirt at the breastbone and pulled her closer, rage ringing in her ears. 'What did you do, you little shit?'

'I mighta mentioned it,' she said, snatching her T-shirt back.

'You told Kai?'

She shrugged. 'Thought he might wanna know who he could and couldn't trust.'

Kim remembered Gemma's words about there being no loyalty out on the streets. Wasn't that a bloody fact?

'Where is she?' Kim demanded.

Again with the slow, lazy smile. 'After what she done, where do you fucking think?'

There was only one place she could be.

Kim turned on her heel and ran.

CHAPTER FIFTY-NINE

Stacey approached the door to the café just as Mariana was turning the sign to closed.

Stacey mouthed the word 'please' around the opening hours sticker on the glass. The girl hesitated and then unlocked the door. Stacey was relieved to step in out of the cold. Dawson had offered to take her home but she had invented a grocery shop she needed to do en route. And when she had, this was exactly what she'd been hoping for. To catch Mariana alone.

After their conversation with Devon, Stacey was convinced that Vasile and his daughter knew more than they were letting on. Especially his daughter.

The Romanian community was a small one and she knew how that worked. The black community in Dudley had been sizeable as she'd grown up but the Nigerian portion had accounted for less than ten per cent and her parents had known everyone.

The Eastern European community was substantial but people gravitated to their own nationality when in a foreign land.

She remembered a weekend away in France in her early teens. Throughout the two days they'd bumped into people they had never met before boarding the coach in the Midlands. But in a foreign country they had become friendly, familiar, almost comrades. On the journey home telephone numbers had been exchanged, drinks nights planned and that was after two days.

Vasile had been here for more than twenty years. She suspected he did know the man at the canal but a bigger part of her wondered if Mariana knew the identity of the mother of the child. She had hoped for just a few minutes alone with the young woman.

'Tata,' she called behind.

Damn it. Clearly that was not going to happen.

'Mariana, may I just ask…'

'What is…'

Vasile's words trailed away as he appeared from the back of the shop. In his hands was a striped tea towel. He frowned at her and then at his daughter who was already backing away. The anxiety in the room was palpable, and Stacey had no idea why. She realised the tension was not coming from Vasile but from his daughter.

Mariana wasn't scared of her father, as Stacey had suspected. Once closer to his reassuring bulk the tension began to leave her face.

He handed her the tea towel and pointed back towards the kitchen. He watched her go with sadness that still lingered when he turned to her. There was a gentleness to this man mountain that she couldn't help but warm to.

'Officer?'

'Sir, I think you know more than you are telling us,' she said, honestly.

He removed two chairs from on top of the table, sat, and pointed for her to do the same.

She did so. 'I understand how minorities within communities work. I really do. There is an unwritten comradeship, code of protection. But we have an abandoned baby and a dead man and we don't know for sure if either of them are Romanian.'

He thought for a moment.

'Seems reasonable based on the evidence,' he said, meeting her gaze.

Stacey instantly understood. He didn't know what evidence they had.

They were correct.

'And we feel that someone at Robertson's is involved somehow.'

He nodded. 'I can understand why you would think that.'

Another correct assumption.

'The girls there seem very frightened of everyone.'

'I suspect they are.'

'Even though they are all legal immigrants.'

'Hmm…' He shrugged.

So, maybe they weren't.

'I think the mother of the child might work there,' she ventured.

'It's possible,' he said, opening his hands.

'Sir, is there no way you can—?'

'I think that the mother of that child must have had a very good reason to give him up. I think she must have loved him very much to do such a thing. It was not a decision she would have made lightly.'

Was he telling her to leave it alone?

'But maybe we could assist the mother; if you would just help us identify her, we could…'

'Do you remember the house raid in Lye?'

She nodded. The one Devon had told them about.

'Someone from the Romanian community was concerned for the safety of the children and made a call to the authorities.'

She nodded her understanding.

'The call was anonymous but three days later the daughter of the confidential informant was brutally raped,' he said, staring out of the window.

A shadow appeared at the doorway to the kitchen.

Stacey's breath caught in her throat as the pieces slotted into place.

'Mariana…' she breathed.

'I feel for that little baby, officer, but Mariana is my *bebelus* and I have to protect her. I can tell you nothing.'

The raw emotion in his voice hit her right in the throat. The investigator in her wanted to pry names and dates and details from him to follow this up and bring the rapists to justice.

As though reading her mind he shook his head. 'It is not what she would want.'

She placed her hand on his arm and swallowed.

'Sir, I am sorry for what you have been through, and I thank you for your time.'

She stood and let herself out of the door. She had no doubt that Vasile had all the answers she sought but she would not return to ask him again.

This small family had suffered enough.

CHAPTER SIXTY

Kim parked outside the maternity entrance of Russells Hall hospital. It was the only access point open once normal visiting was over.

She had chosen to disregard the instruction of the ward sister that she could not visit. The door opened and a woman in a spotted dressing gown and furry slippers stepped out carrying a single cigarette and disposable lighter. Kim took her opportunity and grabbed the door before it closed.

The corridors were eerily deserted with an overpowering aroma of disinfectant. She passed the central concourse and the direction boards. She'd visited the Medical Admissions ward more times than she cared to remember.

She buzzed the intercom and introduced herself as Detective Inspector. The door clicked open and Kim headed to the Nurse's station. Two blue clad ladies pushed aside a half-empty pizza box. Only on the late shift was ten p.m. lunchtime.

'I need to speak with Sally Summers.'

The older woman gave her a knowing look.

'You sound remarkably like the sister I spoke to on the phone half an hour ago when I told you it was too late to visit.'

Kim shrugged. 'I won't cause you any problem. I just need to speak to her.'

The younger nurse said nothing and opened a folder.

'Look, officer, I think you should come back tomorrow when—'

'By tomorrow I may well be visiting a third murder scene.' She paused. 'I'm sure you've seen the news.'

'The prostitutes?'

Kim nodded, and watched the veil of disinterest that closed over the woman's face like a Roman blind. Kim understood the look. It represented much of the population. Prostitutes were less deserving of the rights allowed to other citizens. Somehow they were to blame for their own fate, even if that fate was a brutal, horrifying death. Most people would not voice the thought that slipped into the minds of 'good people'. That she should be working on other cases; solving crimes committed against the worthy. Good people would not say it but the thought would be there nonetheless. A fire fighter killed in the line of duty was a hero, his death a tragedy. A prostitute was simply one less. It all came down to career choice.

'Second room along,' the older nurse said, nodding to her right.

Kim thanked her and passed by the darkened wards. A gentle hum of equipment cushioned the silence.

One wall light illuminated the small room. Sal lay on her back; her eyes closed.

Kim stood for a moment, not surprised that the woman's face was free of injury. The damage done was beneath the crisp white sheets. She quietly moved to the foot of the bed, careful not to disturb the gentle rising of the woman's chest. Kim gently lifted the chart hooked over the edge of the bed. The notes were in medical jargon but she understood the words 'laceration' and 'contusion'. She could also read a body chart.

Kim had seen worse. Sal had been smacked around and would be sore for a couple of days. She suspected the woman was being kept in for observation as one of the blows had been landed to the back of her head. Kai had wanted to teach her a lesson but not put her out of action for too long.

Kim remembered visiting the bedside of a prostitute working the streets of Balsall Heath when she'd been a constable. The girl had kept back £30 of her earnings for the night. She'd read that body chart too. Most of the injuries had been forms of punishment, not intended to kill but designed to cause the maximum amount of pain for the longest period of time. The X-rays displayed a broken rib on each side of her body. The bones could not be set in a cast and had to knit back together in their own good time. The injury to both sides meant that any movement would be excruciating. The bruises across her lower back and buttocks were to ensure that she would be unable to sit or lie down without pain. But the lacerations had been the worst. The girl had been slashed on both sides of her inner thighs. Not one single step could be taken without the agony of the two wounds rubbing together.

Sal had been lucky, Kim thought, as she sat back and watched the rhythmic rising and falling of the woman's chest. Sadly, she still saw traces of the girl she had known as a child. The skin was lost to more burst capillaries than it should have been. The lines around the eyes were about ten years too deep, yet in the woman Kim still saw remnants of the girl.

Their paths had crossed many times during their childhood years. They had met the first time when Kim had been six years old. After her stay in hospital she had been taken to Fairview Hall children's home, an unforgiving grey concrete slab of a building that had reflected the soulless interior. As she'd sat on the narrow single bed beside her bin bag of second-hand possessions a figure had loomed in the doorway. Kim could still recall meeting the curious gaze of the older girl eating an apple.

Sal had stared at her coldly but Kim had refused to look away.

'Want some?' Sal had said, offering the apple.

Kim had shaken her head and the girl had shrugged and walked away.

Eventually Kim had found out that Sal had been voluntarily surrendered to state care following the birth of her younger sister. She'd heard rumours that Sal had tried to hurt the baby but there had been rumours about them all.

'What the fuck you doing here, bitch?'

Sal's whispery voice pulled her back from the past. Her eyes were wide open but dulled by pain.

Kim shrugged. 'Just passing.'

'How'd you find me?'

Kim rolled her eyes. 'You ain't royalty, you know. You weren't signed in under a different name.'

'Jesus, you were a pain when you were a kid and you haven't changed a bit since.'

'I like to be consistent,' Kim said.

'Well, do something useful and pass me some water.'

Kim stood and poured fresh water into the plastic beaker.

Sal narrowed her eyes. 'Look, I don't know what you're doing here but piss off and leave me in peace.'

'It's because of me, isn't it?' Kim asked.

Sal rested her head back on the pillow and shook her head.

'Don't flatter yourself, Kim. It's 'cos I don't like to do what I'm told.'

'I met the little shit that told him. She's a piece of work. Didn't you deny it?'

'Got one of his goons to check my phone, found your mobile number.'

'Jesus, Sal, I'm sorry.'

'For what? I gave you the nod, ya dumb bitch, so take off the hair shirt. It don't suit you.'

Sal was quiet for a moment then shook her head. A sound that seemed like a chuckle escaped from between her lips.

'I saw what you did, you dumb tart. Have you got a death wish or something?'

'I couldn't just let her get in that car.'

'Did she get away?'

Kim nodded. Sal smiled briefly. The expression quickly vanished.

'There'll always be more, you know,' she said, wearily.

Kim nodded. She knew.

If she'd been born a superhero she might have been able to prevent many of the deaths that had coloured her life but she wasn't and she could only fight what was right in front of her.

'You know about Donna?' Kim asked.

Sal nodded and swallowed. 'Heard the news from one of the televisions out there. It didn't name her but I just knew. Stupid cow was determined to go out every night. Said she'd clean up while the other pussies quivered under their warm quilts at home.' Sal shook her head. 'Poor bitch called that wrong.'

There was little compassion or regret in her tone. Kim understood that street life chewed away at sentimentality. It was an existence that left little room for enduring friendships. Bonds were formed through shared adversity but self-preservation always took priority.

'You have to get out of this, Sal,' Kim said quietly.

Sal turned her head slightly.

'And do what, Kim?'

Kim shrugged. 'Anything you want to. You've got a lot going for you. You're an intelligent, attractive woman with a different future if you'd only take the help that's been offered.'

'What the hell is it with you? Just because my life doesn't fit your stereotype you want me to conform to your ideals.'

'No, Sal, I just want you to be safe.'

'I can take care of myself.'

'Bloody well looks like it.'

'Never get injured at work, Detective Inspector?'

'Not by the people I work for,' she snapped.

'Just fuck off, will you?'

Kim stood and touched Sal's left arm. 'Okay, I'll go but I'm not giving up on you, Sal.'

Sal didn't move her arm or speak for a few seconds. When the words came Kim could hear the thickness in her voice.

'Eventually you're gonna have to.'

Kim turned away, thinking that Sal might be right.

But she always came back to the same memory. Foster family three, the Nelson family. Mr Nelson had owned his own hardware business and Mrs Nelson had been a part-time dinner lady. The care workers had been overjoyed at their willingness to take a nine-year-old and an eleven-year-old together. It was the only time they'd ever shared a foster home.

Each Saturday morning Mr Nelson would head off to his premises to tidy up and stocktake his business. The first Saturday he'd taken Sal with him. Upon their return Sal had been quiet and pensive but would not say a word. The following week Mr Nelson had told Kim it was her turn. Sal had immediately stepped in front of her and said she wanted to go again. And so it went every Saturday.

Kim had not fully understood at the time but later she had come to realise what happened at the hardware store on a Saturday morning and that she had been spared because of Sal.

She thought about the woman lying in a hospital bed because she'd tried to help her once again.

So, no, she wasn't prepared to give up on her. Not just yet.

CHAPTER SIXTY-ONE

Dawson pulled onto the drive behind the silver Corsa and sighed heavily.

It was almost eleven and he'd been out of the house since 7 a.m. If Alison was awake there was going to be an argument. He had considered telling her the truth but she wouldn't understand. He shook his head at the thought of the phrase, 'my wife/girlfriend/fiancé doesn't understand me'. But on this occasion it would be accurate.

She'd been cool on the phone when he'd called to explain it was another late night at work. The tightness of her voice had signalled that she didn't believe him. And, of course, she was right. Stacey had left hours ago.

Some nights she chose not to argue at all. She simply deigned not to speak a word. Those nights were worse than the all-out arguments.

He knew that she was tired. He knew that Charlotte was into everything and only yesterday had chosen to shove a red crayon in her ear and call it an antler. He knew that by seven Alison was exhausted and barely able to see straight. Right at the time he should have been coming back and giving her a hand.

He took a deep, preparatory breath and entered his home. As the light switched on he noticed two things: the dining table had been set for a candlelit dinner and there was a pillow and blankets on the sofa.

'I thought you were joking,' she said, quietly.

Damn it, she'd been waiting for him in the dark.

'I really thought you were going to walk in and surprise me.'

He noted the Daniel Wellington box on his side of the table. He'd mentioned a few weeks ago their classic Durham silver watch.

She stood. 'I thought there was no way you'd forget it was four years today since we met, Kev. Obviously I was wrong.'

He could not bear to look at the hurt in her eyes. Even after all the late nights, the arguments, the bitter silences, she had bought him the gift he had wanted. And she was right. He hadn't even remembered.

'What's this?' he asked, sitting next to the pillow.

'Your bed for the night,' she said, leaning against the door frame.

Finally, he looked at her and saw the accusation and pain on her face.

He turned away and removed his jacket. There was nothing to say.

'Whatever it is you're up to you're not bringing it into the same bed as me,' she spat.

He undid his tie and threw it over the back of the sofa.

Alison allowed the silence to build between them. She knew that he could be as stubborn as she was.

Tonight he didn't trust himself to speak.

'You do know we're reaching a point from which we can't return?'

He stared down at the carpet, unable to meet the intensity of her gaze. He wondered if the reason for his deceit was worth this and, damn it, yes it was.

'You're a selfish bastard, Kevin Dawson,' she said, heading towards the stairs.

Oh yes, I'm definitely that, he thought to himself as he lay down to sleep.

CHAPTER SIXTY-TWO

Kim parked her car behind Bryant's Astra outside the crematorium building on Powke Lane in Rowley Regis. The mechanical yellow digger surrounded by white suits beneath the portable floodlights were at the top left-hand side of the site. She blew a kiss to her right and hoped it found her twin brother, Mikey.

She headed up the single-track road as a mixture of grit and ice crunched beneath her boots. Only one entrance to the site had been opened and was being guarded by a police constable.

The temperature had stabilised at -1 °C but was expected to drop to -3 °C before 2 a.m.

'Everyone here?' Kim asked, as Bryant walked towards her.

All parties were already wearing protective suits and face masks. Bryant handed her the last set. Clearly introductions had taken place prior to her arrival and Bryant began to point and name for her benefit.

'Gravedigger, Environmental Health, undertaker and assistant, crem manager, photographer, pathologist, and police,' he said, pointing at Keats and then at the two of them.

The last had not been necessary, she thought, as she stepped into the white overalls.

'And Keats has already grumbled about your time-keeping,' he added.

Kim shrugged. A lot seemed to have happened in the few hours since she'd last seen her partner.

'Are you ready?' Keats asked her shortly.

She nodded as she put the face mask on her head.

Keats instructed everyone to step back as the gravedigger mounted the JCB. The area had been marked out but no headstone had yet been installed. The grave was only ten days old. The photographer stepped in and took a photo.

She stepped forward too, her eyes drawn to the walkway that ran behind the grassed area. She frowned as the digger rumbled into action.

'Stop,' she cried, holding up her hand.

The crematorium manager immediately repeated her action and the digger silenced.

She took another step forward and bent to the ground. 'Was this removed from the grave?' she asked, glancing at the snow-spattered wreath of pine cones, holly and berries.

The manager nodded.

Kim swore under her breath. 'Who touched it?'

The manager looked around. 'Just me,' he said.

Keats reached into his case and produced an evidence bag. She chose a sprig of holly unlikely to have been touched by anyone handling the wreath and lifted it into the bag. Keats took it and marked it up.

'You gonna get a full DNA workup done on that?' Bryant asked, as the digger kicked into life once more.

'What do you think?'

'Woody will be chuffed,' Bryant said.

'Someone valued this girl enough to leave flowers and I want to know who it was.'

They stepped back as the digger broke ground.

'So, where've you been?'

'Umm… home, community centre on Hollytree, and Russells Hall hospital. How about you?'

'Just home for a bite to eat and to reintroduce myself to the wife.'

'Slacker,' she said, watching the bucket make light work of the frozen earth.

Angela Marsons

The Environmental Health rep stepped forward and got in the way of the photographer. Kim was unsure of his purpose. His responsibility was to ensure that the body was treated with respect at all times. They were a good four feet away from a coffin.

Suddenly the digger stopped and the crem manager nodded towards Keats.

Keats took a scoop from his toolbag and burrowed it into the digger bucket.

'We're getting close,' she said to Bryant.

'What's he doing?' her colleague asked.

'Taking soil samples,' Kim answered. He would also take a sample from below and each side of the coffin to ensure the body had not been contaminated by anything from outside the coffin.

'So, who is in hospital?' Bryant asked.

'Sal,' she answered.

'Because of what happened the—'

'Obviously,' she said, shortly. That her actions had caused injury to a woman she had known all her life was not sitting well on her shoulders.

'Listen, guv, she's made her own…'

Kim stepped away from him. There was absolutely nothing he could say that was going to make her feel any better.

The coffin of Lauren Goddard appeared and was placed into the waiting casket that would prevent any liquid from escaping prior to analysis.

For a moment every person present fell silent as they each appreciated the enormity of removing a body from what should have been its final resting place.

The environmental officer stepped forward and checked the name on the brass plate matched the name on the licence. He scribbled something down and then nodded that the process could continue.

'Opened?' asked the crem manager.

Keats shook his head.

Kim knew that sometimes a coffin was opened at site to allow the gases to escape into the air rather than the morgue and for the pathologist to visually check the condition of the bones in case damage occurred in transit. She'd seen the vulnerable points of the hands and feet wrapped to ensure nothing escaped.

But due to the recent burial Keats was obviously happy for everything to take place at the morgue.

The funeral director, his assistant, the crem manager and the gravedigger carried the coffin gingerly to the hearse.

No one spoke until the hearse doors closed.

'I've read the file and studied the report,' Keats said, with a tight expression. 'So what are we hoping to achieve here, Inspector?'

Kim could feel his disapproval. His respect for his customers dictated that someone needed a bloody good reason for disturbing their remains.

'I honestly have no idea, Keats. But someone thinks she's hiding something.'

And he had 48 hours to find out what before Lauren had to be returned to the ground. She could feel the aggravation bubbling within him but was saved by the ringing of his mobile phone.

Kim silently thanked them, whoever they were. She turned away and headed towards Bryant as the hearse slowly pulled away.

'Okay, Bryant, I'll meet you—'

'Not so fast, Inspector,' Keats said, ending his call. 'The lab appears to be working late this evening and I have some news that might be of interest to you.'

She turned back towards him.

'That car, the Toyota, traces of blood were found in the passenger seat footwell.'

'Go on,' she urged.

'Belonging to our first victim, Kelly Rowe.'

CHAPTER SIXTY-THREE

Kim took her temporary new spot at the head of the room. The whiteboard had been updated and divided into three. Lauren Goddard had taken the third column.

'Okay, guys, look lively. We have a lot to get through,' she said. 'As you know, Lauren Goddard was exhumed in the early hours of the morning, and Bryant and I will be heading over to Keats as soon as we can. The lab has confirmed that traces of blood from Kelly Rowe, who was murdered on Saturday night, were found in Roger Barton's Toyota but nothing from Donna Hill who was killed on Monday night?'

'Different killers?' Penn asked.

Kim considered. 'Possible but unlikely,' she said. The murder of two prostitutes in the same week by different killers didn't feel right to her.

'Penn, can you update on Donna's background?' she asked.

He whistled. 'Oh yeah. Donna Hammond-Hill is the daughter of Louisa Hammond-Hill and the late Peter Hammond-Hill.'

'Wasn't he that famous architect who won the contract to design the Grand Tower in the centre of Birmingham?' Dawson asked.

Penn nodded. 'Yeah, died suddenly before he had a chance to get started. Massive heart attack.'

'And Donna?' Kim asked.

'Donna attended Heathcrest Academy from the age of four and a half until five months after her father's death. Expelled for constant fighting. Put a girl in hospital.'

'Guessing she didn't deal with her father's death all that well,' Bryant said.

'And her mother?' Kim asked.

'Is currently on her way to identify the body,' Penn answered. 'She's expecting you to visit the family home this morning.'

Kim was very interested to understand Donna's journey from the carefree, vibrant girl in the photo to the emaciated, desperate young lady in the morgue.

'Okay, we're still looking at Jeremy Templeton. There's something not quite right there, and although he's been warned to leave the area I have a sneaky suspicion that he won't go until he gets what he came for.'

'What's he like? This man who likes sex with young girls,' Dawson asked.

'Not how you'd imagine,' Kim offered. 'Good-looking, athletic, well-spoken and clearly well off.'

He looked nonplussed. 'Then why the hell…'

'Come on, Kev,' Stacey said. 'You know appearances doe count for nothing. Remember Ted Bundy. Not every deviant looks like Fred West.'

'So, his name stays current, and Penn, carry on digging.'

'Nothing incriminating yet.'

'Okay, and keep pinging Ellie Greaves's phone. I promised her mother an update today. And right now the only thing I can confirm is that we don't have an unidentified body.'

'It's been on and off since yesterday but nowhere long enough to get a fix.'

'Keep trying,' she said.

She turned to Dawson. 'Where are you two at?'

She saw his frustration. 'Spoke to the employees at Robertson's, who all spouted the exact same script. We have a thin link from our canal guy to the bag factory.'

'Which is?'

'*Sarmale*,' Stacey answered. 'A Romanian dish of cabbage and meat. Contents were in our guy's stomach.'

Kim raised one eyebrow. 'Is that it?'

They looked at each other and then back at her.

'Yeah, but we did follow the minibus back to where all the girls live. Telling you, boss,' Dawson said, 'something there is not right.'

'Immigration have put out feelers and are suspicious of what they've found,' Stacey offered.

'Or more like what they haven't found,' Dawson explained. 'No complaints, no whispers, no rumours. We're tagging along this morning.'

Giving them the green light to continue to focus on Robertson's was risking a complaint of harassment but she trusted Dawson's instinct almost as much as she trusted her own. The planned raid on the factory would be the responsibility of Immigration but the prompt had come from them.

'Keep on it,' she instructed, looking around the room. 'Anything else?'

Everyone shook their heads.

'Okay, get to it,' she said.

Dawson and Stacey were out of the door first as Bryant reached for his jacket. She did the same and nodded for Bryant to carry on without her.

'Penn, there's something else I want you to look at but it stays between us.'

'Of course, boss.'

'I want you to find me anything you can on Ian Skitt.'

Penn looked puzzled. 'You talking about that young neighbourhood constable guy?'

'Yep, that's the one. But it goes no further, okay?'

Penn nodded his understanding.

There was something there that felt a little off but it was a feeling that was growling in her gut and she was not prepared to muddy his name unless she had a good reason.

And she bloody well hoped there was no good reason to find.

CHAPTER SIXTY-FOUR

Stacey rubbed her hands feverishly to get some heat to the end of her fingers.

'What's the high today?' she asked.

'Two degrees,' he said, turning up the heat in the car.

'Great,' she moaned.

They'd been sitting opposite the trading estate for twenty minutes waiting for Devon and her team. The minibus had entered ten minutes earlier, at 8.55 a.m.

'Stace?'

'Yeah,' she answered.

'Never mind.'

'Okay,' she said.

'It's just…'

'What?'

'It's nothing. Doesn't matter.'

'Jesus, Kev. Go on, ask me the damn question,' she snapped.

'Why the hell did you blow her off?'

It was the question she'd been waiting for. She said nothing.

'She's totally gorgeous.'

'Yep,' she said.

'Sexy as hell.'

'Yep,' she repeated.

'Overdosed on appeal.'

'Yep,' she said.

'Intelligent, articulate, did I mention gorgeous?'

'Yep.'

'I don't get it, Stace,' he said.

'Because of all those things,' she answered.

'You blew her off because she's gorgeous?' he asked, incredulously.

'Look at her and then look at me,' she said.

He turned to her, genuinely confused.

'You've lost me?'

'I just did it first,' she answered.

'Hang on. You finished with her before she could finish with you?'

She nodded. Damn it. It had made sense at the time but put like that it sounded just a little bit childish.

'Fuck me, Stace,' he said, shaking his head as a black van pulled up behind them. 'You finished it because you don't think you're good enough?'

'Leave it, Kev,' she said, with her palm on the door handle.

He growled as he got out of the car. Both doors slammed together as he faced her across the roof.

'Listen, Stace, there ain't a woman alive good enough for you.'

She held his gaze for a second before black uniforms poured out of the van. A second vehicle pulled up behind.

Everyone gathered around the bonnet of the car as Devon headed towards them.

Stacey tried to ignore the feeling in her stomach as the woman strode purposefully their way. Damn, she looked even sexier in a stab proof vest.

'Briefing done at the office. Just finalising now.'

'Did you get the warrant?' Dawson asked.

Devon shook her head. 'We're aiming for cooperation from the owners.'

'Good luck with that,' Stacey murmured.

'Be aware, we're not going in to frighten anyone. The last thing we want is for these girls to be terrified into silence. Myself and Grant will go in first and talk to the owners. One of you can come in but I don't want you both. Not yet.'

She waited for their decision.

'Stacey,' Dawson said. 'The women will trust her more than me.'

Devon nodded and turned her way. 'Don't speak, though. We have to go through a process. Got it?'

'Got it,' Stacey said, grateful to get a bird's-eye view of the operation and hopefully some answers.

'All set?' Devon asked, as a tall blonde man approached. Stacey assumed him to be Grant.

* * *

Stacey was just a couple of steps behind as they crossed the road towards the premises at speed. By the time they reached the reception door she'd caught up.

Melody's smile turned to fear as they entered the building.

Grant immediately held out his hand.

'Grant Chance from Immigration Enforcement,' he said, holding out the identification card hanging around his neck. 'May I speak to the person in charge?'

She nodded mutely and picked up the phone.

Officially that should be Mrs Robertson but Stacey had no doubt that it would be Steven who came through the door.

And as she'd thought Steven appeared immediately, looking flushed and pensive. She guessed he'd seen the vans from the upstairs window.

'What's going on?' he asked, looking across them all.

Grant took a step forward and offered his identification.

'Immigration Enforcement,' he said. 'We've received an anonymous call regarding the employees here.'

Steven looked directly at her. His expression was cold.

'Anonymous, eh?'

'Yes,' Grant confirmed.

Stacey couldn't help but notice that the man's cool, calm demeanour had definitely been ruffled. Each time they'd seen him he had been in control but this surprise visit had unnerved him.

'We have nothing to hide. Please follow me.'

Devon followed Grant and she followed Devon. Melody offered her a tight smile as she passed.

A lot of heads rose with interest as they passed through the factory. Tension crackled in the air as the furtive looks waved along the rows of sewing machines. Foot pedals stopped tapping and hands stilled as their steps to the mezzanine were closely watched.

Nicolae shouted something in Romanian and the heads snapped back down and the noise resumed.

Steven guided them all into his office and closed the door.

'All of our workers are legal immigrants and have every right to—'

'Of course, Mr Robertson,' Grant said, amiably. 'But we have to act on complaints. I'm sure your paperwork will be in order. Now if we could just begin with the full names and addresses of all of your workers?'

Steven sat down and tapped a few keys on the computer. The printer beside him burst into life. Pages began to spit out of its mouth.

Stacey glanced at the first sheet of paper, which held six different names.

Devon removed the sheets and passed them to Grant but not before Stacey had recognised the address.

Devon returned to stand beside her as Grant continued speaking to Steven Robertson.

'Every one of them lives at the property we followed them to last night,' Stacey whispered, as the conversation about documentation continued.

'Not uncommon,' Devon advised. 'These poor women don't normally earn enough to live alone. Sometimes they club together to rent a small house.'

Stacey re-joined the conversation taking place around the desk.

'Well, Mr Robertson, everything appears to be in order here. Our only issue will be to check the passports of the employees, which we can do by visiting the address you've given us.'

'No need for that,' Steven said, stepping to a filing cabinet. His demeanour had returned to the measured, deliberate state she recognised and his movements calm and controlled as he took a key from his desk and unlocked the top drawer. He reached in and produced an elasticated bundle of passports.

Stacey looked to Devon who was frowning, reflecting her own thoughts.

Which was, why did he have their passports at all?

CHAPTER SIXTY-FIVE

Kim couldn't hide her surprise when Bryant pulled up at the childhood home of Donna Hammond-Hill.

A drive along a short lane in Wollescote led them to a modernised farmhouse with a sunroom tagged onto the side. The front of the home had been fashioned with wood and tinted glass. A small Peugeot was the only car on the sizeable drive.

'Honestly, guv, I just don't get it,' Bryant said, shaking his head.

Kim knew he was picturing the tiny space in which Donna had chosen to live. Instead of here.

'We can't judge her reasons, Bryant,' she said. A nice-looking house was not indicative of the life inside. Unhappiness, misery and abuse were not the sole property of the poor and disadvantaged. They had not yet met Donna's family.

Kim knocked and waited.

The woman that opened the door was late forties. Her skin was pale against the red-rimmed eyes and auburn hair. She wore no make-up but her navy trouser suit and court shoes told Kim she had only recently returned from the morgue.

Bryant introduced them both and the woman stepped back from the door.

'Are you alone, Mrs Hammond-Hill?' Kim asked.

She nodded as she guided them through the hallway. 'I was offered a liaison officer or victim support worker or something but I don't want anyone here. I just want to be alone.'

'I'm sorry we have to intrude…'

'Not at all, officer. I am beyond numb right now so it might be best to catch me before it all sinks in.'

Kim saw the tears form in her eyes as she spoke.

It was beginning to sink in.

They followed her into the sunroom.

'My favourite part of the house even in this weather,' she said, taking a single high backed wicker chair.

'A beautiful home you have,' Bryant observed.

A book lay face down on the table beside a china teacup and a pair of reading glasses. Kim wondered if that's what she'd been doing when the informing officers had knocked the door the previous night and destroyed her world.

'It was my husband's labour of love, his childhood home, which was sold off to clear farming debts. He got to enjoy it for a whole year before suffering a fatal heart attack at the age of forty-four. No warning, no previous signs,' she explained as she reached to the side of the chair.

She took out a pair of furry moccasin slippers that immediately looked odd when paired with the smart trouser suit.

'How old was Donna when her father died?' Kim asked.

'Fifteen,' she answered, kicking her court shoes to the side.

'And she reacted badly?' Kim pushed.

'I think we both did, officer.'

This woman had barely had time to grieve the loss of her husband before issues arose with her child.

'After her father died everything changed. We had been so close, doing everything together and somehow the two of us suddenly didn't know how to re-form around his loss. We were like strangers, both unable to reach out and comfort the other. The distance between us grew until neither of us knew how to bridge the gap.'

'It must have been a shock to you, seeing her?' Bryant said.

She bit her lower lip. 'I had to tell myself that was Donna I was seeing. My heart wouldn't believe it even though my head knew it to be true.' She shook her head, bewildered. 'How do I mourn her when I can't process the fact that that poor child is my daughter?' she asked.

'You understand the manner of her death?' Kim asked.

The woman nodded slowly. 'I do understand that she was a prostitute and she was murdered,' she said, as though speaking about someone else.

Kim understood that her brain was connecting the murder to the girl she'd seen at the morgue but that her mind had not yet completely joined the last dot of both of those facts relating to her daughter.

'There is a cruelty here that is unbearable,' she said, dabbing at her watery eyes.

'Sorry?' Kim said.

'That she only called me three days ago.'

Kim sat forward. 'After how long?' she asked.

'It was the first time she'd made contact since she'd left,' the woman said.

Kim thought back through the days. 'She called you on Sunday after more than a year?'

'Yes. It was wonderful just to hear her voice.'

She had called the day after Kelly Rowe had been murdered.

'And what did she say?' Kim asked.

'Not very much. Just that she'd been thinking about me and that she missed me…'

'And?'

'And that she was sorry for what she'd done.'

Kim could hear the heartbreak in her voice.

'Anything else?'

She shook her head. 'I didn't want to push her. I told her I forgave her and that I loved her. I was too scared to say more in case I frightened her off.'

'She would have appreciated that,' Bryant offered, quietly. 'It was probably what she needed to hear.'

'I hope so,' she said, as the tears fell from her eyes.

Kim gave her a moment of silence with her grief before continuing.

'Mrs Hammond-Hill, is there anything at all that changed between yourself and Donna that could explain why she finally chose to leave home?'

After meeting and speaking with this woman Kim was coming around to Bryant's way of thinking. Why the hell had Donna left home in the first place?

After two years of anger, arguments and bitterness, had there been something in that final argument that had propelled her towards the door? What had been in Donna's head to pack some clothes and just leave?

The woman shook her head. 'The argument the night before was the same one we'd been having for months.' She shook her head. 'It ended with the usual line she threw at me before stomping off.'

'And what was that?' Kim asked.

'That I had to learn to see the bigger picture.'

CHAPTER SIXTY-SIX

'I know it's just a saying, Bryant,' Kim said. 'But you don't find it strange that it's come up twice in a couple of days?'

'It's a cliché used all the time,' he argued.

'Our missing girl, Ellie, said it to her mother before running away and now we find out that Donna said it before doing the exact same thing a year ago. What the hell do these kids know about "the bigger picture"?' she asked.

He remained calm in the face of her aggravation. 'I'm just not sure how it helps us find—'

'They were fucking groomed, Bryant. Don't you get it? Some bastard is finding these teenage girls, probably online, and exploiting their annoyance at their parents, manipulating them, weakening them and then taking advantage. It's got to be Kai fucking Lord,' she said, grinding her teeth.

'Steady on, guv. You really think he's the grooming type? There's no shortage of desperate women on Hollytree. I'm not sure he needs to extend his reach beyond—'

'They're young girls, Bryant,' she said. 'They fetch a higher premium. Think about it. Get them away from their parents, maybe hooked on drugs and you've got 'em for life.'

He paused at the traffic island to let a learner driver crawl past.

'You really think Ellie Greaves could be caught up—?'

'Hang on,' she said as her phone started to ring.

'Penn,' she answered. 'Any luck on Ellie Greaves's phone?' she asked, immediately.

He answered in the negative and then offered her the reason for the call.

'Damn it,' she said, pressing the End button as Bryant turned into the hospital. 'No warrant to search Roger Barton's house so we gotta try and get him in without his brief. I want to know why he has Kelly Rowe's blood in his car.'

'Pretty obvious, guv,' Bryant said.

'You think he killed them, don't you?' she asked, as he parked the car.

'I'm thinking that there's something not right with this guy. His house is like something out of Ripley's Believe It or Not! He visits prostitutes but not for sex and now blood from one of the victims has been found in his car.'

She shook her head in the face of the evidence. 'Not feeling it, Bryant.'

'I know your gut is begging to differ, guv, but it might be due its annual service.'

Kim ignored him as she pushed open the door into the morgue.

Keats looked their way and nodded coolly.

The absence of a smart remark told her he was not happy and it wasn't due to the dark circles beneath his eyes. He'd pulled many all-nighters over the years. Just as she had.

'What have we got, Keats?' she asked.

'Absolutely nothing, Inspector,' he replied, tightly.

She understood his irritation. He had spent the night performing a second post-mortem on a victim he felt should not have been exhumed in the first place.

Her colleague was doubting her instinct; the pathologist was pissed off with her decisions. Kim wondered if it might be wise to go back and start this day again.

She used her hands to lift herself backwards onto the stainless steel island in the middle of the room. The body of Lauren

Goddard had been returned to the cooler. She placed her hands either side of her and dangled her legs over the side of the table.

'Keats, stop sulking and talk to me,' she said.

He narrowed his eyes in her direction. 'I fail to understand—'

'Objection noted. Now we've sorted that out, is there any way of deducing from her injuries if Lauren Goddard jumped or was pushed to her death?'

Keats sighed wearily. 'Absolutely not. Falling thirteen floors would eradicate any distinction between the two completely.'

Kim raised herself to a standing position on top of the table, narrowly missing a strip light. She stared down and leaned forward.

'Guv, what the hell?'

She straightened and looked at Keats. 'But surely there has to be something, some kind of calculation based on force or rotation through the air or velocity or—'

'Oh Stone, she has forty-three broken bones in her body. The injuries from that height would be the same if she jumped or was pushed.'

Kim put one foot forward, dangling over the precipice.

'But if she just stepped—'

'For goodness' sake, Inspector, if she fell, dived, belly flopped, stepped, jumped or stood on her head and bounced—'

'Hang on,' she said, easing herself back to a sitting position, a sudden thought in her head. 'Why are we assuming she was standing?' Kim asked. 'If she had no plans to jump, she wouldn't be standing up, would she?'

Keats shook his head in despair and aimed for the desk behind her.

'What if she was sitting, just looking around and then suddenly—'

Kim's sentence ended as she felt herself being pushed forward forcefully from behind.

'Jesus, Keats,' she said, stumbling forward as her feet landed on the floor.

'Like that, you mean?' he asked, innocently.

She stood still for a minute and assessed the instinctive reactions of her own body. She brought her hands up in front of her face.

'Nails, Keats. Check under her nails. My first instinct, without realising it, was to try to grab something, to hang on.'

If Lauren Goddard had been sitting on the edge of the building and had been taken by surprise there was the possibility her nails had scraped on something. With the assumption of suicide she was guessing the nail beds would not have been checked the first time.

He nodded his understanding and then rubbed at his chin. 'I'm taking an hour or two first for breakfast, coffee and rest and then I'll bring her back out.'

She folded her arms and glanced at the pathologist and then back to the table.

'You feel better after that, eh, Keats?' Kim asked.

'Surprisingly, yes,' he said, smiling. 'In the interests of scientific discovery I felt I owed you that.'

'Scientific discovery?' Bryant said behind a cough.

Keats turned towards him. 'Jealousy is an ugly trait, my friend.'

'Next time, Keats, I'm gonna hang you up by the—'

She was interrupted by the ringing of her mobile phone.

'Penn?' she answered.

'Yeah boss, Roger Barton, owner of the Toyota. He's sitting in reception, on his own. No solicitor. Wants to talk to the police and will only speak to you.'

She ended the call and motioned to Bryant to follow.

She hadn't been expecting that.

CHAPTER SIXTY-SEVEN

'Do you believe him?' Stacey asked Devon and Grant once they were outside the building. 'About the women asking him to store the passports for safekeeping – all of them?'

Grant shrugged. 'It's not normal but everything seems to be in order,' he said as Dawson joined them.

'And yet?' Devon said, smiling.

'Yeah, exactly,' he said.

'What?' Stacey asked.

'Instinct isn't limited to you coppers, you know,' Grant said.

'Is that why you asked to take one of the passports?'

He nodded. 'All too tidy. Everything we asked for, at his fingertips.'

'Hmm…' Devon added. 'Almost like they're ready for us to turn up at any time.'

'Thank you,' Stacey said to them both, but especially to Devon.

'Any time, babe,' Devon winked as the two of them headed towards the waiting officers.

'I was talking to the guys there while you were inside,' Dawson said, dragging her attention away from the figure of Devon walking away. 'They raided one property in Netherton which housed twenty-seven people in a two-bedroom terrace.'

'How the hell did they pack that many folks in?' Stacey asked.

'Shifts,' he answered. 'Everyone got an eight-hour shift on a bed and then off to work again.'

'You reckon that's what's going on here?' she asked.

'Wanna go take a look at that address?' he asked.

She nodded distractedly as she got into the car.

'The passport thing bothering you?'

She ignored the question as she got into the car.

Yes, the passports being in the control of the employer bothered her. But there was something else tapping away at the corner of her mind.

But for now it would just have to wait.

CHAPTER SIXTY-EIGHT

'So, Mr Barton, you wanted to talk to me?' Kim asked.

Roger Barton was sitting forward, his elbows on the table and his hands knitted together. She could see a three-layer outfit of T-shirt, check shirt and jacket, which all looked surprisingly clean given the state of his home.

'Yes, officer, I did.'

Silence fell between them.

'And now I'm here,' she prompted.

Bryant laid down his pen.

'It's about that girl,' he said.

'Kelly Rowe?' Kim clarified.

He shook his head. 'The other one.'

'Donna Hill?'

He shook his head more forcefully. 'I told you I didn't meet with either of them.'

'Are you sure?' Kim asked. 'You seem to spend an awful lot of time on Tavistock Road.'

'I was there on Sunday night, when you saw my car, but I haven't been back—'

'Mr Barton, how many of these ladies have you met with altogether?' she asked.

Kim considered asking him about the traces of Kelly Rowe's blood that had been found in his car and decided against it for two reasons: she didn't want to show her hand and she wanted to see why he had come to her. Any mention of the blood would send him running for the hills in search of his solicitor.

'Most of them,' he admitted. 'But only the ones old enough,' he said, colouring. 'I'm not into that kind of—'

'So, if you're not talking about Kelly or Donna, who are you referring to?' she asked, confused.

'The other one. The one on the news. The one you dug up. Jazzy.'

'Lauren Goddard?' Bryant asked.

He nodded.

'What about her?' Kim asked, suspiciously.

'I met with her,' he offered, blinking rapidly.

Kim looked at Bryant who picked up his pen.

Why the hell was he here admitting to contact with Lauren Goddard when they had absolutely nothing to tie him to her?

'Look, I want to tell you something but I need you to believe that I didn't kill anyone. I'm not like that. I wouldn't hurt any one of these ladies.' He looked down at his hands. 'They've been very kind to me. All of them.'

Kim was seriously beginning to wonder if Bryant was right about this man.

'I think you'd better tell us what you know, Mr Barton,' she said, coolly.

He swallowed deeply. 'I met with Jazzy, I mean Lauren, the night before she died,' he said.

Shit, Kim thought. This really was going from bad to worse for her gut instinct. At this rate they'd have this case wrapped up by lunchtime.

She leaned forward as her phone began to vibrate in her pocket. She ignored it.

'And?' she prompted.

'She was acting strange, jumpy. She didn't want to go back,' he said.

Kim covered her pocket with her hand when her phone vibrated again.

'Go back where?' she asked.

'The strip, Tavistock Road. She didn't want me to drop her there.'

'Was she frightened of Kai?'

He shrugged and shook his head at the same time. 'I don't know. She didn't say but she was definitely scared of something.'

'Or someone,' Kim added, trying to hide her irritation at the phone vibrating in her pocket. Damn it, she was interviewing a bloody murder suspect.

'Why are you telling us this, Mr Barton?' she asked.

Was he just trying to distract them from the real truth? Was he scared that they were going to find something in his car to link him to Lauren Jazzy Goddard and thought there would be some advantage to owning up first?

Right now she was more interested in talking to him about the woman who had left a trace of blood in his car and that she could forensically tie him to.

'Mr Barton, I believe you did meet with Kelly Rowe,' she said.

He shook his head vehemently. 'Not for a couple of weeks. I've not seen her out there or I would have—'

'You're lying, Mr Barton,' she accused. He'd only had the car for a couple of weeks, so he was trying to hide something. Kelly Rowe had been in that car.

'I'm not, I swear—'

'You had Kelly in your car the night she was murdered, didn't you?' she pushed.

He shook his head. 'I came here to talk about Jazzy—'

'But we want to talk about Kelly.'

'I don't know anything about—'

'Yes, you do,' she insisted.

'I would tell you. It's no secret I meet—'

'Mr Barton, we found her blood in your car.'

His mouth snapped shut as colour flooded into his face. His eyes narrowed in confusion.

'I think it's time for you to tell us the truth.'

He opened his mouth to answer when a soft knock sounded on the door.

Kim sent a withering glance in the direction of the constable who entered the interview room.

'Sorry, Marm, but one of your team, Penn, needs an urgent word.'

She looked at Bryant and stepped out of the room. She dialled back the number that had called her three times.

'Penn, what the hell?'

'You said you wanted to know the minute I located Ellie Greaves's phone.'

Kim didn't reply. He was right. That was exactly what she'd said.

'Okay, Penn, where the hell is it?'

'That's the weird thing, boss. It's right here in this building.'

CHAPTER SIXTY-NINE

Ellie shivered against the bare stone wall. The garments against her skin had ceased to form any kind of protection hours ago.

She had removed her arms from the sleeves and pulled them inside the T-shirt to use it as a flimsy blanket. She had moved around the black space with her arms thrust out searching for anything that might keep her warm. She had quickly established that the ceiling of the cellar sloped down and that at the end nearest the steps she could just about stand up. She had alternated between sitting on the stone steps and then standing when the cold had worked its way into her bones. Her flimsy shoes offered brief protection for her feet while she stood in one place.

She had tried to keep counting so she could maintain an idea of passing time but as thoughts had rushed in and out of her mind she had lost count. She knew she had been put in the cellar in the evening time and she thought that it was the next day, but she couldn't be sure.

At first she'd cried and begged at the sliver of daylight beneath the door. She had screamed, cried, promised; God only knew what she'd promised, but eventually a towel had been placed along the shaft of light and the thin strip of illumination had been extinguished.

From that point on Ellie had lost all track of time as her efforts had been focussed on trying to keep warm.

Although she could not count the number of hours she'd been in the cellar she did know she had urinated in the corner twice.

Recently she'd thought a lot about the past, the recent past.

She'd thought about school and had laughed out loud with mirth. What she wouldn't give to be in that school right now. She would offer a limb to be sitting in a classroom being laughed at and talked about by Rebecca Weaver and her gang with their cruel comments about her weight, straggly hair and lingering virginity. It would have gladdened her heart. Being cornered in the alleyway behind the school and being pelted with eggs and flour would have been a welcome event. She would have run up to the lot of them and hugged them until they bled.

Until yesterday Ellie thought she'd experienced fear. She now knew that assumption to be false. She may have experienced a heightened sense of anxiety or a mild panic but she had never felt in fear of her life.

Her mind switched back to Roxanne and the beating she'd received yesterday. She knew that Roxanne must have been put in a position of no choice. Roxanne would not have voluntarily lured her into a trap. She'd spent days with the woman. She knew that deep down inside Roxanne was her friend and she'd been forced into this nightmare.

Thoughts of school, college and even what had happened in the kitchen were easier to bear than the thought of her mother.

Ellie did not doubt that the whole situation had been a trap from the very beginning.

Roxanne had befriended her on Facebook, said all the right things to make her feel important and made all the right noises of understanding. But she knew that Roxanne had been forced into it.

Ellie realised how cleverly it had all been done: the home-cooked meals, the flattery of the attention, the subtle manipulation of her anger at her mother. She even guessed that the initial mugging that had left her without money or a phone was no accident.

Every single move, conversation and nuance had been planned, scripted down to the last detail. Ellie knew all of this for a fact just as she knew that Roxanne's involvement was through her fear of that man.

These thoughts had been easier to hang onto when fatigue had been in the distance but not now. Now she knew that if she gave into the exhaustion her body temperature would drop further and the involuntary shivers would not be controlled. The last three shudders had prompted her to jump to her feet and run on the spot for a full minute to generate some heat. Her limbs had turned to stone and the effort of the exertion only exhausted her more. All she knew was that the trembling that she couldn't control was bad.

She had tried to block thoughts of her mother for the whole time she'd been locked away, because every thought brought guilt, love, regret. Every emotion that she could think of and they all came with tears.

Their arguments seemed so ridiculously irrelevant that she could not even imagine the importance they'd held a week ago. Disagreements about her room, her curfew, her dress sense, her taste in music, her refusal to attend college.

Every single one of which she would welcome right now.

Ellie now knew beyond doubt that her mother did not know where she was and had never been given Roxanne's number. How stupid had she been to think that her mum would not have called, even to scream at her? How easily she'd been convinced that her own mother didn't care.

These hours had clarified in her mind that her mother did care. Ellie visualised her sitting at the kitchen table, crying, worried, fearful.

Suddenly, Ellie wondered if she would ever see her mother again. The tears stung her sore eyes and this time she could not hold them back. Just to walk into that kitchen with all her problems that didn't seem like problems any more.

Oh, how grown up she had wanted to be; a maturity she'd been sure of dissolved against her wish to just feel her mother's arms around her, holding her close, just one more time.

Her mind stilled as she heard the click of the cellar door lock. The light burst in and forced her to close her sore eyes.

'If you shout, scream or make any attempt to get away you'll be put back in. Do you understand?'

Ellie nodded and slowly opened her eyes, blinking against the light. The form in the doorway was definitely Roxanne but the harsh tone and facial expression belonged to someone else.

At that point Ellie had no idea for what reason she was being released. Who was out there? Where was she going and with whom?

CHAPTER SEVENTY

Kim left Roger Barton in the capable hands of Bryant and watched as a constable lifted Johnny Banks to a standing position.

The blue jeans rested somewhere around the middle of his buttocks, revealing the Calvin Klein label of his underpants. His Nike trainers had the tongue of a lizard. A black T-shirt sat underneath a hoody topped by a duffled body warmer. Fair stubble was erupting through his shaved scalp.

The constable walked the youth past her. He looked her up and down and sucked the air through his teeth, a mark of disrespect.

'Interview room two,' she advised the constable.

He seated the male, whose legs instantly splayed apart, nonchalantly. His cuffed hands landed in his lap.

The constable stood at the door but Kim indicated for him to leave.

'You sure 'bout dat?' Johnny asked as the door to the interview room closed.

'Yeah, I'm feeling pretty safe,' she said, placing the Samsung phone on the table. 'Where'd you get it, Johnny?'

'I know my rights, bitch. You gotta tape this and I want my brief.'

'Shut up, Johnny. Did you hear me caution you for any offence? We're just talking.'

'I ain't fucking talking.'

'Oh, I think you might.'

'I ain't scared of you, bitch.'

Kim sat back and smiled. 'Where were you lifted from today, Johnny?'

He shrugged. 'Blud's yard.'

'Just a brother?' she asked.

He smiled knowingly. 'Yeah, man, just a brother.'

'Well, I can arrange for the shoplifting charges on your warrant to be dropped and then give you a comfy ride back to your blud's yard in a nice shiny police car. How'd that work for you?'

Any normal person would have clutched that deal with both hands but for Johnny it would be hell. Dropped charges and a comfy ride home would mean he'd been cooperative. His blud wouldn't like that very much.

'Look, I'm not interested in the other petty crap you've been up to. I just want to know about this phone.'

'I found it, fair and square. D'ya get me?'

'Okay, a free ride back it is,' she said, standing.

'All right, all right, some bitch told us what to do. Gave us a ton to take some kid's phone and backpack and scare her a bit.'

A feeling of dread began to form in her stomach. She was right: Ellie had been trapped and possibly by the same person as Donna.

'What did she look like?'

Johnny shrugged. 'About five foot, mousy hair, about sixteen.'

'The woman, Johnny, not the girl.'

He shrugged. 'Never saw her; it was a third party contract.'

'A brother?'

He smiled 'Yeah, you getting it, a brother.'

Kim didn't believe him.

'You're lying,' she said, as she continued towards the door. 'And I'm not in the mood for giving you any more chances, blud. An officer will collect you shortly.'

'Aaah, man, you not even gonna thank me by sucking my—'

'You know, Johnny, you're not the hardass you'd have me believe,' she said, turning back to face him.

'How'd you know what I am, bitch?' His voice had risen an octave.

She took two steps back and rested her hands on the table.

'Because, you've got no gang tattoos and you're not wearing any colours. That means either you've managed to avoid recruitment or you haven't yet managed to perform the initiation task.'

Kim knew that normally included the killing of something smaller that couldn't defend itself.

'So, at this point, you still got a chance.' She locked on his gaze and shrugged. 'Either take it or don't but I'll tell you one thing, matey, if anything happens to that girl you robbed I am going to find you and there ain't no brother gonna be able to save you.'

She walked away and reached the door.

He coughed into his hand and she heard a name.

She turned.

'Excuse me?'

'Just a cough, innit?'

Kim held his gaze for a few seconds before she stepped out of the room.

That was no simple cough. He had offered her a clue.

The name he had coughed was Roxanne.

Roxanne had been a neighbour of Kelly Rowe.

And Kim wanted to speak to her right now.

CHAPTER SEVENTY-ONE

'And yes, the Robertsons do own this house,' Stacey confirmed, putting away her phone.

They'd had no idea of that when they'd followed the minibus here the day before.

'Bloody hell, Stace. What are they up to?' he asked, parking the car.

'So what you wanna do, Kev?' Stacey asked, looking towards the target property. 'Shall we take a look round back?'

Dawson shook his head. All the curtains were closed even though it was lunchtime.

'We're not gonna see anything. We need to try and get a look inside.'

'Yeah but we don't have cause,' she said, stating the obvious.

He ignored her but turned her way. 'You got a notebook in there?' he asked, looking down at her satchel.

'Pocket notebook?'

He shook his head. 'Normal notebook?'

She frowned. 'Why would I?'

He raised an eyebrow. 'Stace, all women's handbags are a mystery to me. You got anything in there, like official?'

'Warrant card official enough?'

He shook his head. 'Exactly not what we're going for,' he said.

She opened the clasp. 'I've got an old electricity bill and a gnarled pencil.'

'Okay, that'll have to do. Now follow my lead,' he said, removing his suit jacket before getting out of the car.

He loosened his tie after knocking the door.

'What are we…' she asked.

'Ssh…' he said, as a bolt slid across the bottom of the door.

A man in his mid-twenties answered wearing stained jogging bottoms and no shirt. Bed hair stuck out from his head.

Suspicion filled his eyes

'Morning, mate, sorry to disturb you. Annual property inspection,' he said, glancing at Stacey.

She nodded and smiled.

The man frowned.

'Won't take more than a minute. Just checking for damp and cracks.'

'Sorry but no speak—'

'It's okay,' he reassured. 'Nicolae…' he added, and gave the thumbs up to indicate that Nicolae had given permission.

The man didn't move.

'Take us ten minutes,' Stacey offered. 'And then you can get back to sleep,' she said, laying her head on her hand.

More hesitation.

Dawson shrugged and turned to walk away. 'Okey-dokey, we'll call Nicolae and tell—'

'Okay, come,' he said, stepping aside.

Dawson walked into a dark, narrow hallway. The walls were covered in Anaglypta wallpaper that had been painted so many times the original design was barely discernible. He had to swallow deeply to quell the gagging from the stench. Body odour and stale food mixed together filled the space. No windows appeared to be open to offer any type of escape from the cloying air.

He stepped into the front reception room and pretended not to notice the four single occupied beds that filled the space. The carpet was littered with burger wrappers and plastic bottles. Every inch of space had been given to mattresses. Items of clothing peeped out from beneath them in the absence of storage area.

Dawson stepped around the gentle snoring and made a show of looking each wall up and down. 'Clear,' he called back to Stacey as his gaze fell on the empty bed. Less litter surrounded that space.

Stacey pretended to make a note of his findings as she followed him to the back room. Three more beds were stuffed into the space. Two were occupied. The male who had let them in reached down to retrieve a half bottle of orange juice, signalling his own area of slumber. He mumbled and then pointed to two strips of wallpaper peeling down from the ceiling displaying water damage from the bathroom above. Stacey pretended to note it down.

Dawson repeated the inspection process and headed towards the kitchen.

From the open doorway he could see an abundance of half-filled carrier bags, A couple of pairs of trainers and more fast food wrappers. Behind the door was a wooden banquette seat normally kept in utility rooms of the wealthy and used for removing dirty boots and clothing before entering the home. A piece of rope was fixed from one side to the other.

He looked at Stacey questioningly. 'Any ideas?' he whispered.

She nodded. 'Extra sleeping space. Sitting up. Rope stops 'em from falling out.'

Dawson decided he'd seen enough. This was exactly the kind of place that Devon had warned them about. Human beings were being packed into tiny airless rooms and treated worse than dogs. He suspected that upstairs was going to be no different.

And he now had a suspicion about what he'd already seen.

'Excuse me,' he said, turning to the only male awake.

He took out his phone and then pointed into the first room he'd entered.

'That empty bed in there. Did it belong to this man here?'

Recognition flashed across his face before he began to nod his head.

CHAPTER SEVENTY-TWO

'You really think she could be in there, guv?'

Kim shrugged and continued to watch the front windows for any sign of movement.

Her phone rang. She answered it and listened to Penn.

'Thanks,' Kim said, ending the call. She looked to Bryant. 'House belongs to Kai Lord.'

'Shit,' Bryant said, and Kim had to agree. This case was turning into a spider's web with strands crossing and stretching across everyone they met.

Finally, her question had been answered on the link between Kai Lord and Kelly Rowe. The intermediary had been this woman named Roxanne.

Kim looked into the rear-view mirror and saw a middle-aged woman pottering along the pavement. As she made her way along she pushed back each recently emptied bin onto the appropriate property.

'Go on, Bryant, get her,' she said.

Bryant jumped out of the car and she followed.

'Excuse me, could we just—'

'Never put these bins back. You'd think they'd be grateful to have a job but no. And why are you sitting here doing nothing?'

Oh perfect, Kim thought. There were certain types of people who proved invaluable to a police investigation and busybodies were right at the top of the list.

'We're police officers but there's nothing to be alarmed about. We've had a report of screaming and shouting from this address.'

The woman frowned. 'I don't think so, officer. It's a very respectable young lady that lives there. Her boyfriend visits a couple of times a week and I have nothing against interracial coupling.'

Kim hid her smile. The deliberate statement to the contrary revealed the exact opposite. And she suspected that the boyfriend was Kai Lord.

'Other than that, Roxanne keeps to herself and causes no bother at all.'

The woman had folded her arms.

'And the charity work she does is commendable,' the woman added.

'Charity work?' Kim asked. So far, this woman did not appear big on helping others.

'Yes, she takes in teenage girls from broken homes who are waiting to be placed in temporary care.'

Kim swallowed as the woman continued. 'You'd think we'd have some trouble with all those teenagers but Roxanne has a way of—'

'How many teenagers exactly?' Kim asked quietly.

'Excuse me?'

'How many would you say Roxanne has taken care of?' Kim asked with her heart rising up towards her mouth.

'Oh, at least ten, maybe more and not one of them has been any bother. In fact, she's taking care of one right now. I saw them come back with handfuls of bags the other day. Laughing and joking, pushing each other up the slippery path.'

Kim's mouth began to lose a little moisture.

'Well, thank you for your time. It seems quiet enough, so I think there must be some mistake.'

The woman nodded, crossed the road and continued her journey of pushing in the bins.

'Guv, I can see what you're thinking and we can't—'

Kim didn't hear the rest. She had already turned to head back to the house.

CHAPTER SEVENTY-THREE

'So, do you wanna head back to the station and start searching missing persons' reports?' Dawson asked.

Stacey shook her head. 'What's the point? We know when he went missing and we also know there have been no reports for a missing male since last Thursday. No one has reported his absence.'

'So what now?' he asked. 'Given that all we know now is that his first name is Andrei. Basically, we're back to the starting point of sweet fuck—'

'Shush,' Stacey said, taking out her phone.

'What are you doing?' he asked, looking over at her screen.

'Thinking,' she said.

He rolled his eyes, dramatically. 'Bloody hell, Stace, don't be changing a habit of a lifetime right now while—'

'It was something Vasile said at the café last night. It's bothering me,' she said.

'From what you told me there was a fair bit that he said.'

'Yeah, but it wasn't anything he meant to,' she said, tapping on her phone.

She searched her email for the electronic copy of the notes they'd given to Cristina and found what she was after. She took the translated notes from Cristina and read them again.

'You know, Kev, there's something not…'

Her words trailed away as her mobile began to ring.

The screen told her it was Devon.

'Hey, I was just—'

'It's a fake,' Devon said, without preamble.

'What?' Stacey asked.

'The passport. It's counterfeit. A bloody good one but definitely fake.'

'Shit,' Stacey said, looking towards her colleague.

'We're heading back over to that factory if you wanna tag along.'

'On our way,' Stacey said, ending the call.

Not least because after what she now suspected that was exactly where she wanted to go.

CHAPTER SEVENTY-FOUR

'Guv, will you just stop a minute?'

Kim was already assessing the side of the house for a suitable access point.

'Will you just hold on? You could get in trouble for this. You know that we have nothing to justify going in there.'

'Ten or more girls, Bryant? Does that sound like a normal social services arrangement? You ever heard of it before?'

He paused then shook his head.

'See, you have the exact same suspicions I do.'

'But she said they were laughing and joking,' Bryant offered.

'Look, we know that there had to be a link between Kelly Rowe and Kai Lord. They would not necessarily have crossed paths.'

She pointed next door. 'Kelly Rowe lived right there and this Roxanne woman lives in Kai Lord's house. There's our link. We have a missing teenager with no money and no phone who appears to have been spending time with this woman. What if Ellie is in there right now? I'm happy to take the shit if I'm wrong.'

'Yeah, you've got me,' he said. 'Let's get in there.'

She assessed the side of the house. There was only one window situated at high level. Kim guessed that was the bathroom. The window was closed making it not worth her time.

A six foot fence prevented access to the rear.

'Okay, there's one choice. Over I go. Bryant, go grab that bin.'

'Guv, hang on. Just stay put, I'll be a few minutes, and try not to scale anything while I'm gone.'

She nodded as he disappeared around the front of the building.

In the meantime she began checking the stability of the fence posts. They were stable enough but the gate was the better option. Although the wood was rotting in places and the paint was peeling off, the horizontal pieces of wood should be strong enough to support her weight to get her leg over the top. It wasn't something she hadn't done before and she'd worry about what was on the other side when she got there. Protruding from the wall was the overflow pipe from the bathroom that she could grip to give her stability when searching for a foothold on the other side.

She gave a gentle kick to the gate, which miraculously opened with Bryant on the other side.

'You were thinking about it, weren't you?' he said, knowingly.

Oh, how well he knew her, Kim thought as she stepped through. 'How'd you get back here?'

'I spoke nicely to the lady next door and asked if I could come through. It's a four foot fence that separates the two properties.'

Woody liked it when she buddied with Bryant and she kind of saw why.

The rear of the house was formed of a set of French doors leading into the kitchen and dining area. Further along was a window with the blinds pulled down.

Kim peered into the kitchen window and found the space to be clean and tidy and eerily quiet.

Bryant knocked loudly on the glass. The sound seemed to echo around the space.

'Just in case, guv.'

They waited for a few seconds before Bryant tried the handle. It was locked.

'Perhaps, if you talk nicely to it,' Kim offered.

Bryant offered her a filthy look and continued to fiddle.

Kim picked up a decorative stone from the rockery.

'Hey, Bryant, look over there.'

He turned to look behind him. She smashed the rock against the glass panel to the right of the door handle.

'Jesus, guv.'

She shrugged. 'And sometimes it's my way.'

She covered her hand with the cuff of her jacket and knocked at the pieces of glass still attached to the frame. She reached inside and turned the key in the lock. There were days when she thanked God for the public's complacency.

Bryant followed her into the kitchen.

She stood for a moment, listening for sounds inside the house. She heard none. She closed her eyes and focussed. All she got was the emptiness of the house.

'Guv, you really are harbouring the heart of a criminal in there.'

She didn't disagree.

'Check upstairs; she's been here, I know it.'

Bryant rolled his eyes and headed out of the kitchen.

'Lord, save me from your gut,' he grumbled.

The kitchen was tidy and smelled of bleach. She opened a couple of cupboard doors and found nothing except tinned foods and cleaning chemicals. She checked the bin but already knew that the rubbish had been collected earlier that day.

Come on, come on, think, she silently instructed herself. Yes, the place had been cleaned and bleached, but why? What had taken place here? And more importantly, had anything been left behind?

She lowered herself to the ground on her stomach and placed her cheek against the floor. Her attention focussed underneath the washing machine. The area closest to the bin. She could just make out a couple of coins, some beads, fluff and debris,

But just in the corner was something else.

She placed her flat hand on the ground and swept as far back as she could. Out came one of the coins, a few beads and a balled-up square of kitchen roll.

'Oh, shit,' she said, as she got a closer look. The kitchen roll was stained with blood.

She jumped to her feet and met Bryant back in the hallway.

'Only evidence of one room being used, guv; the master bedroom. The second bedroom is stripped bare and the box room is just full of junk.'

She showed him the kitchen roll. 'There's something here, Bryant, I can feel it.'

'Well, whatever it is wins the hide-and-seek game,' he said. 'That tissue could have been a simple nosebleed,' he offered logically. 'Now, can we get back to investigating our own case before we're both arrested for breaking and entering?'

Kim stepped back into the kitchen.

Beyond the small utility room was a door. Kim strode to it and opened it. She looked down into the darkened space.

'Just a cellar, guv,' Bryant said from behind her.

Kim hit the light switch but nothing happened.

'Shine your torch,' she said.

The shaft of light illuminated a space approximately six feet long by four feet wide. The ceiling sloped down reducing the amount of usable space.

Kim took one step down and wrinkled her nose.

'Do you smell that?' she asked.

Bryant shook his head.

'Someone's used this cellar for a toilet.'

'Takes all sorts, guv,' Bryant offered.

Kim stood on the second step and focussed her mind.

No one chose to urinate in a cellar when there was a perfectly good toilet upstairs.

Ellie had been locked in this space. Probably for refusing to comply.

Kim turned and headed back up the steps.

Bryant lowered his torch to aid her footing. Something glinted at her from the stone.

She reached down and retrieved the tiny object.

'Take out the photo, Bryant,' she said, quietly.

Bryant took the folded copy from his inside pocket.

Kim stood beside him. She held the black stud earring against the photo. It was a match.

'Dammit,' Bryant said.

Kim took one last look into the cellar and summarised what was now staring her in the face:

She knew that Ellie Greaves had been imprisoned in this cellar.

She knew that the young girl had left a clue in removing her earring.

She knew the kid was way out of her depth and scared to death.

And she knew she'd arrived too damn late.

CHAPTER SEVENTY-FIVE

The van was already parked twenty metres away from the property when they arrived.

Seven immigration officers were huddled around Devon and Grant.

'Okay,' Grant said, pointing around the circle. 'You two secure the entrance and exit. Devon, take three with you onto the factory floor and I'll take Neale and Dixon up to the mezzanine to speak to the owner.'

Stacey hadn't considered the entrance and exit points but she guessed it wasn't unusual for illegal immigrants to make a run for it.

'Be calm, courteous and respectful,' Grant said, casting his eyes around the circle.

Once he'd received an affirmative nod from each one, he continued.

'Okay, all set?'

A joint sound of assent rumbled around them.

'Go,' he instructed.

'Stay behind us and let us do our thing,' Devon said to them both.

'Understood,' Dawson said, as they followed the uniformed officers to the door. Dawson caught her gaze and nodded towards the operation leader, indicating that he would head up to the mezzanine. Stacey would remain with Devon.

Grant charged into the reception and continued around the reception desk with a stream of officers behind him.

Melody already had the phone in her hand.

Although he'd spoken to his team about conduct, Stacey guessed the initial show of force was intended to take the occupants by surprise, giving less time to plan, form a story or make an attempt to escape.

'I need to speak to one particular girl,' Stacey said to Devon as they thundered through the corridors.

Devon nodded her understanding as she exited onto the shop floor. The officers fanned out around the room and began speaking to the employees.

The sudden ceasing of the sewing machines was startling as the room fell into silence.

The women looked at the officers and at each other.

Cristina was looking directly at her.

Devon followed her gaze and nodded.

Stacey approached the second workstation in the middle row and touched the girl's arm lightly.

'Cristina, can you come with me, please?' Stacey asked, gently.

The fear flooded into her face as she pulled her arm away.

'I haven't done anything,' she screamed. 'Leave me alone.'

'Cristina, I just want to talk. That's all,' Stacey said, calmly.

Many of the other girls had turned to see what the shouting was about. Stacey caught the look of satisfaction on Natalya's face. She didn't agree with it but she now understood it.

'Please, come with me,' she said, gently guiding Cristina into the corridor and the small break room where they had conducted the interviews.

Stacey tried to offer a reassuring smile as she closed the door. She waited for Cristina to sit before voicing the suspicion that had been growing in her mind since the night before.

'He's yours, isn't he?' Stacey asked. 'The baby at the police station?'

Cristina began to shake her head vehemently but the emotion that had gathered in her eyes told a different story.

'And Andrei was your father?' Stacey asked.

That's why Nicolae had been watching Cristina so closely. She knew exactly what had been done to her father.

'I don't know what you're talking about,' she said, making a move towards the door.

'Sit back down, Cristina,' Stacey said.

Despite her denial, Stacey knew she was lying and Natalya's expression had confirmed it. When questioning the women, Natalya, who was a mother, had launched a bitter, accusatory attack at Cristina, unable to believe that she had abandoned her own child. They had been reliant on their translator, Cristina, to tell them what each girl had been saying. She could have told them anything.

'It's time to tell the truth,' she said, softly. 'You've carried this fear for way too long.'

The head shaking stopped and her eyes reddened with emotion.

'How did you guess?' she asked, brokenly.

'The word "bebelus" was missing from your translation of the pages we gave to you. I heard it somewhere else this week and realised I'd seen the word in the book pages, yet your translation made no mention of a baby or a child. You are that child. Your father, Andrei, travelled all the way from Romania. With you.'

'And I hated him for it,' she cried. 'I never felt comfortable here,' she said. 'I always felt that I was in the wrong place. I never went to school. I learned the language along with my father. He taught me to read and write. He would go to work and some Romanian woman from one of the houses would take care of me.'

'Tell me about it, Cristina,' Stacey urged. She wanted to understand the circumstances that had led to her abandoning her child.

'Eventually we managed to get two rooms next door to one of the houses. A lady named Alanna lived downstairs, spoke no English but would bring us back leftovers from the factory. I worked at a hotel in Birmingham just changing beds and cleaning but my money was my own. That's how we got the two rooms.'

She shook her head sadly. 'I loved him so much but hated him too for the life he had chosen for us. I begged him to let us return to Romania. I suspect I showed him the hate more than the love.'

Stacey heard the regret in her tone.

'And now?' she asked.

'He never told me what he went through to get us here. I don't even know how he kept us alive never mind together. I realise now that although I didn't have a lot. I always had him.'

Stacey felt compelled to match the girl's honesty. 'I have to tell you that your father had received many injuries over a long period of time. He was regularly beaten...'

The tears fell from her eyes. 'I know,' she breathed. 'He would try to hide it from me. He always tried to protect me but I could tell when he was suffering. And there was nothing I could do about it.'

'He suffered a horrific injury to his leg. Cristina. Almost every bone was broken.'

Cristina cried out and then buried her face in her hands.

Stacey looked around and spied kitchen roll beside the sink. She ripped off a square and waited for a moment until the deep sobs had subsided.

'Where could that have happened?' she asked, gently.

Cristina wiped at her eyes and nose. 'He mainly worked on a farm in Worcestershire. I don't know which one.'

Stacey guessed that he had sustained the horrific injury and just been cast aside like a broken, worn-out hand tool.

'He was taken to the canal and left to die,' Stacey explained but she could see that this came as no shock to Cristina.

'I understand,' she said, quietly. 'He was unable to work and was no longer any use to Nicolae. He would have ordered it.'

The tears rolled unchecked over her cheeks. The grief was finally allowed to break free from her tight control.

'How did you know he'd died?'

'Nicolae threw me his payment book and told me where to report to the next morning.'

'Robertson's?' she asked. Stacey still didn't fully understand why Cristina had abandoned her baby.

'Your father managed to work and keep you…'

Stacey stopped speaking as fresh pain filled the girl's eyes.

'My father was bonded,' she said, taking a battered notebook from her pocket.

Stacey took it, and leafed through.

'Upon his death, his debt falls to me.'

Stacey got to the end and gasped.

'It stands at £49,000. You will never pay that off,' Stacey said.

She smiled sadly. 'I know, and any remaining debt would fall to any child I might have.'

Cristina had not abandoned her child at all. She had tried to free him from the bonded debt.

'Cristina, we'll get all this sorted out, I promise. You'll be appointed a lawyer and you can—'

'I will never claim him,' she said, clutching at Stacey's arm. 'I will never admit to being his mother. Look around you. What can I give him? He deserves a life free of fear and isolation. He will grow up as a British baby. I love him so much but I have to let him go.'

'What about the baby's father?' Stacey asked. She suspected this girl was not the type to sleep around and the relationship could have been serious.

Cristina shook her head. 'He can not help. I will not reveal—'

'He's illegal, isn't he?' Stacey asked. Cristina had previously worked in the hotel trade, well known for employing illegal immigrants.

'He can not help,' Cristina repeated.

Stacey frowned and pulled away her arm. 'But the two of you could be…'

'Do you think this will end with Nicolae?' she asked, urgently. 'Do you think they will lose all this money so easily? Nicolae will never give you any names. I don't know who they are but they will know me and they will come looking. I cannot protect my baby.'

Stacey felt torn.

There was a part of Stacey that loved curling up on the sofa with a Disney film. A part of her that still believed in happy endings, that believed mother and child could be reunited and live happily ever after.

'I am also illegal,' Cristina reminded her.

'Please understand, he is my child and it is my sacrifice to make. I have nothing to give him but fear and uncertainty,' she said, thickly, clearly remembering her own childhood.

Stacey swallowed the emotion down. She could hear voices approaching the door. Cristina heard them too.

'Please, I beg you, for the sake of the child, don't tell them that he is mine. He has a chance at a better life. He will not have to run or hide. He will be a legal citizen.'

The tears rolled over her cheeks. She had no fear for herself, only for her child. This poor girl had spent her entire life looking over her shoulder, frightened of discovery, never fitting in or belonging. Her only crime was wanting something better for her own child.

Stacey felt the emotion gather in her throat.

'Please, I beg you for the future of my child.'

She felt the girl's terror, her torment. She was willing to sacrifice anything for the sake of that little boy who had not chosen this life. She had the power right here and now to change that child's life for ever.

So many questions were rolling around her mind as the door opened and Devon stepped in.

But ultimately there was only one question that really mattered.

CHAPTER SEVENTY-SIX

'Turning into a bit of a maze, this case, eh, guv. I mean we've kinda stumbled across Ellie by accident.'

That fact did not make the discovery any easier to bear, she thought, as she stared at the front of the house. A young girl had been seduced, flattered, befriended and trapped, and she suspected she knew why.

'She's gonna be taken to Templeton,' Kim said, voicing her worst fears. 'And it's because of me.'

'How so?' he asked.

'That one stupid action the other night of scaring that girl away,' she said, shaking her head. 'Got Sal beat up and another young girl moved up the food chain quicker.'

But how the hell did you prioritise who you were going to save?

'Guv, listen, you can't blame yourself for—'

'I don't, Bryant. I blame you. You're supposed to stop me from doing these things,' she said.

He ignored her. 'You gotta pass it on, guv?'

Kim knew what he meant. Protocol dictated that she inform missing persons so that another team could be dispatched to deal with what they suspected about Ellie Greaves.

'You really think they'll find her before we do?'

'Guv, we got two dead bodies in one week. That's our case.'

'You know what's gonna happen to her?'

'I've got a pretty good idea.'

'And who else is gonna give a shit? Mispers aren't gonna jump all over it because she's sixteen years old. And we know where she was. We're already way ahead. We can't just pretend it's someone else's problem. She's someone's daughter, for God's sake. You think I can just walk away?'

Bryant sighed heavily. 'You already got something in mind?'

'Not quite, Bryant, but I'm getting there.'

CHAPTER SEVENTY-SEVEN

'Jesus, Stace, that sounds intense,' Dawson said, once she'd finished recounting her conversation with Cristina.

His own journey upstairs with Grant had elicited statements of 'no comment' from the business owners and a speedy call to their solicitor. It was clear from the guilt written all over their faces that they knew the workers were illegal and that they had probably arranged the fake passports themselves.

Grant had requested evidence of BACS payments or wage slips being produced and issued directly to the workforce. The efficient Mr Robertson had not been able to magic those documents onto the printer quite so easily.

Despite their assurances of lessons learned in the past, and the thin veil of respectability and legitimacy, it was clear that the Robertsons had learned nothing and were the same dishonest, underhand family they had always been.

The two of them continued to watch from the car as the employees were led from the building into waiting transportation. A police car awaited Nicolae Rachnovich.

'So, what did you do?' he asked. 'What was the question?'

She sighed. 'Can't you guess?'

He thought for a minute and then smiled. 'What would the boss do?'

'Yep,' she answered.

'And?'

'It ay my choice, Kev. It's not up to me what truth gets told or to whom. My job isn't to give everyone their happy ever after. My job is to enforce the law and ultimately Cristina abandoned her baby. I cor allow her reasons for her actions to dictate how I do my job.'

'Easier said than done, though, eh?'

'Oh yeah,' she agreed, as a shadow passed over her face.

He knew that Stacey would have sympathised with the woman who had felt that she had no other option. Cristina's life had been unenviable to this point and the temptation for Stacey to keep the knowledge to herself must have been overwhelming. If only for the sake of the child.

He nudged her as the vehicles began to pull away. 'I'm proud of you, Stace, talking and acting like a police officer and a grown up.'

She turned towards him. 'Yeah, Kev. I am a grown up and some stuff is hard to deal with,' she said. 'And I have been letting fear get the better of me recently, but not any more.'

'Good,' he said, patting her arm.

'So, it's time to knock it on the head now, Kev,' she said.

'What's that?' he asked.

'Parking up outside my flat at night to keep an eye on me.'

'Don't be bloody ridiculous, woman, I—'

'Kev, I've seen you and I'm okay. I'm not scared any more. I know what it's costing you at home and you've got to stop.'

He swallowed. 'Stace…'

'Let it go, Kev. I know you think you should have been able to prevent what happened but you couldn't, no one could. It happened and it's over. We gotta move on.'

He nodded and stared out of the window. Yes, he had felt responsible when Stacey was abducted by those evil, racist bastards. Every minute she'd been held captive had weighed on him heavier because he'd taken his eye off the ball. He'd been too busy fighting and squabbling with Bryant instead of making sure his colleague was okay.

He hadn't told anyone in case they'd tried to make him stop. He wasn't prepared to stop until he knew she was okay. While there was breath in his body he would not allow anyone to harm her again.

He only hoped he hadn't pushed his relationship with Alison beyond repair.

'Tell her the truth,' Stacey said, reading his mind.

'You think?'

'Yeah, she'll bollock you but then she'll be so relieved you were out late being a good guy instead of a cheating wanker there'll be some decent sex in it for you.'

He laughed out loud.

Tell her the truth? Well that was a novel idea but he might just give it a go.

He fired up the engine as Stacey's phone signalled receipt of a text message.

'Uh oh,' Stacey said as she read the words. 'Boss says to drop whatever we're doing and get back to the station. She wants us back there, like now.'

CHAPTER SEVENTY-EIGHT

'Okay, Bryant, I'm pretty sure it's your turn to go get the coffee,' Kim said once she'd read the text message from Stacey. Even allowing for rush-hour traffic they were only a few miles away.

He pointed to the full percolator. 'But, guv, I just…'

'Please leave the room so I can have a private word with Penn.'

Bryant walked past her and huffed.

Kim waited until he'd left the room.

'Any update on Ian Skitt?'

Penn shook his head. 'Not a lot, boss. He is one tight little clam. All I've got so far is that he's twenty-five, transferred out of the Met two years ago, lives alone and has not dated or shown interest in anyone at the station in the time he's been here. He's pleasant and professional, never makes lewd jokes or treats anyone disrespectfully.'

'Regular Boy Scout, then?'

'Appears so. The lack of female partners is not due to a shortage of interest. Every available woman in the control room has thought about it, but any attempts on their part have been politely but pleasantly rebuffed.'

'How'd you find all this out?'

Penn shrugged. 'Took the lovely ladies in the control room a cup of coffee and a few muffins.'

Kim smiled at his ingenuity. The control room operators worked in a sterile environment and didn't get company all that often.

The simplest methods were always the best.

Ian Skitt was clearly a private person who did little to get himself noticed. He was a background player, the type of officer who would retire a nonentity. There would be no anecdote that would travel the annals of history on the back of his name. And that was okay. There were plenty of officers just like him. And yet most of them did not turn up with an armful of fried chicken for sex trade workers each week.

Still her gut told her that there was something not quite right with the constable. There was an instant distrust for her when a person failed to make eye contact.

The activity at the doorway disturbed her thoughts.

'All right, boss?' Dawson asked, rushing in, followed by Stacey, followed by Bryant with coffee.

'Everything okay?' she asked, aware they'd been involved in the raid at Robertson's.

He nodded. 'We'll update you later.'

Kim took a marker pen and stood at the second wipe board.

She wrote the names: Tim, Roger Barton, Roxanne, Kai Lord, Jeremy Templeton, Kelly, Donna and Lauren at random points around the board and circled each name.

Dawson turned to get a better look.

She talked as she drew lines linking the circles.

'So, we know that Tim has been in contact with all our victims at one time or another. Roxanne works for Kai Lord and was also the next-door neighbour of Kelly Rowe.'

She drew another line from Templeton to Kai. 'We know that he is a client of Kai Lord.'

She drew another line from Roger Barton to Kelly Rowe and wrote the word 'blood' along the line. She added Ellie's name in the corner and drew lines to Roxanne and Kai Lord. She added a dotted line to Jeremy Templeton.

Kim stood back. 'Any more links?'

They all murmured in the negative. It was not difficult to see that all lines led back to Kai Lord.

'So, on paper, he's our guy?' Bryant observed.

Kim perched on the edge of the desk and turned to her team.

'But where's the motive? Yeah, we know Kelly was thinking of bouncing, but by killing her, Kai loses out on either her income or transfer fee. And Donna was in no danger of bouncing anywhere.'

She stood back and tapped the marker pen against her lips.

'There's something here we're just not spotting,' Kim said.

'Too many bloody suspects,' Dawson said, still looking at the board.

And yet not one that she'd stake her house on.

Kim frowned. 'This cannot just be about sex. There is something more going on here and Ellie Greaves is at the centre of it. But because Ellie is just a runaway there's no way I'll get authorisation for surveillance. And we wouldn't even know where to start. She's no longer at Roxanne's house.'

'So, if she's been moved, Templeton could be meeting her tonight?' Stacey asked.

Stacey had a point.

It was time to go and see Woody.

She stepped away from the table as her mobile phone began to ring.

'Keats,' she answered.

'You were right about her nails,' he stated, without greeting or preamble.

'Damn it. Go on,' she said.

'Rushed through the request and I have some preliminary results. Her nail bed holds traces of dust and bitumen: a substance used for—'

'I know what it is, Keats,' she said. It was a black semi-solid material found in different forms and used most often for roads and roofing.

'So, Inspector. I don't think Lauren Goddard jumped from that rooftop. It is safe to say she was pushed.'

CHAPTER SEVENTY-NINE

Kim knocked the door and waited for the low rumble.

'Got a minute, sir?' she asked, already closing the door behind her.

'What do we have, Stone?' he asked.

'Not as much as I'd like,' she said honestly. 'We're still considering our Scout leader even though we can only link him forensically to one victim,' she said. 'He admits to contact with Lauren Goddard, but definitely nothing with Donna.'

He tipped his head. 'I'd be hopeful of a positive result but for the reservation in your tone.'

'I know, I know, but my instinct doesn't react to him at all.'

'Although there's no forensic link to Donna Hill, he did have access to both victims and possibly Lauren as well,' he said, informing her he had already read the confirmation email from Keats about his findings.

'What about the male who runs the community centre? Isn't he linked to all three girls as well?'

'As is Kai Lord?' she offered.

She could tell that he was beginning to see her problem.

'Okay, so what next?'

Kim took a deep breath. 'Sir, I want to do a sting, tonight.'

'Stone, are you being serious?'

Kim held up her hand. This was the response she'd expected. A sting was usually an interdepartmental operation forming a diverse task force with clear and concise objectives. Such an operation was subject to stringent planning, risk assessments and authorisation from the superintendent. None of which could be achieved in the two hours she had available.

'Sir, please hear me out and then give me your refusal. Jeremy Templeton is a ruthless, cold man who preys on young girls. Kai Lord and his associates groom and supply the young girls, and I think Ellie Greaves is the young girl that's about to be traded.'

He indicated for her to continue.

'Jeremy Templeton has still not left the area even though he was suitably warned against staying, so he has to be reasonably confident that he's not going to get caught. I think the transaction is going to happen tonight and I have the opportunity to get two of my main suspects at the same time.'

'You think Kai Lord will accompany her personally?'

'Oh yes, my interference the other night cost him a lot of money. He will have jumped through some hoops to get another opportunity, so he's certainly going to want to make sure it goes to plan tonight.'

'What's the plan if you manage to get them?'

'Bring them in on lesser charges and then rattle them. If either one knows anything about any involvement in murder, they'll soon give it up.'

'Shaky plan.'

Kim sat back. He was right but at this stage it was the best she'd got.

He looked at his watch and thought for a moment.

'This can be done but only if it's completely off the radar. Your team must understand the risks involved before they agree. Do we understand each other?'

'Of course, sir,' she said.

Her team always understood the risks involved.

CHAPTER EIGHTY

'Listen up, folks. Before we start I have to be clear that we have no official authorisation for this operation at all. You all know that means no radio comms, no backup and no plan B. All communication will be done by mobile phone, and there will be no support team in place. It's just us lot.'

'Does Woody know?' Dawson asked.

'It's an unofficial op, Kev. The buck stops with me.'

'Yes, boss.'

'Now, none of you need to take part. It's now six o'clock on a Wednesday night. You're all officially off shift. If you want to leave feel free to do so. There will be no repercussions, I assure you.'

'Wife's at bingo, anyway,' Bryant offered.

'It's been a slow day for me,' Stacey joked.

'One more late night ain't gonna kill me,' Dawson said, winking at Stacey.

'Boss, I'm here if you need me,' Penn said.

Woody's instructions had been clear. Her own team did understand the risks involved in off-air operations but she couldn't ask the same from a seconded officer. His assistance on the murder case had been invaluable while Dawson and Stacey worked the child abduction case, but they were back now, and Penn was probably desperate to return to his own team.

She stepped towards the spare desk and offered her hand. 'Thank you for your help on this case, Penn. I'll let you know how it all goes but I'm sure Travis is starting to miss you by now.'

He returned her handshake and stood. 'It's been awesome working with you guys,' he said, offering a wave that encompassed them all. And then he was gone.

Suddenly the office felt emptier but strangely normal. She took her place perched on the spare desk.

'Stace, any info on other addresses for Kai Lord?' she asked. She'd asked the constable to check before she'd hotfooted it up to Woody.

'Umm, yeah, boss, I've got five other addresses registered to Kai Lord.'

'Oh, fabulous. Just what we need right now is more choice. Where are they?'

'Four are in various areas of Birmingham, student accommodation mainly, but the fifth is on the outskirts of Wombourne.'

'That's the beginning of the green belt, guv,' Bryant offered. 'Nothing but derelict farmhouses.'

'I'll take that,' Dawson said.

Kim nodded.

'Stace, I want you on Tavistock Road, just to be sure. They have to know we're onto them by now, so I don't think they would be stupid enough to use the same location for the pickup but we have to be sure. Stay out of the way and that goes for you too, Kev. Stay in the car and call if you see anything suspicious.'

'Yes, boss,' they said together.

'Bryant, you're with me.'

Silence was the response.

'Hey, teacher's pet,' Dawson called. 'You daydreaming?'

Bryant tore his eyes from the ceiling.

'You know, guv, there's something been bothering me. We find it strange that Templeton hasn't left the area yet despite the warning.'

Kim frowned as Dawson groaned.

'Catch up, Bryant,' he said, and Kim had to agree.

'We all feel that whatever he's waiting for has got to be better than sex?'

'Bryant, for goodness' sake, where have you been for the last…'

His eyes met hers. 'Where are they all, guv?'

Kim felt anxiety begin to rise in her stomach. She didn't like the intense expression on her colleague's face.

He continued. 'That neighbour of Roxanne's said she'd fostered more than ten young girls. Well, we know they're not on the strip 'cos we know most of them, so where did they all go?'

A piece of the puzzle clicked into place when realisation dawned on them all. But only Kim said the words out loud.

'Kai isn't taking Ellie Greaves to be raped at all. He's taking her to be sold.'

CHAPTER EIGHTY-ONE

It was almost eight when Kim started her welfare calls.

Stacey answered on the second ring.

'You in place, Stace?'

'Yeah, boss. Pretty quiet here on Tavistock Road, just two girls out tonight, huddled together in the newsagent's doorway.'

'Describe them,' Kim said.

'One older, blonde hair, bleached, blue coat, black shoes—'

'Pink handbag?' Kim asked, fearing the worst.

'Yep.'

'That's Sal,' Kim said, shaking her head. Damn that woman for being out of the hospital and back to work so quickly.

'The other one is almost a foot shorter, jeans, trainers, curly blonde hair…'

'Sounds like Gemma,' Kim said. 'Keep an eye on them at all times, Stace. Anything suspicious call me straight away.'

'Will do, boss.'

Kim ended the call and immediately called Bryant.

'Can you hear me?' she asked. She had an earpiece attached to her phone and the microphone nestled on the inside of her helmet pushed against the cheek cushion.

'Loud and clear, guv.'

Bryant was on hands-free in his car and they had agreed to maintain an open line.

'Ready?' she asked.

'When you are. Got a perfect view of the driveway,' he answered.

Kim lowered the stand on the bike and placed her feet on the ground.

'Guv, if we're right, we really gotta stop this,' Bryant said, quietly.

'I know,' she responded.

Somewhere in this equation was a young girl who had been tricked from her home and manipulated into a world that was completely alien to her. Kim had no idea what awaited Ellie if they failed tonight but what she did know was that she would not be coming back.

Her best-case scenario was getting Ellie to safety while grabbing both Templeton and Lord in the exchange and drilling them both for information on the murders of Kelly Rowe, Donna Hill and Lauren Goddard.

Her instinct did not favour either of them as murderers but one of them knew something and she suspected that someone was Kai Lord. Threats of kidnap and trafficking might help loosen his tongue.

'Got movement, guv,' Bryant said, much sooner than she'd expected, confirming her suspicions.

'It's Templeton's BMW, turning left out of the property.'

'Okay, Bryant, stay on him.'

Kim waited for ten seconds and kicked the bike into life. She moved slowly around the van and squeezed between two parked cars a few spaces down from where Bryant had been parked. Now all she could do was wait and hope that the hunch about a decoy car had been correct.

Kim always remembered that she was not dealing with stupid men. Whatever Templeton and Kai had been up to they had so far remained unidentified.

'Where are you, Bryant?'

'Just heading down Harris Road. Can't see who's in the driver's seat but he's not doing anything out of the ordinary. Observing all the speed limit changes, stopping in plenty of time for traffic lights. Nothing erratic.'

'Okay, keep talking. Tell me where you are.'

'Okay, guv. We're just at the island on the Kidderminster road. He's taking the dual carriageway. Increased speed but still staying within speed limit.'

'If he goes straight over at the next island…'

'Yeah, guv, first exit heads towards Romsley. Third exit goes through Fairfield. Straight over goes to the motorway island.'

Kim was visualising the stretch of road.

'He's in left-hand lane so it's either Romsley or… it's straight over, guv. I think our guy is heading for the motorway to go home.'

It was looking that way but Kim was not so sure.

'Okay, guv, he's indicating to join the motorway. What do you want me to do?'

'Stay with him, Bryant,' she said.

She glanced up the road at the uneventful driveway and just hoped, for Ellie's sake, she'd made the right call.

CHAPTER EIGHTY-TWO

Dawson fiddled with the dial on the radio. Although he was just out of Wombourne the trees had pretty much killed the radio reception. Finally, he gave up. Sick of half sentences, clutches of songs and a lot of crackling he turned it off. The display died bringing the outside darkness into the car.

He'd been parked up on the single-track road for fifteen minutes and nothing had passed him either way.

The silence was complete.

He could hear no traffic and the last street lamp had been left a quarter mile behind.

He'd already driven up ahead to scope out the access/exit points and had ended up at the narrow driveway of a property called The Briars. The wooden gate had been closed. After completing a nine-point manoeuvre to turn the car around he had eased back down the hill to the target property, safe in the knowledge that any exiting vehicles would have to pass him.

The entrance to the property was not gated but the space beyond was dark. Dawson was convinced that this was the ideal place to keep a secret. There was no one to see the comings and goings. There were no neighbours close enough to notice anything suspicious. It was perfect.

But, the guv had told him to stay in the car and that's what he had to do even though there was a young girl in the clutches of a ruthless, sadistic bastard.

He thought of his own daughter, Charlotte, not even two years old, born to fighting parents who were doing their best to work it all out. He knew that he'd felt love in his life of varying degrees. He'd loved his family, he'd loved his first car. He'd even loved one or two girls in his thirty-one years. But what he hadn't known was the love he had felt the first time he'd seen his daughter.

And that was the cause of his concern now. What if the boss was wrong? What if Ellie Greaves was somewhere beyond that darkness being subjected to unspeakable acts. What if he'd arrived too late and Templeton was already back there somewhere?

Ellie had a parent too. A mother who was losing her mind to worry.

If the boss was wrong, he could be sitting feet away from what they all feared.

Dawson shook his head and opened the car door.

And that's when he heard the scream.

CHAPTER EIGHTY-THREE

'Bryant, where are you now?' Kim asked.

'I think we're pulling into Frankley Services. Shouldn't need to stretch his legs yet.'

No, he shouldn't, Kim thought. He'd only driven a few miles up the road.

Kim spotted a set of headlights descending down the target drive. She lowered her head and viewed through the glass of a couple of cars.

'Bryant, I've got movement. A light Mondeo saloon on an 03 plate. What you got?'

'My guy has parked up at the western edge of the car park. Engine is turned off but no one exited the vehicle.'

Kim watched the Mondeo head to the end of the road, and turn left.

'Go ask him for directions, Bryant. We need to know who's in that car.'

She waited at the end of the road for five seconds allowing three cars to insert between herself and the Mondeo.

'Okay, walking across the car park, guv. Trying to look confused.'

Kim bit back the quip in her mouth as the Mondeo drove slowly through the heart of Kinver village. One car left the convoy leaving only two vehicles between her and the Mondeo.

'Stay on the phone,' she said.

Kim could hear talking in the background. To be fair Bryant could do both confused and affable in equal measure very well.

She heard Bryant thank the man for his help as the Mondeo turned left onto the Bridgnorth road. Damn it, the way back to civilisation was a right turn.

'Okay, guv. I got the wild goose. This guy is Templeton's gardener… told… check…'

'Bryant, you're cutting out,' she said, indicating left as the car headed towards Halfpenny Green Airport.

'Where… you…'

'Bryant, if you can hear me I'm just entering Bobbington… heading towards the airfield.'

Kim heard the click as the line went dead. Damn it. She had no idea if Bryant had heard her or not.

Right now she was well and truly on her own. And so was he.

Every minute of training she'd ever received told her to pull over and wait. Her own personal safety came first. She must not risk her own life. Problem was, every situation in her training had been fictional, every crime a scenario. This was no hypothetical desktop exercise. Ellie Greaves was not a name made up in a PowerPoint presentation.

And if she wasn't prepared to risk herself for the sake of a young, innocent girl then what the hell was the point of the training in the first place?

The Mondeo turned left into the darkened airport.

And she turned left too.

CHAPTER EIGHTY-FOUR

Ellie tried to scream against the gag as the car hit a pothole in the road. The impact of the jolt forced her back against the edge of the boot.

Ellie guessed she'd been forced into the boot approximately half an hour earlier. Initially the car had stopped and started often. She'd heard voices, traffic, shouting, even a siren that she had prayed was coming for her. But like all the other sounds it had gradually faded away.

At first the pungent oily smell had threatened to overpower her until she'd realised that it was coming from a rag that was sticking to her cheek. She had managed to use her chin to push it away from her nose and now her face rubbed against a harsh piece of carpet.

Tears of frustration had rolled over her cheeks as she had tried to kick and punch at her metal coffin but the boot lid remained out of reach to her bound hands and feet.

And now the car was moving faster, matching the pace of her heart as it beat against her chest.

Now there were no sounds, no stopping and starting but the ride was bumpier. She guessed that they were on country roads. A large vehicle occasionally roared as it passed on the other side of the road, shaking the car from side to side.

She didn't even know the type of vehicle she'd been put in when Roxanne had taken her out of the cellar and handed her over to Kai. And no amount of begging on her part had changed the woman's mind.

Seeing the complete lack of emotion on her friend's face, Ellie had been forced to accept that there was no bond, that Roxanne hadn't cared for her even for a moment. Every kind word, gesture had been bought and paid for by Kai Lord. Every comment, compliment and sympathetic sound had been perfected and designed to suck her in. The hurt she felt at the betrayal was matched only by her anger at her own gullibility and willingness to believe her mother couldn't care less.

Every emotion that she'd felt during the journey paled against the fear. It was now as much a part of her as any of her vital organs. Other emotions and feelings visited but the terror never left her side.

Suddenly the journey changed again. The car slowed and was taking one sharp turn after another. Her head bounced off something metal behind her.

She tried to ignore the pain in her thighs from being forced into the foetal position but she knew they were going to cramp at any minute. She tried to shake life into them. She wanted to be ready for any opportunity to escape. Her calf cramped and she cried out as the tears filled her eyes.

Her logical mind told her that Kai Lord would never let that happen but she had to try and hold onto the hope. Otherwise she would have to accept that she may never see her mother again.

She knew the trip was coming to an end. They were close to their final destination. She could feel it. The car was about to stop and Ellie had no clue what was going to happen once it did.

CHAPTER EIGHTY-FIVE

The only remaining car disappeared as the Mondeo turned into the airfield.

She followed the Peugeot that had been in front of her and allowed the Mondeo to continue along the entrance road alone. Remaining behind would have given her away completely.

As she looked to her left she saw the brake lights illuminate on the vehicle just short of the car park at the edge of the site. The headlights rested on a car already parked.

Shit, this was the exchange and she was on her own. The whole thing could be over in minutes.

She took the next left turn and quickly parked at the edge of the airfield and dismounted.

Better known as Wolverhampton Business Airport, the site was a small 400 acre airfield constructed in the mid-forties and now catered to private aircraft, business jets and helicopters.

She took a moment to get her bearings. She knew this field. She'd been brought here to open-air markets with Keith and Erica when she was twelve years old. She could short cut across the field towards the hedge that lined the east side of the car park.

She hung her helmet from the Ninja's handlebars and began to sprint through the icy grass that was crunching beneath her boots. She trod more quietly as she approached the dense hedge as muted voices met her ears. The wall of trees obscured her vision but she could clearly hear the voices of Jeremy Templeton and Kai Lord.

'Any problems, man?' Kai asked.

'No, any watching police officers would have followed the Beema. My gardener must be wondering what the hell is happening,' he said, smugly.

Despite her quickening heartbeat Kim had the luxury of rolling her eyes. She was insulted that they really thought she was that stupid.

'You?' Templeton asked.

'Nah, man, that bitch got no clue where I was coming from.'

'Okay, let's make this quick. After this one I want to lie low for a while. I don't like that woman copper one little bit.'

Score one for Templeton, Kim thought, but was alarmed at the speed this transaction was taking place. And they had the advantage of numbers.

'I got the photo you sent,' Templeton said. 'This one's bound for Ukraine.'

Kim swallowed as she heard a boot pop open.

A single strangled cry reached her ears and Kim closed her eyes.

The sensible thing to do was return to her bike and wait for the Mondeo to exit. She knew that Ellie would be in that car but she couldn't risk the Mondeo getting away from her. Then she would have no Kai, no Templeton and, more importantly, no Ellie.

Kim heard a muffled cry before a shout.

'You fucking bitch,' Jeremy Templeton shouted.

Whatever Ellie had done earned her a smack around the face.

'Quiet down, man,' Kai said.

'Bitch kicked me in the balls,' Jeremy said.

Kim had to think quickly. This had to end right here, right now, but she was at a gross disadvantage. They had brute strength, possibly weapons and the motivation to get away. If she played this wrong, her body would be found amongst a pattern of tyre tracks in the snow.

Suddenly the thunder of an aeroplane engine shattered the silence.

Her heart lurched. She had assumed the car park was just the drop off point. Never had she suspected that Jeremy Templeton had a bloody plane. The choice had been whipped away from her. If Jeremy Templeton got on that aircraft they would never see Ellie again.

She silently prayed that Bryant had heard her last transmission.

The sound of the aeroplane engine had dulled to an idling growl.

Kim realised she had to use the only thing available to her. She stepped out of the shadows and placed her hand on her hip.

'Hey boys, did you miss me?'

CHAPTER EIGHTY-SIX

Kim quickly assessed the scene before her. Kai stood to the left of the Mondeo boot and Templeton to the right. Ellie was kneeling in the middle, her hands tied. Tear stains were evident on her cheeks.

Three startled faces looked towards her, which gave her a chance to speak.

She looked at Kai meaningfully. 'Thank you, Kai. I can take it from here and I'll be true to my word. Those charges against you will be dropped.'

Templeton looked at Kai in shock.

Kim took the opportunity to offer the terrified girl what she hoped was a reassuring smile.

Kai held up his hands and shook his head.

'You crazy bitch.'

Kim was straight-faced. 'Kai, leave it now. You did what we asked you to do, now step away. Jeremy's got the idea. He knows we want him more than you.'

Templeton looked from her to Kai. His mouth started to turn upwards and Kim saw that her ploy to buy herself more time wasn't working. She had to try harder to convince him, to get extra minutes.

'You were right, Kai,' she said, 'when you told me to let the first car go and to follow the second.'

Now Templeton looked back at Kai and his face was thunderous.

'You sold me out, you bastard?'

Kai was no longer smiling.

'Get real, man. This deal's worth far more than snitching to the fucking police. And whatever petty charges she's talking about—'

'I'd hardly call abduction and kidnap petty, Kai, but I am a woman of my word. And then there's your involvement in the recent murders—'

'Fucking murder?' Jeremy screeched. He took two steps away from the boot of the car.

'Man, don't listen to her. She talking shit. She's got nothing. Think about it.'

She cut in quickly. The more opportunity she gave Kai to speak the more dangerous this situation became for her. 'Yeah, think about it, Jeremy. How would I have known what to do? How would I have known that this exchange was going to take place tonight? Jesus, I would have needed some help to put this together.'

Kim played into Jeremy's opinion of women. She couldn't possibly have worked this out on her own.

The three of them stood in a triangle.

Kai's expression was murderous and then amused.

Dammit, he'd realised there was one clear way he could prove he hadn't snitched.

He began walking towards her.

'What are you doing?' Jeremy asked.

'Silencing this bitch once and for all. I'm fucking sick of her costing me money.'

'Hey, what are you going to do?'

Kai took a flick knife from his pocket.

'No way,' Templeton said. 'I am not killing a fucking police officer.'

He stepped towards the driver's door of the Mondeo.

'This just got way too complicated. Just let me get out of here and then do what the hell you like. I'm not getting involved in this shit.'

'Stay where you are,' Kai said to Templeton but his eyes were on Kim.

'I'm gonna sort this bitch out once and for all and then we will conclude our business.'

Kim stepped back, away from the advancing blade. She saw Ellie swipe her legs for Kai's ankles but missed by a good foot.

Kim could step back no further. Her back was against the wall of trees. Her eyes remained fixed on Kai. She would not back down. She would not show any emotion. She was not one of his fearful girls.

He stepped closer so that only a foot of space existed between them.

'I like ballsy women,' he whispered. 'Up to a point.' He raised the blade so that it glistened between them. 'And this is the point.'

Kim knew she could have run as he had advanced towards her. She'd had just a few seconds to make that decision but there had never been a choice. Not when a teenage girl lay bound and trapped on the icy ground right in front of her.

'You've been a pain in my fucking ass for months,' he said.

'Fucking hell, Lord, back off,' Templeton shouted.

He stroked her cheek with the blade.

'You've cost me money and lost me trade but I'm done, now, bitch.'

Another stroke.

Kim didn't look at the blade. She continued to stare into the hard cold eyes. He would get nothing from her. Any effort on her part to make a grab for the knife would end in serious injury to her, or worse.

But she had to at least try.

She flexed her right hand and splayed it, ready to make a move for the knife.

She closed her eyes and said a silent prayer as she felt the weight of Kai Lord's torso fall against her.

CHAPTER EIGHTY-SEVEN

'Stuuurike,' Dawson shouted.

Kim turned quickly to see her colleague stepping out of the bushes to her right. In his hand was a second rock, much like the one that now lay beside Kai's head.

Kim had never been so happy to see anyone in her life.

She stamped on Kai's wrist as Templeton made a run for the car. This time Ellie's aim and timing with her foot swipe was spot on and he tumbled to the ground.

'Oh no you don't, sunshine,' Dawson said.

Dawson flipped him onto his front and put a knee in the small of his back. He grabbed Templeton's wrists and cuffed him.

Kim did the same thing with Kai who was groaning. There was a gash to the back of his head that was not bleeding enough to be life-threatening.

Kim and Dawson both reached Ellie at the same time. Dawson used Kai's knife to cut through the tape binding her wrists and Kim ripped the cloth from the girl's mouth.

Ellie burst into tears and scooted into Kim's arms.

Her arms automatically closed around the trembling form. 'It's okay, Ellie, you're safe now, I promise.'

The girl inched further in and Kim had to steady herself not to fall backwards.

'Did they hurt you?'

The girl didn't answer so Kim quietly stroked her hair soothingly.

'How'd you find me?' Kim asked Dawson over the top of the girl's head.

'Bryant called. He got your last message and knew I was only four miles away. Glad to get the call. Those fox cries were scaring the shit out of me.'

Kim allowed herself a small smile of triumph. There were two scumbags cuffed on the floor and a young girl sobbing in her arms, instead of embarking on the next leg of her journey to Ukraine.

She'd take that.

Kim guided the trembling girl to the back seat of the Mondeo. 'Sit in there. You'll be fine now, I promise.' She reached into her back pocket and handed Ellie her mobile phone.

'Ring your mum and tell her you're safe.'

Ellie took the phone and sat sideways on the back seat so the door couldn't be closed. Kim could understand that.

'How'd you stall them?' Dawson asked.

'Tried to convince Dumb over there that Dumber over here had ratted him out.' She nudged Templeton's arm with her foot. 'And you were stupid enough to fall for it, weren't you, hot shot?'

Templeton squirmed and called her a few names.

Dawson nudged his other arm. 'The boss was asking you a rhetorical question.'

Dawson turned back to her. 'Risky though?'

'It was all happening too quickly. I couldn't risk them getting away with Ellie.'

In truth, it had given her no more than a couple of minutes but thanks to her team that had been long enough.

And talking of her team she turned to the young detective sergeant.

'Kev, enough already. Stacey's a big girl and it wasn't your fault.' He smiled. 'Yeah, pretty much what she said, too.'

Kim laughed. 'She caught you?'

He nodded and raised his eyebrows.

She'd seen him parked up a couple of times. Just when she'd been doing the odd drive by herself.

'You know, Kev, you're not nearly as much of a selfish bastard as you think you are,' she said, meeting his gaze.

'Hey, boss,' Dawson said, looking behind her. A set of headlights dimmed and then died.

Bryant stepped out of the car as the noise of the aeroplane died away. Someone had clearly informed the pilot that his fare had been delayed.

'Better late than never,' Dawson called to his colleague.

'Transport van is a few minutes away,' he said as he approached.

'Bryant, check his pockets,' she said, nodding towards Kai. 'Dawson, check Templeton.'

'Forty-five quid,' Dawson said.

She looked at Bryant who was still counting the contents of a white envelope from Lord's pocket.'

'Forget it, Bryant. We can safely assume that the money changed hands.'

She walked over to Templeton. 'Get him up.'

Dawson and Bryant lifted him. His face no longer held any of the boyish charisma that had almost drowned her the previous day. Gone was the overt sexual confidence and what was left was an unattractive, spoilt, scared little boy.

He didn't even have the bollocks to glower at her. His mind was already trying to calculate damage limitation.

She stepped over to Kai. 'Leave him where he is. Kev, over here.'

Dawson came over to stand beside her.

'So, what do you think of the guy that didn't have the bollocks to take you one-on-one?' she asked.

Dawson tipped his head and sighed. 'You know, he's much smaller than I remember,' he said, pulling his eyebrows together.

'Say that again, you fucking—'

Dawson laughed and walked away, giving his threat the attention it deserved.

She knelt down closer to Kai Lord so she could see the murderous look on his face.

'Kai Lord—'

'Don't,' he said

'Don't what?'

'Do something you're gonna regret.'

Kim laughed.

'How am I gonna regret putting away a piece of shit like you? Once I get you two back to the station we'll find out who has been murdering those poor girls.'

Kai surprised her by laughing out loud.

'Yeah, good luck on that.'

Kim felt the rage swirl in her stomach. She didn't like his confidence.

'Excuse me, officer,' said a small voice behind her.

She turned to find Ellie wrapped in Bryant's long overcoat. She was holding out Kim's phone.

'A lady named Stacey wants you.'

Kim took the phone.

'Sorry, Stace, meant to call. We're all done here. You can stand down and—'

'Not yet, boss,' Stacey said, breathlessly.

'What is it?'

'I only looked away for a minute and—'

'And what, Stace?' Kim asked, urgently.

'It's Sal and Gemma, boss. They've disappeared. Both of them.'

Immediately the whiteboard back at the station flashed into her mind. The names, the thick lines, the dotted lines linking all the players. Nausea rose in her throat as she realised there was one crucial line missing.

'Oh shit,' she cried, running towards her bike.

CHAPTER EIGHTY-EIGHT

Kim tried the handle of the metal door. If she could get one piece of luck she prayed for a quick entry to the premises.

The knob turned in her hand. Of course, they were not expecting visitors.

Kim closed the door quietly behind her. She blinked three times to adjust her eyes to the darkness. She could make out vague shadowy shapes and that she was in a small reception area no bigger than her bathroom. An open door led into a larger area filled with metal racking. Kim's sight was assisted by a shaft of light from a doorway at the far end of the warehouse.

She traversed a path through the narrow corridors of shelving. Odd boxes of discarded nails and tacks littered the shelves from when the hardware business had gone into liquidation.

She neared the lit doorway and saw evidence of a struggle. A box of tacks had been spilled all over the floor.

Kim attempted to step around them as she heard a voice from the other side of the door.

'You'll look like a suicide, just like poor little Lauren,' said the voice that ripped at her heart.

Kim closed her eyes for a moment.

She took a deep breath before she pushed open the door.

'How the hell could you do it, Sal?' Kim asked, walking into the room.

She instantly saw Gemma. The girl was standing on a chair, gagged, her throat in a noose tied to the light fitting. Her old friend was standing perilously close to the chair.

'What the fuck are you doing here?' Sal cried, turning towards her.

'I'm here to stop you taking the life of anyone else, Sal,' she said, taking a step forward.

Sal moved closer to the chair, so Kim stopped moving.

'Don't be ridiculous, Kim. I've not killed anyone. Me and Gemma was just having a little game here. I've always protected these kids, just like I protected you.'

The fear in the girl's eyes and the blood dripping down her right arm disputed that fact.

Kim stood still but had to maintain Sal's attention. One good kick of that chair and she would be adding another name to the board.

'You put the £5 notes in the handbags of Kelly and Donna, didn't you? We were focussing on their last customers and you pointed us right towards Roger Barton. But it was you that was waiting for them when they came back to the strip.'

Sal was regarding her with interest, so she continued.

'I wondered about the locations, Sal. First one behind a Chinese takeaway and the second in a ladies' public convenience. Both very easy places to lure your fucking friends,' she said, bitterly.

'And the blood in the car of Roger Barton. Kelly Rowe's blood was in the passenger seat footwell. He hadn't been with Kelly Rowe recently but I saw you get into his car on Sunday night. You had the woman's blood on your shoes from the night before when you killed her. And you left it in Roger Barton's car.'

Sal shrugged and turned back towards Gemma. It was like she'd been accused of taking too many biscuits from the jar.

'What the hell happened to you here, Sal?' Kim asked and she didn't mean the obvious.

The same memory she'd had earlier in the week had returned to her again as she'd run towards her bike. And that's when she'd known where to find her old friend.

'You weren't protecting me when we were kids by stepping in to prevent me from being brought here by Mr Nelson. You were getting rid of the competition.'

'He brought me presents,' she said, proudly. 'And all I had to do was let him put his small, limp dick inside me for a few minutes. Fucking easy. And even better when I learned that if I moved around and made groaning—'

'Stop it,' Kim cried, unable to stand the thought of the child with the apple groaning and grinding to earn herself a few presents.

'What's the matter, Kim. Can't you stand the thought that I saw an opportunity and exploited it?'

Sal looked around. 'This is where I learned my craft, where I finally understood what I had that I could use and it was so bloody simple. It didn't cost a fucking penny.'

'You weren't helping when you alerted me to that young girl on the corner, were you?' Kim asked. 'You just wanted her gone.'

Sal grinned. 'Yeah but you didn't know that.'

'But why kill them? They were your friends. What did Lauren do?'

Sal blew air through her lips. 'Slag was only at it for a few months; fucking bitch was getting all the business. The minute Kai put her out on the street no one else could get a fucking look in.'

'And then Kelly Rowe, you started that rumour that she was planning to bounce, didn't you?'

Sal's face didn't change one bit. These women meant nothing to her.

'Even Donna?' Kim asked.

'What's your fucking shocked indignation about, Kim? I don't give a shit about any one of these bitches. Why would I?' she asked. 'You tell me what we learned about loyalty and lasting friendships growing up. Fuck all. We learned how to take care of ourselves and my rent just keeps coming around.'

'Fuck your rent,' Kim spat. 'It has nothing to do with it. You can't stand the fact that the punters were choosing the other girls over you, could you?' Kim baited.

Sal took two steps towards her, which sent her two paces away from the chair beneath Gemma's feet. Kim saw the relief on Gemma's face but Sal was not yet far enough away for safety. She needed to bait the woman closer.

'Even Donna, who in your mind was a lice-infested druggie, was getting more business than you.'

Kim finally understood that this was not just about murdering her competition. Sal had given away something of herself in this room almost thirty years ago. She had allowed something to shrivel up and die, and that had been okay. Until now. Sal's age was working against her every single day. And if, before she'd even reached her forties, her golden gift was gone, had it been worth it?

'Face it,' Kim taunted. 'You're finished. No one wants to fuck an old cow when there are young, fresh kids out there.'

Sal came hurtling towards her but Kim was ready. She lunged forward bringing her right arm around Sal's front at the neck. Sal continued to move forward, stepping out of her heels, reducing her height by a few inches, bringing Kim's arm level with her mouth.

Sal snapped her head to the left and managed to capture the fleshy heel of Kim's hand in her mouth. The teeth punctured her skin and burrowed down into her flesh. The jaws locked on like a pitbull.

Kim screamed out in pain and tried to shake her hand free. Sal shook her head like a terrier. Kim reached up with her left hand and grabbed a handful of hair to pry her head away. Sal's head craned backwards. She spat out Kim's hand and lurched forward with brute strength.

Kim felt the hair tear from Sal's scalp as the woman got free.

Gemma cried out as Sal moved towards her precarious position. One good kick and it was all over.

Kim stumbled forward, realising that only twenty feet separated Sal from Gemma and the woman was advancing all the time. She sprinted forward with only one target on her mind. She launched herself through the air aiming for Sal's body to bring her down.

Sal fell to the ground with Kim on top of her. She tried to scrabble forward beneath Kim's body, desperate for those extra inches.

Kim knew if she moved up the body they could roll into the chair and snap Gemma's neck.

She punched Sal in the head. The pain shot through her hand all the way to her brain.

But the woman was stunned enough that Kim could climb over her. She clasped Sal's ankles and dragged her across the floor, away from Gemma. Sal shook off her hand and sprang to her feet. She looked towards Gemma and back towards the door. Kim saw the indecision and kicked at the back of Sal's calves. Sal fell to her knees but like a sprinter from the blocks she managed to advance towards the exit.

But Kim was ready and pushed Sal back to the ground.

Every movement was taking them closer to the door and away from Gemma.

Kim rounded on Sal and kicked her in the left kidney. The woman clutched her side but continued the forward movement. Kim took a second to get her breath.

'Where the hell do you think you're going?' she said, leaning down.

She grabbed Sal's right arm and turned her onto her back, lodging her knee into Sal's back.

'Nooooo,' Sal screamed, and with one almighty push managed to dislodge Kim's right knee.

Pumped by hatred and adrenaline and a life behind bars Sal managed to throw Kim to the side but her focus was no longer on escape. Her eyes were filled with hatred as Kim felt herself being thrown backwards. The back of her head bounced off the concrete floor.

Sal was on top of her. Her hands closing around Kim's throat.

'You fucking bitch, you fucking interfering bitch…'

Kim felt the air leaving her body. She gulped wildly but nothing could get past. Her head began to swim. She heard sirens in the distance. She knew she could not hang on until they got there. She would live for less than a minute.

Her hands scrabbled at her side trying to push herself away from Sal's grip as her vision started to fail.

The darkness brought clarity into her mind's eye. She suddenly knew exactly where they were. She opened her eyes but her vision was now gone completely. Her lungs were starved of oxygen. And she had one chance to save her own life. She gathered every ounce of determination she possessed and rolled to the left. Taken by surprise Sal rolled with her and toppled to the ground.

A piercing scream filled the space.

The pressure on her throat suddenly loosened. Kim opened her eyes but her vision was blurred.

Sal's hands were reaching all over her body. She rolled again as though covered in flames. The tacks stuck out of her back like a pincushion.

Kim hungrily gulped in the precious oxygen.

Sal fell to the side and Kim scrabbled to a sitting position. Her lungs ached but her vision was returning.

The sound of the metal door exploding open was the sweetest sound she'd ever heard. She shouted her location and Bryant was beside her in a second. He quickly appraised the situation and the marks around her neck.

'Jesus Christ, guv,' he exclaimed.

'Get Gemma, both of you, she's in there.'

Two uniformed officers stomped into the scene.

Kim raised her hand and pointed at Sal who still writhed around the floor.

'Cuff her,' she managed to say, before she passed out.

CHAPTER EIGHTY-NINE

Kim came around to find herself being held hostage by a tall green alien.

She struggled to free herself.

'Easy, guv,' Bryant said. 'It's just the paramedic, checking you over.'

'Where's Sal?'

'On her way to hospital under police guard. She's not going anywhere.'

Kim nodded her understanding.

'Gemma?'

Bryant smiled. 'Waiting to speak to you.'

Kim pushed herself up from the stretcher in the back of the ambulance.

Her head felt woozy but she pushed herself forward.

'Guv, you need to go to the—'

'Bryant, stop fussing and get out of the way.'

Bryant stepped aside to reveal a sea of strobes that lit up the area like a blue version of the Northern Lights. Her eyes fell on Gemma and Dawson, standing closely together by Bryant's car. Dawson's overcoat was draped around Gemma's shoulders.

Kim could see the kid was still trembling.

Gemma turned before Kim reached her. The fear in her eyes instantly disappeared.

'Kev, give us a minute,' Kim asked.

Dawson nodded and stepped away.

'You okay?' Kim asked, placing her left hand on Gemma's arm.

Gemma nodded covering the hand with her own.

'Are you?' she asked.

Kim smiled. 'I am now you're no longer hanging around.'

She turned to Kim. Her eyes glistened and her voice was thick. 'Look, what you did in there…' She shook her head. 'No one has ever… I just don't…'

'What else was I supposed to do?' Kim asked.

'I tried to kill you,' Gemma said, hoarsely.

'No, you didn't,' Kim said, smiling sadly.

'I was in your house, ready and—'

'You were in my house two days before eating my bloody oven chips but you didn't try then, did you?'

'I hadn't had the instruction then,' she answered, honestly.

Kim folded her arms and tipped her head. 'So, how exactly were you gonna do it?' she asked.

'Well, I… err…'

'Shit, that makes me frightened for my life. You didn't even have a bloody plan.'

Gemma surprised her by throwing back her head and laughing out loud. 'Now that you come to mention it, I actually didn't.'

They laughed together and then sobered.

'Listen, Gemma, the problem with you is that you're not as bad as you think you are. You're not as stupid as you think you are, and you're not as worthless as you think you are.'

Gemma guffawed and then lowered her head.

'Hey, look at me,' Kim said.

Gemma raised her head and Kim saw the tears rolling over her cheeks.

'Yeah, kinda proving my point there,' she said, gently.

Kim couldn't help the sudden rush of tenderness that coursed through her. Jesus, what was it with this kid?

A paramedic appeared beside her. 'Need to get her off to be checked...'

'Yeah, yeah, no problem,' Kim said, stepping aside. She tipped her head at Gemma. 'Now, don't go giving them any shit. They're trying to look after you.'

Gemma wiped at her eyes and blew a raspberry.

The door was almost closed before Kim pulled it back open.

'And if you're passing mine some time, drop in if you like.'

'Seriously?' she asked with wide eyes.

'Yeah, but bring your own food. You've seen my fridge.'

She heard Gemma chuckle right before the door was closed for good.

She watched the vehicle drive away before striding towards her colleagues.

'Ellie?' Kim asked.

'In a police car on her way home,' Bryant said.

'Boss, boss, are you—?'

'I'm fine, Stace,' she reassured the detective constable barrelling towards her.

'Your neck...' she said, staring.

'Honestly, Stace. I'm good,' she said.

They all looked around at each other. The smiles were wide and genuine.

'Good job, guys, bloody good job.'

They all nodded.

'Guv, there's an ambulance waiting to take you...'

Kim rolled her eyes. 'Please send it off to deal with sick people.'

He shook his head and motioned for the ambulance to leave.

'You know something, Bryant?' she said.

He turned to her, clearly waiting for some kind of profound statement about the events of the evening.

She turned to him and smiled. 'I bloody love this job.'

CHAPTER NINETY

Kim enjoyed the peace of the office as she stared at the wipe board.

Bryant was interviewing Sal, Dawson and Stacey were interviewing Jeremy Templeton, and she'd just finished up with Kai Lord who had remained silent and glowering throughout the process. Roxanne was waiting in a cell, and Ellie was safely back home with her mother.

All that remained was to wipe the board. An action that went hand in hand with the settling of her gut. It was the final act to signify that the case was solved.

It was a literal and symbolic gesture of wiping away.

And she wasn't quite ready to do that yet.

She really should have seen it sooner. She should have seen that every line on the board somehow led to Sal.

Kelly Rowe had been forced into a corner by circumstance. The sex trade had been a temporary measure for her and, despite the cliché, from what she had found out about Kelly it had been true. She was a loving mother who wanted to do the best for her child.

Donna Hill had been a lost soul, battling addiction and doing whatever she could to survive. She had been lured from an angst-ridden relationship with her mother by a ruthless, soulless, ambitious woman who had no capacity for empathy. And she had very nearly scored again with another innocent soul.

Poor Lauren Goddard had been cruelly sacrificed into the sex trade by her own mother and then pushed off the edge of a building by someone masquerading as a friend.

All three of them had been working the streets for different reasons, befriended by Sal, a woman of more experience, compassion, protection. And she had been none of these things. Instead they had found a woman who had been twisted as a child. Her own perception of value distorted by abuse and cruelty. Kim had assumed the seeds had been sown during her years in care, but now she couldn't help wondering if there had been some truth to the rumour that Sal had tried to hurt her newborn sister. Perhaps she had feared competition right back then. She suspected she would never know.

And then there'd been Ellie. Innocent, naive and desperate to grow up, she had been trapped and exploited, groomed by Roxanne for the streets and then sold – destined for Ukraine.

She thought about the case Dawson and Stacey had been working. About Cristina, who had been willing to sacrifice anything for her child. Would suffer never seeing or holding her baby again to give him a better life than she'd had. The child was still safely placed with the foster family, who were growing more attached to him every day. Already his life was complicated but she trusted that social services would ensure the child's welfare whatever the outcome.

Through Cristina and her father, Dawson and Stacey had exposed a network of illegal workers being exploited, beaten and abandoned. People being treated like dogs or farm animals with no proper accommodation, meals or healthcare. Individuals who had been deceived and then bought and sold like cattle.

And then, finally, there was Gemma. Defensive, rebellious, hardass Gemma who was still selling her body to get a meal. The kid that had once been manipulated into trying to kill her but hadn't quite been able to pull it off.

Would coming this close to losing her life change anything about the way she chose to live it? Kim wondered, acknowledging the smile that teased at her lips.

Her team, as ever, had surprised her. They had welcomed a near stranger into the fold and adapted professionally to his involvement. Penn was not the warmest of characters but he was intelligent, intuitive and a little bit quirky. And he had been a great help.

She smiled as she thought about Dawson's determination in keeping his colleague in sight, guarding her flat until he was sure she was safe. She admired Stacey's bravery in getting back out into the real world. And then there was Bryant, the glue that held the team together, and he didn't even know it.

She couldn't help the feeling of pride that surged through her as she heard the tentative footsteps approaching the doorway.

This was the person she'd been waiting for.

'Come in,' she said to the young constable.

Ian Skitt stepped in and automatically looked to the wipe board, where his reaction told her he saw a name he recognised.

His white shirt was open at the collar and his eyes bloodshot from a night shift. He put his hands in his pockets, uneasily.

'You put that note through my door, didn't you?' she asked.

He nodded.

'Lauren Goddard was your younger sister. You were one of the children taken away.'

'Thank God,' he muttered.

'Sorry?' Kim asked.

'Nothing, it's…'

'Go on,' Kim urged.

'I did okay. I was fostered long-term by a middle-aged couple that kept me for nine years. They were my parents. I was lucky.'

Kim understood. The three years she'd spent with Keith and Erica had formed the building blocks for her entire life.

'Did you ever get to see her?'

'Yes. I found her on the roof of the flats just two weeks before she died. I wanted her to come with me, leave her mother, but she refused. Said I'd abandoned her.' He looked down to the ground. 'She said she hated me and never wanted to see me again.'

'So you started visiting the community centre, trying to see her?'

'I didn't want to crowd her. I just wanted to be close by.'

Kim understood.

He had been removed from the family home through no fault of his own and had made the most of the opportunity. He had taken that gift and made a decent life for himself. Kim knew he was carrying the guilt for all that he had been given and all that Lauren had not.

'There's nothing you could have done,' she offered.

His expression thanked her for the sentiment but, in reality, that acceptance was a long way away right now. There was only one final thing she could give him.

'Lauren's body is being returned to the ground, right now. She was your sister, and I'd like you to come with me.'

He swallowed. 'I'd like that.'

Kim grabbed her coat and paused. There was something she had to know.

'Skitt, why didn't you just come and speak to me about your sister's death?'

He thought for a few seconds. 'I just didn't think she would matter to anyone.'

Kim offered him an acknowledgement and a smile before glancing once more at the board.

'In this office, I can assure you, everyone matters.'

A LETTER FROM ANGELA

First of all, I want to say a huge thank you for choosing to read *Broken Bones,* the seventh instalment of the Kim Stone series.

What began as an idea about working in the sex trade developed into a story about grooming, prostitution, entrapment and the modern day slave trade. The unbelievable horror of people ownership still existing today and affecting generation after generation is a subject that I felt compelled to explore. Thank you for joining me on this emotional journey. I hope you enjoyed it.

If you did enjoy it, I would be forever grateful if you'd write a review. I'd love to hear what you think, and it can also help other readers discover one of my books for the first time. Or maybe you can recommend it to your friends and family...

To keep up to date with the latest news on my new releases, just click on the link below to sign up for a newsletter. I promise to only contact you when I have a new book out and I'll never share your email with anyone else.

www.bookouture.com/angela-marsons

In *Broken Bones* I enjoyed learning more about the friendship between Dawson and Stacey and offering them an opportunity to work a case together. After separating Kim and Bryant in the previous book there was a welcome familiarity in pairing them back up here. I definitely missed their banter.

It was interesting to present Kim with a situation completely alien to her right at the beginning of the book and I must admit to having a little fun at her expense with regard to her maternal instinct. I can promise that no babies were harmed in the writing of those chapters!

There are six other books in the D.I. Kim Stone series – *Silent Scream*, *Evil Games*, *Lost Girls*, *Play Dead*, *Blood Lines* and *Dead Souls* – so if you enjoyed *Broken Bones* and haven't read the other books, I hope you'll love reading them too.

I'd love to hear from you – so please get in touch on my Facebook or Goodreads page, Twitter or through my website.

Thank you so much for your support, it is hugely appreciated.

Angela Marsons

www.angelamarsons-books.com

 angelamarsonsauthor

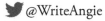 @WriteAngie

ACKNOWLEDGEMENTS

As ever, my first acknowledgement must be to my partner, Julie. If there is blood, sweat and tears from the author this must be doubly so for an author's partner. She feels every emotion of the process along with me from the excitement of the initial idea to the inevitable despair and self-doubt along the way. And yet she always manages to dispel my fears and fan my joy. She never lets me forget the reasons I love to write.

Thank you to my Mum and Dad who continue to spread the word proudly to anyone who will listen. And to my sister Lyn, her husband Clive and my nephews Matthew and Christopher for their support and a really cool photo of one of my books in Harrods.

Thank you to Amanda and Steve Nicol who support us in so many ways and to Kyle Nicol for book spotting my books everywhere he goes.

I would like to thank the team at Bookouture for their continued enthusiasm for Kim Stone and her stories. In particular, the incredible Keshini Naidoo who never tires in her encouragement and passion for what we do. To Oliver Rhodes who gave Kim Stone an opportunity to exist. To Kim Nash (Mama Bear) who works tirelessly to promote our books and protect us from the world. To Noelle Holten who has limitless enthusiasm and passion for our work.

I can not write a book without acknowledging the growing family of Bookouture authors. Their enthusiasm for each other is genuine and provides an environment of friendship, advice and support. Thank you to the fantastic Kim Slater who has been an incredible support and friend to me for many years now and to the fabulous Caroline Mitchell, Renita D'Silva, Sue Watson and Mel Sherratt without whom this journey would be impossible.

My eternal gratitude goes to all the wonderful bloggers and reviewers who have taken the time to get to know Kim Stone and follow her story. These wonderful people shout loudly and share generously not because it is their job but because it is their passion. I will never tire of thanking this community for their support of both myself and my books. Thank you all so much.

Massive thanks to all my fabulous readers, especially the ones that have taken time out of their busy day to visit me on my website, Facebook page, Goodreads or Twitter.